Acclaim for Kathleen Fuller

SOLD ON LOVE

"Kathleen Fuller writes an 'opposites attract' romance that will leave you with a wonderful sigh and a silly smile. Harper Wilson overworks to cover up her insecurities, but when tenderhearted and gentle grease monkey Rusty Jenkins enters her life to save her Mercedes, an unexpected friendship grows into something both of them need: love. Authentic and sweet, this small-town romance with wonderful heart and a delicious male makeover will have you cheering for two people whose lives look very different on the outside but whose hearts are very much the same."

—PEPPER BASHAM, AUTHOR OF *THE MISTLETOE COUNTESS* AND *AUTHENTICALLY, IZZY*

MUCH ADO ABOUT A LATTE

"Fuller returns to small-town Maple Falls, Ark., (after *Hooked on You*) for a chaste but spirited romance between old friends with clashing entrepreneurial goals . . . The cozy atmosphere and spunky locals will leave readers eager to return to Maple Falls."

—*PUBLISHERS WEEKLY*

"You've heard of friends to lovers; now get ready for childhood friends, to coworkers, to fake-dating coworkers, to business rivals, to lovers. *Much Ado About a Latte* has it all—charming and sweet with delectable dialogue and just enough biting tension to keep you on the edge of your seat. I fell in love with Anita's determined spirit, Tanner's kindness, and their slow-burning romance. A wide cast of side characters, including Anita's complicated but loving family, build the delightful feel of the town. Readers will love the beautiful setting of Maple Falls, the gratuitous food descriptions at Sunshine Diner, and Anita's adorable cat, Peanut."

—CAROLYN BROWN, *NEW YORK TIMES* BESTSELLING AUTHOR

"Something's brewing in Maple Falls, and you're going to be rooting for the romance every step of the way. Kathleen Fuller has created a wonderful small-town setting for this sweet reunion romance. How these two first-kiss kids ever kept their distance until now is beyond me! Just goes to show if true love is meant to be, there's no escaping it."

—NANCY NAIGLE, ECPA BESTSELLING AUTHOR OF *THE SHELL COLLECTOR*

HOOKED ON YOU

"Sign me up for a one-way ticket to Maple Falls. If you love small towns, charming characters, and sweet, swoony romance, *Hooked on You* is your next favorite read. Kathleen Fuller has knit one wonderful story yet again."

—JENNY B. JONES, AWARD-WINNING AUTHOR OF *A KATIE PARKER PRODUCTION* AND *THE HOLIDAY HUSBAND*

"A charming story of new beginnings, family ties, love, friendship, laughter, and the beauty of small towns. Fuller invites you into Maple Falls and greets you with a cast of characters who will steal your heart, make you want to stay, and entice you to visit again."

—KATHERINE REAY, BESTSELLING AUTHOR OF *THE PRINTED LETTER BOOKSHOP* AND *OF LITERATURE AND LATTES*

"A sweet, refreshing tale of idyllic small-town life, family, and unexpected romance, *Hooked on You* is the perfect read to cozy up with on a rainy day."

—MELISSA FERGUSON, MULTI-AWARD-WINNING AUTHOR OF *THE CUL-DE-SAC WAR*

"The quaint Arkansas town of Maple Falls could use a little sprucing up, and as it turns out, Riley and Hayden are the perfect pair for the job. What neither of them is counting on, of course, is that their hearts may receive some long overdue TLC in the process. Kathleen Fuller has knit together a lovable cast of characters and placed them in a setting so rich and dear you may find yourself hankering for a walk down Main Street on a warm summer's evening. I loved every minute of my time in Maple Falls, and I can't wait to return to visit the friends I made there."

—BETHANY TURNER, AWARD-WINNING AUTHOR OF
HADLEY BECKETT'S NEXT DISH AND *PLOT TWIST*

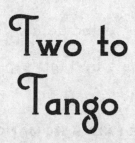

Two to Tango

Other Contemporary Romance
Novels by Kathleen Fuller

THE MAPLE FALLS ROMANCE NOVELS

Hooked on You

Much Ado About a Latte

Sold on Love

Two to Tango

Two to Tango

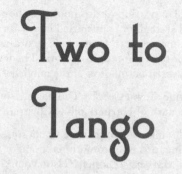

A
MAPLE FALLS
ROMANCE

KATHLEEN FULLER

THOMAS NELSON
Since 1798

Two to Tango

Published in Nashville, Tennessee, by Thomas Nelson. Thomas Nelson is a registered trademark of HarperCollins Christian Publishing, Inc.

Thomas Nelson titles may be purchased in bulk for educational, business, fund-raising, or sales promotional use. For information, please email SpecialMarkets@ThomasNelson.com.

Library of Congress Cataloging-in-Publication Data

Names: Fuller, Kathleen, author.
Title: Two to tango : a Maple Falls romance / Kathleen Fuller.
Description: Nashville, Tennessee : Thomas Nelson, [2023] | Series:
    Maple Falls romance novels ; 4 | Summary: "Librarian Olivia
    Farnsworth isn't looking for love. Pediatrician Kingston Bedford
    is more than ready to get married. When the entire town of Maple
    Falls schemes to get them together, sparks fly"--Provided by
    publisher.
Identifiers: LCCN 2023000511 (print) | LCCN 2023000512 (ebook) |
    ISBN 9780840715968 (paperback) | ISBN 9780840716019 (epub) |
    ISBN 9780840715821
Subjects: LCGFT: Romance fiction. | Christian fiction. | Novels.
Classification: LCC PS3606.U553 T96 2023 (print) | LCC PS3606.
    U553(ebook) | DDC 813/.6--dc23/eng/20230112
LC record available at https://lccn.loc.gov/2023000511
LC ebook record available at https://lccn.loc.gov/2023000512

Printed in the United States of America

23 24 25 26 27 LBC 5 4 3 2 1

To James. I love you.

Prologue

Olivia Farnsworth always had a plan. Every Monday for five years, she had been precisely thirty minutes early for the Sunset Cinema's monthly Vintage Movie Night. As always, she ordered a Diet Coke—no ice, please—then entered the theater and headed straight for her seat. Seventh row, tenth seat, square in the middle of the room. Although all the Vintage Movie Night features could be seen on TV or a streaming service or purchased for her personal collection, viewing the classics at home couldn't compare to sitting in a darkened theater, the characters larger than life on a massive screen, the surround sound resonating through huge, albeit outdated, speakers. That was an *experience*.

But as she settled onto the nearly threadbare cushion and waited for Sunset's yearly showing of *The Quiet Man* to start, her mind wasn't on the movies. She was in a rut. A Grand Canyon of a rut. That fact had been pointed out to her last week when Aunt Bea dropped a less than subtle hint that she needed to "step out of your comfort zone, dear." And Flo, one of her assistants at the Maple Falls Library, had once again offered to introduce her to her grandnephew, a "charming" young man who was still "finding himself."

A thirty-eight-year-old guy without a plan? No thanks.

She stared at the empty screen. Over the past five years, she'd seen a variety of films in numerous genres. Noirs, musicals, World War II epics, farces, westerns, and the occasional foreign flick with subtitles. But *The Quiet Man* was her favorite. She watched it at least twice a year. She should be eager to see it for the thirteenth time.

Instead, she was restless, and not only because of her aunt and coworker. For a single second she'd considered not coming tonight and doing something different instead. What that would be, she had no idea. Diverging from her plan wasn't part of the plan, and her five-year habit of sitting in the seventh row, tenth seat was a hard one to break. So here she was, attending vintage movie Monday again. And after the movie was over, she would go home alone . . . again.

She glanced around and noted a few college-aged students sprinkled among the seats, most likely students from nearby Henderson and Ouachita Baptist universities. To her left, three rows back, she noticed a couple sharing their drink. The girl leaned her head on her date's shoulder, her expression blissful.

Olivia faced forward again. When was the last time she'd been on a date? Much longer than five years.

Talk about a rut.

A man plunked down on one of the chairs two seats

over, a bucket of popcorn cradled in the crook of his arm and a drink in his other hand. Curious, she glanced at him. This was the first time anyone had sat near her in five— Wait. She knew this guy. "Kingston?"

His light-brown eyebrows furrowed over cornflower-blue eyes. Then he grinned. "Olivia?"

She returned his smile. Kingston was her best friend Anita's older brother, and Olivia hadn't seen him since last summer, when he'd made a rare appearance at one of the church's softball games. She inwardly cringed, remembering that despite her determination to overcome her exceptional lack of athleticism, she'd been awful. Oh well; this was Kingston. She wasn't out to impress him.

He glanced at the empty seat beside her. "Are you waiting for someone?"

She shook her head and motioned for him to join her. He quickly moved to the seat as she took another sip of her drink.

Kingston balanced the popcorn on his knee and set his drink on the floor. The Sunset had been constructed before the dawn of built-in cupholders. "I didn't know you were an old-film buff."

"Every third Monday night," she said. *Sigh.*

"Me too. When I'm not on call, that is. Usually I'm running late, so I sit in the back. Popcorn?" He tilted the bucket toward her.

"No, thank you."

"I can't eat all of this. I should have gotten a medium."

She was a little hungry, having skipped lunch this afternoon to work on the youth spring program at the library. As head librarian, she had a variety of jobs and tasks to do, but planning the programs for the kids was her favorite. "Just a few." She picked three kernels and ate them. Hot, buttery, salty. Yum. Why hadn't she gotten popcorn before now?

Because I always get a Diet Coke, and only a Diet Coke.

He shook the bucket a bit. "How's the library business going?"

"Good." Better than good. After years of hard work, and plenty of near begging for extra funds from stingy Mayor Quickel, the Maple Falls Library was finally where she wanted it to be, especially the children's and young adult programs. She'd even had nearby librarians ask her for advice on how to implement her ideas into their own systems. "Still busy with your practice?"

"Yep. I do some volunteer work at the health department too. And a bit of teaching on the side at Henderson." He shoveled a handful of popcorn into his mouth. When he finished chewing, he asked, "Have you seen this movie before?"

She glanced at the straw poking out of the plastic top of her cup. "Once or twice."

"I haven't."

"Really? And you call yourself a film buff?"

"I guess I'm an aspiring film buff, when time permits." He settled back in his seat. "This is a nice spot. Much better than the back row."

Olivia nodded. As she turned to him, a sudden pleasant shiver danced down her spine to her toes. She froze. Kingston had always been good-looking. Through the years even she'd noticed—when she bothered to take her nose out of whatever book she was reading. But she'd never *felt* anything when she saw him. Until now. He'd taken off his charcoal-gray puffer jacket without spilling the popcorn, and his blue-and-white checked shirt paired with khaki pants and tan dress shoes looked good on him.

Very, *very* good.

Normally she wouldn't care that one of the—if not *the*—most eligible and desired bachelors in the greater Hot Springs area was sitting right next to her, especially since he was Anita's brother. But good gravy on a biscuit, was he *gorgeous*. And as she kept looking at him, she experienced something nice. No, *nice* wasn't the right word. More like *delectable*.

Her cheeks heated, and she stared straight ahead. Where had all that come from? She'd never put *Kingston* and *delectable* or *gorgeous* in the same sentence.

"Have some more." Kingston set the popcorn bucket between them.

She snuck another glance at him. *Delectably gorgeous.* She jerked her head away and pinched the top of her straw closed.

"Do they show commercials here like they do in other theaters?" he asked.

"Uh, what?" she replied, still grappling with the unfamiliar thoughts and sensations he was causing.

"You know. The previews before the previews." He frowned. "When was the last time you saw a current movie?"

She thought about it, grateful to have something different to focus on. "Eleven years ago." That had been a group outing with her fellow students when she was in college getting her master's in library science. She would have preferred to continue studying—she had fast-tracked both her bachelor's and master's degrees—but her study partners insisted she go with them. She couldn't recall what the movie was, only that she'd found it dull and preferred her classics.

"Wow, that long," Kingston said. "I don't blame you. Most of them are garbage anyway. So what do you and your dates do for fun, then?"

"Dates?"

"You know." He gave her a wry look. "Guys you go out with?"

"Oh, I don't have any dates." Her cheeks flamed.

He scoffed. "You're kidding."

She shifted in her chair. How had they ended up on this topic? She'd never been bothered by her lack of a dating life before . . . for the most part. *Thanks, Flo.* "No. I'm not."

Kingston paused. "Always the serious librarian."

"I'm not always serious—" Wait. That was exactly true. She was a serious person, in addition to being in a serious rut.

"Hey, it's not an insult. I've been accused of the same thing myself."

"By your dates?" She arched a brow.

He glanced away. "Um, a couple. There haven't been that many for a long time."

He said the last words so quietly that she barely heard them. Shocker. She knew he was busy, but she figured he'd made time to date.

He was smiling again. And once again, she couldn't look away. He appeared relaxed, almost boyish, making him even more attractive. Her spine started tingling.

Oh no. This wasn't good. It felt good, but she wasn't

supposed to tingle around Kingston. She wasn't twelve. She was twenty-seven, and he was her best friend's brother, not some teenage crush.

But the sensation inside her wasn't adolescent. It was definitely *adult*.

Thankfully the lights dimmed, and images hit the screen. She could pay attention to the movie and not the tingle. She faced the front and, without thinking, shoved her hand into the bucket. Instead of popcorn, her fingers brushed against his.

Tingle. Tingle.

She jerked away, tipping the popcorn to the floor. "Sorry!"

"Shhh" came from several directions in the theater.

"Sorry," she whispered. She reached for the bucket as he scooped it up, leaning close. Their shoulders touched.

Tingle tingle tingle. Three tingles now?

"Don't worry about it," he whispered back. "There's still plenty to share."

A steam engine appeared on-screen, smoke billowing out of the top, the wheels chugging, horn blowing. But it was all background noise. Her ears were tingling now too.

None of this made sense. This was Kingston, Anita's brother. A guy she'd known all her life but admittedly knew little about. And this was her favorite movie, in her favorite theater, on the third Monday in January. She wasn't about to be distracted, not when Wayne and O'Hara were on the screen. She would ignore Kingston, enjoy the movie, and stay away from his popcorn. Afterward, they would say goodbye and go back to their busy lives, two classic-film buffs passing through the night. The tingling would disappear, and although she might give a few minutes of thought to why she'd even tingled to begin with, she would go back to her rut.

Just like she always did.

Kingston had experienced several surprises so far this evening. First, he'd gotten off work early—which was more a miracle than a surprise. Second, he'd arrived at the theater before the feature film had started, something that hadn't happened for at least a year. Two, now that he thought about it. Coming to the Sunset was his secret indulgence—it gave him a chance to relax with very little risk of running into a parent of one of his patients.

The third revelation was finding out that Olivia Farnsworth was a vintage-movie fan.

And the fourth—and most confusing—surprise was that he couldn't take his eyes off her.

The Quiet Man continued to play on the big screen, accentuated by the scents of salty popcorn and ancient upholstery. Currently an aggravated John Wayne was arguing with a spunky Maureen O'Hara, but Kingston had no idea what the fight was about. He was trying to figure out when he'd last seen Olivia and if at that time he'd had such an intense . . . Well, he wasn't sure how to define his reaction. *Attraction* seemed too strong a word, and *curiosity* didn't quite fit. All he knew was that for the first time in months, maybe close to a year or so, he was in the company of a female who didn't

work for him, wasn't related to him, and wasn't the mother /
aunt / grandmother / legal guardian of one of his patients. It
was nice.

He tried to focus on the screen again. He'd known
Olivia since she was a young girl and he was a goofy—in
his opinion, anyway—yet driven kid. Even then she'd had
chin-length stick-straight black hair and flawless olive skin,
and she had always seemed older than her chronological
age. She and Anita were usually inseparable, and she had
stayed for dinner and/or spent the night more times than he
could count during those years. Often, he'd been too busy
with school, sports, church activities, and whatever else his
mother expected of him to pay attention to either of them.
The other times she was just Anita's little friend, both in
stature and in age, and he'd barely noticed her.

For some mystifying reason, he was noticing her now.

Although he tried to stop from looking at her again, he
failed and watched as she mouthed the movie's words:

"Don't touch me. You have no right."

"What'ya mean, no right?"

Kingston glanced up at the movie to see the two leads
standing in front of an Irish cottage, the woman in a wedding
dress. Huh. When had they gotten married?

*"Until I got my dowry safe about me, I'm no married
woman."*

He'd spent so much time thinking about the past and
gazing at Olivia that he'd lost the plot of the movie, and he
couldn't exactly ask her what was going on without looking
like an idiot. He grabbed another handful of popcorn and
watched as the couple continued to fight.

"This is my favorite part," Olivia whispered, more to the screen than to him.

Wayne had just kicked down the bedroom door. Now he was kissing O'Hara, and quite passionately—for the 1950s anyway. Kingston looked at Olivia again. She stared at the screen, mesmerized, her hand gripping her soft drink.

Her favorite part was the make-out scene. *Interesting.*

Wayne scooped O'Hara up into his arms, carried her to the bed, and plopped her down on it. *Snap!* The bed broke.

Kingston jumped, not expecting the result. The woman was unharmed—and had kind of gotten what she deserved, considering her petulance.

Olivia softly chuckled.

He looked at her again, the light from the screen illuminating her smile. Had she always had such a pretty smile?

He must be overworked (always) and overtired (ditto), because he was paying way too much attention to her and not the movie. Using the laser focus that had made him Maple Falls' valedictorian and gotten him through an Ivy League college and medical school in under seven years—including his internship—he set his mind to watch *The Quiet Man* and his not-so-quiet lady.

When the credits started to roll, he thought he heard a sigh coming from Olivia. "I guess you enjoyed the show," he said, picking up the almost-empty bucket of popcorn.

"I always do. Especially when it's this movie." She gathered her purse and coat, then stood.

He rose as well. "How many times have you *really* seen it?"

"Thirteen. And a half. Aunt Bea interrupted me the third time I saw it."

"With a phone call?"

"No. Blackberry cobbler." She glanced at her shoes, smiling a little. "I can't resist it, and she doesn't allow food in the living room."

"Neither does my mother." He picked up his coat and exited the row, then waved for her to go ahead of him. When she passed, he detected the scent of "clean laundry." An actual scent—he'd seen the words on the detergent bottle in the laundry room growing up. How such a utilitarian fragrance smelled almost irresistible on Olivia, he had no clue.

They walked up the aisle and out of the theater door. He tossed the popcorn bucket in the nearby trash can as she started to slip on her black coat. Partly out of good manners and mostly out of the unexpected need to be closer to her, he said, "Allow me."

She nodded and he took her coat. When she turned around, he noticed her outfit—a dark-green sweater with a collared white shirt underneath, a black skirt that hit below her knee, black tights, and flat black shoes. If she had a pair of glasses, she would be the picture of librarian chic.

"Thanks," she said, putting her arms into the sleeves.

"No problem." He draped the coat over her shoulders, catching that scent again. Her scent.

What is the matter with me?

Olivia turned and faced him, having to look up because of her short height. He figured he was about a foot and a few inches taller than her. The last girl he'd dated, eons ago, had been closer to his height, making it easier to kiss her. Wait, had he kissed her? He literally couldn't remember. But now that he was thinking about kissing—

"I guess I'll see you around," she said. "At Anita's wedding for sure, right?"

Right. His sister's wedding. His other sister, Paisley, had gotten married last year to her lawyer husband, Ryan. He was a good guy, as was Tanner, Anita's fiancé.

Wait a minute; the wedding was in August, wasn't it? Hopefully Janine, his admin, had put it on his calendar. "Are you a bridesmaid?"

"Maid of honor." A touch of pride shone in her dark-brown eyes. "Lonzo is the best man."

"Yes." It was coming back to him now. In addition to Tanner's younger brother, he, Hayden, and Ryan were the other groomsmen. Riley, Hayden's wife, and Harper, one of Anita's good friends, were the other bridesmaids, along with Paisley. "I guess we'll see each other at the rehearsal dinner." Eight months away.

She nodded, and the lights started dimming in the lobby. He glanced at the empty popcorn machine and glass candy case. Apparently, the old man running this place was in a hurry to get home. He opened the door for Olivia, and she walked out in front of him. "Where did you park?" he asked.

"There."

She pointed to the first car in the parking lot, approximately twelve steps away from the front door, give or take a few. That was disappointing. He'd parked his Audi in his usual spot, at the back of the gravel lot that sat adjacent to a large field. At one time the Sunset had also had a drive-in screen, but that had been torn down sometime in the late eighties, according to his father. He hadn't needed to park so far because he'd been early for once, but old habits died hard.

"See you later." Olivia waved and started for her car.

He moved to wave back. He would head for his car as well and drive to the condo he'd rented four years ago in Malvern. He'd intended to live there for only six months and then buy something permanent. The location was convenient—between his Hot Springs and Malvern clinics—and not too much of a drive to the Garland County Department of Health, where he volunteered every other month. But time had gotten away from him, and he was still living in his rental. And like his mother constantly, *constantly* reminded him now that she had one daughter hitched and another engaged, thus leaving him the only target for her matrimonial pestering, if something didn't change, he'd live there for the rest of his life. Alone.

"Alone, Kingston. Utterly alone." Mother had pointed out that depressing fact to him yesterday afternoon at his parents' monthly Sunday brunch. Being in his thirties and *utterly* alone was a little disheartening now that he thought about it. Usually he was too busy to think about anything related to his personal life.

As he watched Olivia walk away, a cute bundle of black heading to her small vehicle, he didn't wave. He didn't head for his car either. Eight months. That was a long time to wait to see her again. They used to attend the same church, but he'd started watching an online pastor on the Sunday mornings he wasn't working, so he hadn't been to Amazing Grace in a while. And with his schedule, he couldn't count on bumping into her here next month.

"Hey." He sounded like a frog with a pack-a-day smoking habit. He cleared his throat. "Olivia."

She turned around. The lone lamp in the parking lot highlighted her surprised expression. "Yes?"

He moved to stand in front of her, and his words disappeared. That had never happened to him before. He was nuts. Had to be. Or his mother had gotten under his skin, something that was happening more often lately. Or he was dealing with the lingering aftereffects of a good romance movie—one he'd enjoyed once he started paying attention to it.

"Is something wrong?" Olivia asked.

Her soft voice brought him back to reality. He couldn't stand there much longer in silence, not unless he wanted her to think he was off his rocker.

I probably am.

What was the worst she could say? No? It wasn't like he hadn't heard that word a million times before, especially when dealing with some of his more precocious and, let's face it, spoiled patients.

But he'd never been turned down by a woman before. Ever. And for some reason, he knew if Olivia turned him down, it would bother him. A lot. "Would you like to go out?"

Her eyes widened. "Out?"

"Yeah. Like to . . ." Uh-oh. He hadn't thought that far. Where could they go? Coffee. That would work. "There's a coffee shop a couple miles from here. We can get a cup and catch up."

"I don't drink coffee."

Oh. He probably should have known that. But then again, how would he? He didn't know that much about her, which was surprising since she was Anita's closest friend. But he hadn't been that close to Anita lately either.

She looked at her watch. "And it's past nine p.m. I'm always home by nine thirty on Mondays."

Ouch. He should have just driven home to his empty condo. That would have been less painful. Nothing like getting rejected by a childhood acquaintance, even if it was just an invite for coffee. "Yeah," he said, backing away and forcing a smile. "It's pretty late." He gave her a half wave before turning to leave. "See ya."

She nodded and turned toward her car again as he headed for his. He'd taken half a step when he heard her say his name. He stopped and whirled around.

"I . . ." She tugged on one of her coat cuffs. "I suppose I can stay out a little later tonight."

He grinned. She sounded like a teenager on a curfew. Oddly enough, he was feeling a little like a kid himself right now. "Hang on. I'll pick you up." He started to turn.

"I prefer to drive."

"Okay. I'll meet you there—"

"Wait." She paused, then nodded. "I'll ride with you."

He stuck his hands into his pockets, unable to stop smiling as they walked to his car. Sure, this was Olivia. And they weren't going on a date or anything. It was also nice not to have to go back to an empty house just yet. But that didn't mean anything either. They were two friends who hadn't seen each other in a long while, getting coffee after a movie. Simple as that.

Considering Dr. Kingston Bedford was highly successful at everything in his life, Olivia would have easily guessed he'd be good at kissing. That is, if she'd ever thought about *kissing* and *Kingston* in the same sentence. But as of two minutes ago—or was it three? She had no idea—she was discovering exactly how phenomenal he was. Not that she had anything to compare . . . him . . . to . . .

Whatever thoughts were left in her head, they disappeared.

Minutes or hours later—again, no idea—he finally pulled away and leaned his forehead against hers. "That was . . ."

"Amazing." She sighed, her pulse hammering in her chest, throat, and everywhere else. Her clasped hands rested at the base of his neck. Every single second in his arms had taken her breath away, literally. And she found herself hoping he'd take it away again.

Then she blinked. Moved her forehead from his and looked around. How had she ended up sitting on the hood of his Audi? She barely remembered getting out of the car, because he had started kissing her the minute they'd returned to the Sunset parking lot and he'd opened the passenger door. Her face, already hot despite the thirty-degree temperature outside, flamed.

Kingston's eyes widened, as if he'd finally figured out where he was and what he'd been doing. He dropped his hands from her waist at the same time she unlocked her legs from around him. He stepped back and threaded his hand through his hair.

Please don't say you're sorry.

"I'm sorry." He shook his head and looked to the side. "I . . . I don't know what happened."

She kicked herself for being so stupid. When Kingston asked her to go to the coffee shop with him, she should have listened to her gut. Instead, she'd second-guessed herself, seeing his offer as a prime opportunity to stick her little toe out of her comfort zone and ignore her evening schedule of being in bed no later than ten thirty. It was well past that time, and all she had for her trouble was sheer embarrassment. She couldn't even enjoy the memory of those amazing kisses, not when regret was splashed all over his face.

And now she had to come up with something to say, some way to explain why she'd been perfectly fine sitting on the hood of Kingston's car, kissing him with reckless abandon, without giving a single thought to any repercussions. She had to clarify that this wasn't her modus operandi. Not even close.

"I just want you to know—" they said in unison.

He chuckled, but it sounded awkward. Probably the first time in his life he'd ever experienced such a thing. Her feet dangled over the side of the hood as he moved a few yards away, putting plenty of distance between them.

Then he was suddenly closer, though not as close as he'd been a few minutes ago. Before she could decide whether she was relieved or disappointed, a half smile formed on his lips. "I want you to know that I don't go around inviting women out for coffee so I can make out with them."

"I didn't think you were." Which was true. She couldn't imagine him being anything but the perfect gentleman. Although she'd just discovered firsthand that he was a little wicked around the edges.

"But . . ." He shoved his hand through his hair, leaving

the ends messy and sticking out all over. She almost lost her mind and reached over to smooth them down, catching herself at the last second.

"I really enjoyed the movie," he said. "And the coffee, and tea. I didn't know you were an Earl Grey girl."

She had to smile at that.

"And . . ."

If he apologized again, she was going to kick him. Softly, though. Just a light tap on the side of his leg. She didn't want to hurt him. "And?"

He surprised her by cupping her cheek with his large hand, the palm covering half her face. "And I thoroughly enjoyed this." He bent down and kissed her, lightly this time, before he drew back. Then he held her gaze. "Are you okay?"

If "okay" meant floating on a cloud while melting into a flustered, boneless puddle, then she was absolutely okay. She nodded.

He moved his hands to her waist. "Probably not a good idea for you to stay here," he muttered, lifting her with ease and setting her on her feet.

"Thank you," she said.

"You're welcome."

So formal, when less than a few minutes ago they'd been anything but. She glanced at her car parked next to them. And because she'd always believed being straightforward was best, she looked back up at him. "Where do we go from here?"

Confusion flashed in his eyes, then disappeared. He smiled again. "How about an official date?"

Surprised, her pulse tripped again. The idea of a date with Kingston would have seemed ludicrous even two hours ago.

But was it? The time they'd spent talking at the café had been nice, easy, and comfortable, even if she was still tingling from sitting next to him during *The Quiet Man*. But it wasn't long before she'd forgotten her physical reaction to him and discovered they had a lot in common other than watching old movies. He was extremely smart and well read. Being a true nerd, she appreciated his interest in reading and learning. She already knew he was devoted to his family—when he had the time to be. And when he enthusiastically told her about his volunteer work—without revealing any patient information—he almost had her convinced that she should volunteer at the health department, too, even though the sight of blood made her feel faint.

Then on the drive back to her car, she'd wished the evening didn't have to end so soon. She'd gotten her wish— and they'd extended their time in the best way possible.

"Olivia?"

His handsome face came into focus, the uncertainty in his eyes surprising her. Confident Kingston Bedford was worried she'd say no. She probably should. She'd gone out of her comfort zone enough tonight, and she didn't want to end up hurt. But this was Kingston, the most upstanding man she knew.

Not to mention those kisses. "Yes." She drew in a deep breath. "I'd like to go out with you."

He grinned and pulled out his phone. When she realized her purse still sat on the passenger seat, she opened the door, grabbed her bag, and shut the door with her hip. Quickly she took out her cell.

"The earliest I have is next Tuesday," he said, scrolling. "Will that work?"

"Our monthly staff meeting is Tuesday evening. I usually order takeout from the diner while we work. We won't wrap up until eight thirty."

He ran his finger over the screen. "Next Wednesday?"

"Church. And I have to be at the library early Thursday morning to set up our biweekly homeschool workshop." She looked at her calendar. "What about a week from Friday?"

"I'm on call." He frowned. "How about I call you? I might be able to switch some stuff around, but I need to check with my admin. She'll kill me if I mess with the calendar without her permission."

Olivia understood. Calendars were sacred. "Here's my number." She told it to him as he entered it into his contact list.

"Cool." He slipped the phone back into his pocket. "Until next time." He took her hand and kissed the top.

She almost sighed out loud. Corny, but the perfect gesture. And he waited as she got in her car and pulled out of the lot before getting into his vehicle.

On the drive home, butterflies danced in her stomach. Kingston Bedford. Who knew? She certainly didn't, and she doubted Anita had ever put the two of them together either, or she would have brought it up to Olivia before now.

But she wasn't going to tell Anita anything until her and Kingston's first official date. And maybe not even after that, since the wedding preparations were taking up a lot of Anita's time, thanks to Karen. Anita and Kingston's mother could test the patience of a saint, even though she meant well.

No, best to keep things to herself until the right moment. She grinned. Aunt Bea would be so tickled that Olivia had taken her advice.

Next time, she might even try the coffee.

Chapter 1

Eight months later

Kingston yanked at the collar of his white dress shirt while the other groomsmen talked to Tanner, the nervous groom. As the bride's brother, he knew he should have some words of wisdom to impart to the man who would be his brother-in-law in less than an hour, but he had zip. How could he think about marriage advice when (a) he was still single, and (b) all he could think about was how mad Olivia must be at him?

Sweat broke out on his brow, and he stepped outside of the preschool Sunday school room at Amazing Grace. The women were using the larger third- and fourth-grade classroom to get ready, as was fitting. What was Olivia doing right now? Probably organizing everything and everyone. Maybe if she'd overseen his calendar, they would have gone on their official date.

If he could physically kick himself, he would. After

he'd asked her out for coffee—and subsequently found his equilibrium after their incredibly impulsive and incredibly incredible make-out session—the natural next step had been to ask her out on an actual date. He'd hesitated for only a second, mostly because he knew the next few weeks would be chaotically busy for him, but he had asked her anyway. In that moment, he'd wanted to see her again more than anything. And he had fully intended to call her and set up a time to take her to a steakhouse in Hot Springs that had a filet so tender you could cut it with the side of a spoon.

But he didn't call her, and they never went out. Instead, he did what he always did. Worked. And by the time two weeks flew by, he realized he'd forgotten his promise.

At that point he should have called her the moment he remembered. But it had been 10:04 p.m., and he knew she liked to keep a strict bedtime schedule. And in the morning when he'd gotten a call from his nurse about one of his patients who had been admitted at Children's Hospital in Little Rock, Olivia was far from his mind and his appointment calendar.

By the time he had a break in his work, almost a month had gone by, and yet he'd still considered calling her to explain himself. But he kept putting it off, and by June it was too late to apologize.

Before he knew it, Anita's rehearsal dinner was upon him, and he'd fully intended to go and face the music with Olivia somehow. But he'd been called to the hospital at the last minute, earning a well-deserved haranguing session from his mother, who afterward had instructed him on what to do the day of the wedding. His father was a cardiologist, and his family usually wasn't completely bent out of shape, having gotten used to short-notice cancellations over the years. But missing the rehearsal dinner? That had strained their goodwill.

"Mark my words, Kingston," Mother had said in a stern, harsh voice he hadn't heard her use on him since he'd gotten a B in art in sixth grade—his one and only B. "If you don't show up tomorrow, you're going to break Anita's heart. You'll break all our hearts."

He kept to himself the fact that he'd been to three weddings already this summer. But those were for his clinic partners' kids, who had all seemed to get engaged and plan their nuptials at the same time. He only made an appearance at those and left as soon as he could, his obligation finished. But he didn't dare mention that to his mother. She'd have an epic conniption.

So here he was, ready for his sister's big day and still unprepared to see Olivia again.

"It's time." Hayden clapped him on the shoulder. "The bridesmaids are already in front of the sanctuary. Except for Harper. She's running late."

Whew. That took a little pressure off since he wouldn't be the only one in Olivia's bad graces.

When he got to the foyer in front of the sanctuary, he tried to make eye contact with Olivia. She wouldn't acknowledge him. Pressure back on.

Harper finally showed up and took her spot by his side. The two of them were paired up, and with her sky-high heels, she was only a few inches shorter than he was. After twenty minutes of being ignored by Olivia, then listening to her and Harper bicker for the last five while they waited for the cue to walk down the aisle, he turned to them. "Ladies, can this wait?"

"Sorry," Olivia murmured, staring down at her pale-green low-heeled shoes. Then she looked straight ahead and straight through him.

He clenched his jaw and faced forward as the couples in front of him started to move. First Hayden and Riley, then Ryan and Paisley. Then it was his and Harper's turn. As he took his place next to his brother-in-law, Ryan, he forced himself not to watch Olivia as she moved down the aisle with Lonzo. This was Anita's day, and he had to set his personal issues—and failings, in this case—aside.

Less than forty minutes later, they were congratulating Mr. and Mrs. Tanner Castillo.

His stress eased a bit seeing his sister so happy. He'd long suspected she had a crush on Tanner, and that had ended up being the case. As for Tanner, he was a great guy. Anyone could see how much he loved Anita.

The bridal couple and attendants formed a reception line in the foyer and received congratulations from the guests. That all went smoothly until Erma McAllister and her crew, including Olivia's aunt Bea, stopped in front of him and Harper.

"My stars, look at the two of you," Erma said. She leaned over to Bea, along with Peg and Myrtle, the other two ladies with her. "They look straight out of a fashion magazine, don't they?"

"They sure do," Bea said before leaning forward and whispering, "Maybe you two will be the next ones to get married."

He heard Harper laugh, but he didn't find the comment amusing, especially coming from Bea and stated right in front of Olivia. He frowned and glanced at Olivia to gauge her reaction. There was none, as if she hadn't heard what Bea had said. What a relief. Erma and her friends were dead wrong about him and Harper. He'd known her for a few years and liked her well enough. She was stunning, and Erma was right—she did look like she'd stepped out of *Vogue*. But she wasn't his type, and he'd never gotten the indication that he was hers.

After the receiving line ended, everyone dispersed for the reception at the Maple Falls Community Center. He saw Olivia heading for the door, and he thought about catching up with her. But what could he say? Sorry for being a schmuck? He was sorry for so many things—for letting work get in the way, for shoving her off to the side, and for being a coward and not calling her the first moment he'd had free, which would have been the very next morning after their coffee date and before he took a shower. He could have called her while he was *in* the shower. His phone was waterproof. It would have survived.

But most of all, he was sorry he hadn't followed through. Because even though he'd set her aside in his mind to attend to his patients and other work responsibilities, he still felt her. Felt her lips on his, felt the way she'd sighed when he swooped her up and set her on his Audi so they would be at eye—or rather, mouth—level. Felt the warmth of her smile when she said she'd go out with him. Felt so many other things, some confusing, some demanding.

He felt so ashamed for ignoring her.

As if sensing his gaze on her, she turned before stepping outside. She was so beautiful in her bridesmaid's dress—a pale green that complemented her olive-toned skin, with a demure neckline and fabric that flared a little around her hips. Her hair was swept up in a simple updo straight out of a classic film, and her light makeup made her look like a glamorous librarian—and that was a compliment.

He made a move toward her, then stopped, seeing the shields go up in her eyes. She quickly went outside.

It's what I deserve.

The emotional part of him wanted to chase after her, but the logical part of him refused. There were still people in the parking lot, and he didn't want to air personal business in front of any of them and risk being the next topic on the Maple Falls grapevine.

He was heading for the door when Harper appeared beside him. "Can you give me a ride to the reception?"

"Sure."

"Thanks. I just need to get my purse."

When she returned, he held the door open for her. Thick, humid heat hit them, and he pressed the automatic start on his key fob to cool the interior of his car. As they walked, she explained that her Mercedes was in the shop, and that Rusty Jenkins, a local mechanic, was working on it. Harper was always easy to talk to, and as they left the church lot, he said, "I can't believe both my sisters are married."

"That means you're next."

He tried to be good-humored but flopped. "Stop sounding like my mom. Like I told her, I'll get married when I'm ready."

"Okay."

Nuts. He hadn't meant to snap at her. It wasn't her fault his mother wouldn't let up on bugging him to get married, or that the one woman who'd caught more than his passing interest wasn't speaking to him—with good reason. "Sorry." He fought for a smile, and this time he was on point. He explained that being teased at weddings for being single was getting old. She agreed.

He pulled into the lot of the community center, and they both got out of the car. "Thanks again for the ride," she said.

"Anytime." And he meant it. Helping someone in need, even something as simple as a six-minute ride to the community center, usually put him in a good mood. He wasn't in the best of moods right now, but doing a good deed helped.

When they got inside, he saw his mother engaged in a conversation with a caterer that looked like it was quickly heading south. "Uh-oh," he said. "She looks ready to pop off."

"How can you tell?" Harper said. "She looks fine to me."

"That's the calm before the storm. Better go rescue that guy."

"Good luck."

He walked over and lightly put his hand on his mother's back, his fingers brushing the gray silk fabric. Her dress probably cost more than his first year of medical school, and he figured the only reason they were having the reception in Maple Falls instead of at the Hot Springs Country Club was because Anita had insisted.

His mother continued to berate the young man about the color of the napkins. "We agreed they would be eggshell," she said.

"That's tan, right?" The caterer's brown eyebrows flattened. He couldn't have been older than twenty-one, if even that. "My boss said they were what you ordered."

"As if!"

"Mother," Kingston said, knowing she liked formality in front of others. "May I talk to you for a minute?"

She turned to him, as if just realizing he was there. "Now?"

"Yes. Now."

"Fine." She glared at the young man, then allowed Kingston to guide her away. "I hope this is important," she said. "The napkins are a disaster."

"No one will notice them," he said. His sister couldn't care less about napkin color.

She glanced up at him. "I just want everything to be perfect."

"I know. And it will be. It is." For Anita and Tanner, anyway. For himself . . . totally different story.

She smiled and brushed the lapel of his gray suit jacket. "You look handsome, as usual."

"Thanks, Mom."

"You'd be even handsomer if you wiped that sourpuss expression off your face."

He thought he'd successfully masked his feelings. He mustered a smile. "Better?"

"Yes." A small frown. "Aren't you happy for Anita and Tanner?"

"I am. I'm sorry, I was just thinking about . . . I've had stuff on my mind."

She gave him a pointed look. "You know how proud we are of you, King, and how important your job is. But sometimes you have to set work aside and enjoy yourself."

He almost laughed at that. He hadn't thought about work since he'd gotten up this morning. All he could think about was Olivia. "Agreed. On one condition."

"What's that?"

"You take your own advice and stop harassing the staff."

She lifted her chin, diamond earrings dangling against her short, stylish silver hair. "All right," she said, relaxing a bit. "Touché." A gleam entered her eye. "You and Harper Wilson looked stunning walking down the aisle."

"Mother—"

"Wouldn't it be something if you married one of Anita's best friends?"

He paused. It would be something, all right. But Harper wasn't the friend filling his thoughts. "I have one more condition," he said.

She frowned. "It isn't like you to be difficult, King."

He nearly groaned out loud. He hated being called King. What a pretentious moniker. And stating a second requirement wasn't being difficult. Then again, when had he ever pushed back at his mother's requests? Seldom, if ever. "No matchmaking. No mentioning my marital status. And absolutely no harping on me being *utterly* alone."

Her perfectly groomed eyebrows compressed as she squinted at him. "I'm just concerned about you, dear."

"I know." And she did mean well. "Just let it go for tonight. Okay?"

She eyed him a little longer, then nodded. "I will." She rose on tiptoe and kissed his cheek. "Go have fun."

For the next hour or so, he followed his mother's edict and tried to enjoy the reception as much as he could. He worked the room, something that came easily to him, especially with the residents of Maple Falls. He'd grown up with these people, but as soon as he graduated from college, he'd moved to Little Rock and gone to med school. He never exactly reconnected with his hometown the way he'd fit in when he lived there before, and when his parents moved to Hot Springs after Paisley graduated, he was even less involved. But today he visited with everyone, answered their questions about his work, heard a few more compliments about him and Harper, and ended up dancing with her for the bridal attendants' dance.

His duties were done. He would have left if he could, but his mother—and probably at this point his father—would never forgive him.

But he could get some fresh air.

He started to leave the main room, intending to go outside even though it was probably still ninety-nine degrees and 100 percent humidity. He was surprised to see Harper coming back indoors, and that gave him an idea of how to pass the time until he could make his exit. He held out his hand. "Dance?"

"Um, not right now. I hurt my foot a little while ago."

"Want me to take a look at it?"

She waved him off. "I'm sure it's fine."

"You should probably stay off it to keep it from swelling." He looked at her feet. "I'm sure those heels aren't helping."

She nodded. "Thanks for the advice, Dr. Bedford."

"Anytime. Just save me a dance at the next wedding. Maybe you'll be Maple Falls' next blushing bride."

"Hey," she said, feigning offense. "I thought this was a no-teasing zone."

"No teasing *me*," he said, glad to have some lighthearted conversation. "You, on the other hand, are fair game."

She smirked. "Laugh it up, Chuckles," she said, slipping off her shoes. They were back at the entrance of the main room, and she glanced at the bridal table where Olivia was sitting. Alone. "Olivia's free. Why don't you dance with her?"

The exact person he was trying to avoid, and he'd been successful most of the evening. He was sure she was dodging him too. He was about to tell Harper no, then realized he'd have to explain why he was refusing when he'd just asked her to dance. "Uh, sure."

Wait. Maybe this was his chance to make amends. He wasn't completely certain he could, but it was worth a shot. He walked over to the bridal table where Olivia sat alone, staring at one of the small vases of flowers that decorated the long table. He gulped, his palms turning damp. After another deep breath, he said, "Olivia?"

She looked up at him, surprised, then averted her gaze.

"Uh . . . would you like to dance?"

Anger flashed in her eyes, and it was clear she was primed and ready to tell him to buzz off. Or worse. But then she nodded. Perhaps she'd realized the same thing he had—better to let everyone think things were nonchalant between them than to draw attention. After all, he'd already danced with Harper, both his sisters, and Erma McAllister. No one would guess he and Olivia had any sort of history together. She rose from the table and followed him to the dance floor.

The song was a fast disco number, and they weaved their way to the center of the crowd. For a moment neither of them moved, and she spent the time looking in every direction but his. Finally, he started dancing. He wasn't the best dancer, but he could cut a decent rug and pretend he was having fun. Not an easy feat when Olivia looked like she'd just eaten a bag of lemons, skin and all. Her feet barely moved.

This wasn't going to work. He had to settle things between them, and he couldn't do that while half of Maple Falls surrounded them, shaking their behinds to the beat. He took her hand.

"What are you doing?" she said above the noise of the music and dancers.

"Come with me." He tugged, half expecting her to pull back. She didn't, but her hand went limp in his as he led her out of the hall, through the small kitchen where the catering company was starting to clean up for the night, and to a hallway. Then he halted. He'd never been in this part of the community center before. Where was a private place they could talk?

"Kingston—"

He spied a door and walked toward it, still holding her hand. When he tested the knob, it was unlocked. He opened it and found a supply closet. Good enough. He tugged her inside and shut the door, plunging them into darkness.

Uh-oh. Where was the light?

"Kingston," she said, her tone sounding like broken glass. "If you don't tell me what's going on, I'm going to scream."

Frantically he searched for a switch on the wall. Nothing. What kind of closet didn't have a light?

Suddenly he heard a *click*, and light spilled over the confined space. Olivia stood down from her tiptoes, and he noted the single bulb with a long silver chain dangling from it. "How did you know that was there?" he asked.

"The library has sponsored several events at the center." Her tone was crisp as she crossed her arms over her chest. "Now, why did you drag me in here?"

"I, uh . . ." There went his words again, although he still hadn't landed on the right thing to say to her. He'd just taken advantage of the moment to talk to her alone. He looked down at her. Even with her heels, she only reached his chest. He liked it better when they were eye level.

Like on my Audi.

He shoved away the thought and glanced around. When he saw a tall, old-looking stool a few feet away, he grabbed it and sat down. Now she was a little taller than him, but he didn't mind.

She blew out a breath. "Kingston, what are you—"

"I'm sorry," he blurted. "I'm sorry I didn't call you. I'm sorry I didn't set up a date. I'm sorry for being a jerk, and I'm sorry I missed out on the best opportunity of my life."

"Wait, what?"

He inhaled, trying to remember what he'd just said. "I'm sorry I didn't call—"

"No. The last part. What do you mean, the best opportunity of your life?"

He smiled. "A date with you."

She rolled her eyes. "That's laying it on thick."

It might have been, but he meant it. "Olivia, I really am sorry. I was so busy with work, I just . . ."

"Forgot. Right?"

He nodded. "Yeah. I did." He was also ashamed that he hadn't called her when he did remember, and he was about to tell her that when he caught her staring at him under the sallow light of the antiquated bulb. He couldn't get a read on her. She was completely impassive.

"It's okay," she finally said, her tone as limp as an overboiled spaghetti noodle. "It wouldn't have worked out anyway."

Good. She accepted his apology and didn't seem angry with him. He should have been fine with that. Grateful, even, that she was so amenable. But her emotionless declaration bothered him, and he couldn't end things on that note. "I disagree."

Her eyebrows flattened above sharp eyes.

He stood, and due to the small size of the closet, only a fraction of distance separated them. "I think we could have worked out."

"And what makes you say that?"

"Because we fit together." The thought just came to him, but now that it was out of his brain, it made sense.

"You figured that out after a movie and coffee?"

"Well, there was something else that clued me in." When he saw her cheeks flush, he smiled. She wasn't as cold as she appeared. "You felt it, too, didn't you?"

"I . . . ," she whispered, not looking at him.

He brushed away a stray lock of hair that had loosened from her updo. "Maybe we should give this . . . give us . . . another try?"

She looked up at him, and what he saw in her eyes was far from emotionless. It was passion, pure and simple. And quite unexpected from her typical staid demeanor. Pleasantly unexpected, and it made him want to hold her again. But he didn't dare. He'd already been a cad, and he wasn't about to make things worse by taking advantage of her again.

He was lucky she wasn't furious with him for kissing her in the Sunset parking lot. He had never kissed on the first date, and they hadn't even officially had that. But he'd had so much fun with her at the café, and the undeniable connection he'd felt made him lose his marbles. He'd only meant to give her a quick peck on the cheek.

Next thing he knew, she'd been in his arms, kissing him, and he was in heaven.

"Are you serious?" she said, her voice featherlight and tentative. "About us?"

He couldn't stop himself from moving closer. "Yes. I am. And I promise this time, Olivia Farnsworth, I won't let you down."

"You used my last name." A smile played on her lips. "That must mean you're serious."

He chuckled. Touched a lock of hair, then rubbed it between his thumb and forefinger before letting it go again. This intelligent, serious, cute woman with a subtle sense of humor and the softest hair imaginable was knocking him off his feet.

Who would have thunk it?

Her fingers touched his teal necktie. "How do I know you'll keep your word?" She lifted her gaze, a miniscule twinkle in her eye.

He swallowed. "Maybe we should shake on it?"

"Hmm." She placed her palms on his chest. "I'm not sure that will be enough."

His arms circled her waist. "Have any suggestions?"

She stood on her tiptoes and whispered, "A kiss will do."

She didn't have to ask twice. He bent down and kissed her, holding back as much as he could. She'd given him a second chance, and he didn't want to blow it. "Believe me now?"

Olivia nodded. "Yes," she said. "I do."

"Good. Because I'm going to call you tonight after the wedding, and we'll set up a date. And I promise you, Olivia *Farnsworth*, it will be the best one you've ever had."

He never called.

Chapter 2

One year later

$\mathcal{B}$eau's thinking about coming for a visit."

Olivia glanced up from her computer behind the library checkout counter. She, Flo, and her other assistant, RaeAnne, were closing for the evening. "Who's Beau?"

"My grandnephew." Flo straightened the stack of bookmarks Olivia had ordered for the after-school students who hung out in the library until their parents picked them up. School was starting in a week, and there was still so much to do.

"He's the one you've been trying to fix Olivia up with, right?" RaeAnne said. She was straightening the New Arrivals display a few feet from the desk. "Is he still living in his mother's basement?"

Flo scowled. "He's still—"

"Finding himself," Olivia and RaeAnne said at the same time.

"Very funny. I'm sure if he met the right woman, he'd make her a wonderful husband."

Olivia tuned Flo out. She had books to order and snacks to unpack for the vending machine in the seating area away from the bookshelves, and she had to catalog the shipment of magazines they'd received earlier in the day. And she had to get all that done before she met up with her friends at Knots and Tangles in—she glanced at her watch—less than ninety minutes. The Chick Clique, they called themselves. Well, Riley, Anita, and Harper did. Olivia hated the cheesy name.

"Olivia? Olivia?" RaeAnne said.

She continued typing. "What?"

"Maybe you should give Beau a chance."

"Exactly what I've been telling her for over a year now," Flo huffed.

"Not interested." She tapped on the keyboard.

RaeAnne sighed. She was ten years older than Olivia and married with two young boys. Blissfully married, as she liked to remind Olivia and Flo at least twice a week. "I don't understand. You're cute as a button. You should be hitched to some handsome man by now." She turned to Flo. "Is Beau handsome?"

"I think so. His mother does too."

Olivia resisted the urge to roll her eyes.

"You know who she reminds me of?" Flo went to stand next to RaeAnne. "The actress in that mummy movie. What was it called?"

"*The Mummy*?" RaeAnne supplied.

"Yes, that's it." Flo snapped her pudgy fingers. "She was

a librarian too. Very smart. Knew Egyptian. She was also pretty. Had dark hair, right?"

"Yes." RaeAnne rearranged two of the hardback books. "But she was English, not half Hispanic."

"I'm a quarter Hispanic." Olivia continued to type, unable to let the error pass. "Puerto Rican. On my mother's side."

"The English librarian was also taller," Flo pointed out.

"And adventurous," RaeAnne added.

"Well, we all know Olivia's not adventurous."

Olivia glanced up from the computer at Flo's regretful tone. "Not everyone has to be adventurous. There's a lot to be said for staying close to home."

"You mean staying in a rut," RaeAnne mumbled.

Olivia winced. The rut thing again. It had been a year and two weeks since she'd taken a chance on getting out of her rut and ended up crash-landing into heartache. *Twice.*

"You know," Flo said, turning off the lights in the children's section of the library, "maybe what Beau needs is an adventurous woman. That might be just the thing to get him out of—"

"His mother's basement?" RaeAnne chuckled.

"His *rut.* I've been reading about analysis paralysis in this month's issue of *Psychology for Everyone*, and some people overanalyze everything that might go wrong. Therefore, they never take a risk. Sometimes they don't move forward at all."

Olivia's back teeth clenched as she shut down the computer. "It's 5:30 p.m.," she said, eyeing both busybodies. "Quitting time."

RaeAnne saluted her. "Off to the store I go. Trent and I are taking the boys to Lake Catherine for the weekend, and

I have a mile-long list of things I still need to get. At least we have the tent and two coolers already."

"Don't forget the sunscreen." Flo fell into step beside her as she headed for the break room next to Olivia's office in the back of the library. "It's going to be a scorcher on Saturday."

Olivia took a box cutter off the shelf under the counter and walked over to the vending machine. As she opened the box, she tried to ignore RaeAnne and Flo's remarks. First off, she wasn't going out with Beau. She didn't even want to meet him. While he might be a nice guy, even if she was interested in going out—and she absolutely, positively wasn't—she couldn't see herself with someone who didn't have the gumption to move forward with his life. She might be in a rut, but hers was comfortable. Necessary. And she owned her own house.

Her conscience kicked in. For all she knew, Beau could be living in the basement for legitimate reasons that Flo didn't know about. Who was she to judge?

She made quick work of filling the machine with various chips, crackers, and candy, then broke down the empty box and took it to the back storage room. Two words kept coming to mind—*analysis paralysis*. She didn't have the same interest in psychology that Flo had, but she had heard of the term, and it didn't apply to her. She wasn't paralyzed. She liked her life the way it was. And the last time she'd listened to people who thought they knew better, she'd made a mistake. A huge mistake, one she would never repeat again.

Ignoring the pricking in her heart, she went to her office.

RaeAnne and Flo had already left, but she saw a sticky note attached to a flyer and recognized Flo's handwriting.

Forgot to pin this on the bulletin board. Ms. Abernathy dropped it off today.

She peeled off the note as she read the flyer.

LET'S DANCE!

Learn the rumba, waltz, swing, and tango.
Six weeks of fun-filled lessons for ages 18+.

**Put on your dancing shoes and join us
at Abernathy's School of Dance!**

The flyer featured a silhouetted graphic of a couple pressed against each other in a dance pose, the woman in a sheath dress, the man in a trilby hat. In the bottom corner were the date and time—Mondays at 6:30 p.m., starting next week. Hmm. That sounded like fun . . . for someone else.

She went to the front of the library and pinned the flyer on the board. Ms. Abernathy had opened her dance studio last month, renting the building Rusty and Harper owned in downtown Maple Falls across from the Sunshine Café. She taught ballet and tap lessons for toddlers up to high school, but Olivia had no idea she knew how to ballroom dance. She wondered if anyone in Maple Falls would even be interested.

Good luck, Ms. Abernathy.

At six forty-five, she turned off the laptop on her desk, checked the front entrance and emergency exit to make sure they were locked, turned off the lights, and left through the back door. By six fifty-five she was pulling into a parking spot behind the Knots and Tangles yarn shop. Erma McAllister, Riley's grandmother, owned the shop with Riley, and every Tuesday night the Chick Clique—Olivia shuddered—met here. She grabbed her satchel, got out of her two-door car, which hadn't even had time to cool down inside from the oppressive August heat, and entered the back of the shop.

"Hey." Riley was pouring a bag of rippled potato chips into a plastic bowl. All around sat yarn in various stages of being dyed—blank yarn, some drying, some waiting to be twisted into hanks, and some hanks lying next to the yarn winder to be wound into cakes. Different colors, half solid and half variegated. All beautiful.

Olivia pulled a bag of pretzels from her satchel and poured them into another bowl. Anita would bring the coffee and tea from her café two doors down, and Harper, who had now started baking full time after completely leaving the real-estate business this past spring, would bring something sweet and delicious.

Olivia and Riley took the bowls and sat down on the lime-green couch in the middle of the large dyeing area. "How has your week been going?" Olivia asked.

"Busy." Riley yawned. "Extremely busy. We had the yarn crawl last week."

"Oh, that's right." Their weekly meeting had been canceled because of the crawl. Knots and Tangles was on a list of Arkansas yarn shops, and for one week customers could get a map, visit the shops all over the state, and receive a stamp for their passports and small button pins from each retailer. According to Riley, the yarn crawl was one of Knots and Tangles' biggest events. Olivia enjoyed knitting, but not enough to make a weeklong trek around Arkansas, especially right before school started. "Was it successful?"

"Very." Riley leaned back against the couch as Anita walked in the back door, followed by Harper. She waved at the two women and turned to Olivia. "It's going to take me a month to fully recover. But so worth it."

After setting out the beverages—Earl Grey for Olivia, coffee and water for everyone else—and oohing and aahing over Harper's latest confectionary creation of cookie-dough dip with scratch-made chocolate graham crackers, the four women settled with their needles and hooks and worked on their latest yarn project, a lacy shawl. Even Harper, who had always eschewed crafts, was learning how to crochet, having asked Erma to teach her three weeks ago. She had progressed from making a chain and single crochets to now practicing with cotton yarn to make baby-size washcloths.

Anita suddenly dropped her project to her lap. "I can't take it anymore."

Olivia looked at her. "Take what?"

Excitement entered her amber eyes. "I have news."

Harper grinned. "Me too!"

Riley laughed. "I have some as well. Who wants to go first?"

"Anita." Olivia knitted two stitches together. "She spoke first."

"Okay." Anita leaned forward. "I'm pregnant!"

Harper gasped. "Me too!"

"Really?" Anita jumped up, her knitting falling to the

floor, and gave Harper a huge hug. "We're gonna have babies together?"

"Yes!" Harper hugged her back. "I found out last week," she said as Anita sat back down. "I'm only a month along, and Rusty and I were going to wait to tell everyone—except Senior, we had to tell him—but I can't keep it from my besties."

"What did Senior say?" Riley asked with a smile, referring to Rusty's grandfather, who lived with the two of them.

"Oh, he was thrilled. Of course he said if it's a boy, he'll be named Russell Jenkins IV." She paused. "Negotiations are still ongoing." Then she turned to Anita. "Okay, your turn. Spill."

"Well . . ." Anita had picked up her knitting and was glancing at it in her lap. Unlike Harper, she was more reserved. "We weren't exactly trying—"

"Oh, you were doing *something*," Harper cracked.

The tops of Anita's cheeks reddened. "You know what I mean. If it happened, it happened. And . . ."

Riley grinned. "It happened. When are you due?"

"January."

Olivia stilled. Anita had been pregnant for almost four months?

And she's just now telling me?

Anita leaned against the chair. "It feels so good to spread the news finally. Tanner's been wanting to let everyone know for a while now, but I needed to be sure everything was, you know, okay. And it is."

"This is amazing." Riley lifted her coffee cup. "To babies!"

Harper and Anita followed. So did Olivia, but she barely made the toast. No one noticed.

"Okay, Riley, your turn." Harper dipped a graham cracker into the cookie-dough dip.

"Are you pregnant too?" Anita said, hope in her eyes.

"No. You two are a hard act to follow, by the way." But Riley was still smiling. "Hayden's officially running for mayor next year."

"Oh," Harper said, crunching on the dip and cracker.

Anita nodded. So did Olivia.

Riley's grin faded. "All right, I know it's not as exciting or wonderful as having a baby, but come on. A little enthusiasm would be nice."

"We're enthusiastic." Harper grinned. "But that's not really news, is it?"

"The whole town expects him to," Anita added. "Mayor Quickel—ew—needs to go."

"And Hayden is the perfect man for the job," Olivia pointed out.

"Yeah," Riley said, pushing her toes against the rug underneath the coffee table. "He is."

"But?" Harper said.

"I'm not sure I'm ready for all that entails. The campaigning. The time and money he—I mean we—will have to put in."

"I'd be happy to help you with organization and scheduling," Olivia said. "And I can put campaign collateral on display in the library."

"I'll make phone calls and put flyers in the café window," Anita said. "Obviously Tanner will do the same at the diner."

"And I'll handle the PR." Harper grabbed another cookie. "And put together a bake sale or three."

"But you'll both be pregnant," Riley said, then looked at Olivia. "And you're so busy as it is."

"Not too busy for this." Olivia smiled.

"Never too busy for a friend and her soon-to-be mayor husband." Harper lifted her mug again. "To the future Mayor Price!"

"To Mayor Price!"

"And Mrs. Mayor Price," Anita added.

They all toasted, then went back to their yarn work. Now Harper's baby washcloths made sense.

Riley tucked her legs underneath her and wound a strand of purple yarn around her forefinger. "Do you have any news, Olivia?"

"No." Olivia continued with her brioche stitch. "Just the usual."

"Ready for all the school munchkins next week?" Harper asked. "It's hard to believe school is almost in session."

"Yes. I finished all the planning last week."

"Are you taking another class?" Riley asked.

Olivia nodded. Last year she'd received her second master's degree, this one in art history, but she had decided to continue taking at least one college class a semester since most of them were online and fit into her schedule. "I start Eighteenth-Century English Literature on Thursday."

"Sounds thrilling." Harper winked at her.

"I enjoy studying and dissecting literature," Olivia said. Although, truth be told, she had glanced over the syllabus, and the topics did look a bit dull. But she'd never dropped a class before, and she wasn't about to now.

No one said anything for a few seconds. Then Harper

and Anita turned to each other and began to exchange pregnancy notes.

Riley's phone rang. She grabbed it off the coffee table and slid her finger over the screen. "Hi . . . No, it's okay, Mimi. You're not interrupting anything . . . I'm not sure if we have that colorway in stock, but I can check." She stood.

"Tell Erma I said hi." Olivia turned her needles to knit the next row.

Riley gave her a thumbs-up and disappeared to the front of the store where the yarn was displayed and available for purchase.

As Anita and Harper continued to discuss their early-pregnancy experiences, Olivia tried to focus on her project. Why hadn't Anita told her first? She was her best friend . . . or so she'd thought. But the more she mused, she realized that other than their Tuesday-night meetings at Knots and Tangles, they hadn't spent much time together lately. True, they were both busy. All of them were. But couldn't Anita have at least called?

She couldn't remember the last time they'd talked alone. Even at church Anita was always with Tanner, and they taught the preschool Sunday school class together. During the service the friends all sat together—Harper and Rusty, Riley and Hayden, Anita and Tanner. Olivia always sat at the end of the pew. Alone.

"How far in advance do I have to book an appointment with Kingston?" Harper asked, selecting a large potato chip from the bowl. "Naturally I want him to be our baby's doctor."

Olivia's ears perked.

"He hasn't been taking new patients for a while." Anita frowned. "At least that's the last I heard. I haven't talked to him lately."

"Does he know you're pregnant?"

"Not yet. He's so hard to pin down." She grinned. "But I'm sure it won't be a problem for both of us to get on his schedule."

Harper took another chip. "Have you been hungrier than usual? I sure am. Any weird cravings?"

"Yes! Cream cheese and sardines are my favorite."

Harper tilted her head. "That sounds pretty good, actually."

"It's delicious."

The yarn and knitting needles in Olivia's hands came back into focus. She'd dropped seven stitches listening to her friends, and she was glad they'd moved on from the Kingston topic. She'd listen to them talk about disgusting food combos for the rest of the night if it meant she didn't have to hear that man's name again.

But as she tried to fix her mistakes, a tiny part of her mind wouldn't shut up. Was he busy solely because of work? Or was he dating someone? Or more than one someone? She wouldn't put it past him.

Her chest tightened, and she gripped the needles. Over the last year she'd been able to keep him from her mind, mostly because she was too busy to think about him, even when she was hanging out with her friends. Nights were harder, but eventually she could fall asleep without thinking about—or feeling—him. Reminding herself how badly she'd misjudged him helped. His good-guy facade made her stomach roil.

She would never admit that to Anita, or anyone else. No one needed to know she'd been fooled by him.

"This is for Bea."

Olivia looked up to see Riley standing by her, holding out two skeins of sunny yellow yarn.

"Mimi said she'd forgotten to give these to her on Sunday. You're seeing her tomorrow, right? She and I won't be at church this week. We have a contractor coming to give us an estimate on replacing these old wood floors." Riley lightly stomped her foot for emphasis.

Olivia nodded and took the skeins. She always had supper with her aunt Bea and uncle Bill before Wednesday-night church. "I'll make sure she gets them."

For the next hour the women continued to knit and crochet while talking about babies, interspersed with some campaign planning. Olivia wondered if Riley was feeling left out of the baby talk. She didn't seem to be. Olivia kept quiet and focused on fixing her project, which somehow ended up even more of a mess than it was before.

As they packed up to leave before 9:00 p.m.—Olivia always kept track of the time—Anita walked over to her. "Is everything all right?" she asked in a low voice.

"Of course." Olivia put the knitting in her bag.

"You seemed quiet."

"I'm always quiet."

"More so than usual."

She looked at Anita, still fighting her resentment. "I've had a long day." Not exactly true. Her day wasn't any longer, or any busier, than any other Tuesday.

"Good, then." Anita tugged on the hem of her Sunshine

Café T-shirt. "I thought you might be upset. About my news."

Guilt over hurting her best friend snapped Olivia back to her senses. "Oh, Anita. I'm not upset. I'm so happy for you and Tanner."

"Really?" Anita stepped back, still looking unsure.

"Absolutely." She smiled and meant it, pushing away her petty resentment. "I can't wait to organize a shower for you. Harper too. This is so exciting."

"Isn't it?" Anita beamed. No, she glowed. But her smile faltered a bit. "I'm a little scared," she admitted. "Okay, I'm a lot scared."

"Don't be." Olivia held her hand. "You're going to be an amazing mom."

"That's what Tanner said too."

"Listen to him. He's right."

Anita nodded, smiling fully again. "I'll listen to both of you. And if I have any questions or run into trouble, Kingston can help."

Another twinge. *Don't ask . . . Don't ask . . .* "What's he been up to lately?" Ugh. Why couldn't she obey the smart part of her brain when it came to him?

Anita shrugged. "Working, for sure. Other than that, I don't know. Mom hasn't talked to him much either. She's pretty put out with him. She called his admin last month to schedule a phone call." She chuckled. "I'm sure he got an earful. Oh well, that's Kingston. Always busy. I do miss him, though."

Me too.

Olivia drop-kicked the thought out of her mind as Riley turned off the lights.

"It's nine fifteen, Olivia," Harper joked as she opened the back door. "Sure you won't turn into a pumpkin?"

The three women laughed.

Olivia didn't respond. Normally she didn't mind their teasing her about her passion for punctuality. But tonight it grated. She followed them out of the shop and to her car, waved goodbye, and put her bag on the passenger side as she sat down behind the wheel. She turned on the car and flipped the air conditioner to medium, leaving the window cracked to let the hot, humid air escape.

As the interior cooled, she tried to think about work. School. Church. Aunt Bea. Even Flo and RaeAnne, despite their incessant chatter and nosiness. But Kingston kept rolling around her mind, like a pebble she couldn't get out of her shoe.

So she employed the strategy that had gotten her through the weeks after he'd ghosted her a second time: she tried to be thankful. Even if they had dated, he would have eventually hurt her. She didn't even rate an apology from him. He'd had an entire year to do so. No excuse.

She put her car into Drive and headed home, welcoming the bitterness enveloping her. Anything to short-circuit her brain and extinguish any thought of him. Who cared what Kingston Bedford was doing with his life? She sure didn't. Not. One. Bit.

A short while later, after she'd dressed in her pajamas and prepared a warm mug of milk and honey, she called her mother. Once a week they alternated calling each other, the calls lasting no longer than twenty minutes. That had started when her parents moved to Asheville, North Carolina, after she graduated from high school, and their relationship had settled into a true long-distance one. There were the perfunctory visits on holidays, but other than that, they didn't see each other. Her parents were both academics—her father was a professor of ancient Mediterranean studies, and her mother taught anthropology, both at UNC. They had always been consumed with their careers.

As usual, after the first ring, her mother picked up. "Good evening, Olivia."

"Hi, Mom." She sat down on her love seat and curled her legs underneath her. "How are things in North Carolina?"

"The same as they were last week, dear." Her mother's standard answer.

"Have the leaves started changing yet?"

"You know they don't change until late September."

Olivia fiddled with her mug. "How's Dad?"

"He's looking forward to teaching his Greek classes this year."

"Is there something different about this semester?"

"No. He always looks forward to teaching them."

Her parents were the most predictable people on the planet. "And how is your semester shaping up?"

"The way it always does, dear."

The rest of the conversation consisted of Olivia talking about her library programs as her mother listened and said *Yes* and *That's good* at the appropriate junctures. "Aunt Bea is doing well," Olivia added, checking the time on the large round clock on the opposite wall. Five minutes left. "She and Uncle Billy are taking a cruise next year for their anniversary. I think one of her Bosom Buddies convinced her to go. Myrtle seems to be a big fan of them."

"That's good." Pause. "Have your fall classes started yet?"

"This Friday," she said. "I didn't realize I'd mentioned it to you before."

"You didn't."

"Then how did you know?"

"You haven't stopped taking classes since kindergarten. Your pursuit of education has always been admirable. What degree are you working toward now?"

Olivia smiled. That was as close as she'd get to a compliment from her mom. "No degree. I decided two masters were enough, so I'm taking a single class. Eighteenth-Century English Literature."

"Interesting." Pause. "Our time is up, Olivia. It's been nice talking to you."

"Nice talking to you, too, Mom. Tell Dad I said hi."

"I will. Goodbye."

"Bye."

Olivia ended the call and put her phone on her lap, then took a sip of the milk, which was almost room temperature now. She didn't mind, just like she didn't mind the perfunctory conversations with her mother. There was a time when she'd wished her parents were more . . . normal. But long ago she had come to terms with the fact her mother and father were who they were, and they couldn't be anyone else. They weren't emotionally demonstrative, but they were attentive and supportive—when they were around. Often they were abroad doing research or working overtime teaching classes and writing grant proposals. Aunt Bea had practically raised her, always eager to give her what her parents couldn't—hugs, kisses, quality time, and, of course, something delicious to eat.

Olivia knew her parents loved her in their own way, and she accepted that. But there were also times, especially when she was spending the night with Anita and her family, that she longed for the closeness her friend had with her parents. Karen could be overbearing, and Anita's father, Walter, was often busy with work, yet they had always been close with their kids.

Thinking about the Bedfords' tight-knit family brought a forgotten memory to mind of when she and Anita were in their teens. Paisley was spending the night with a friend, Karen and Walter were out for the evening, and Kingston was also out, although Olivia couldn't remember why. Anita had fallen asleep on the couch, and Olivia was watching TV when Kingston came home, and he'd motioned for her to meet him in the kitchen. He'd fixed a snack and brought out a deck of cards.

"Do you know how to play gin?" he'd asked.

"No."

"It's easy. Someone as smart as you will pick it up in no time."

Olivia stared at her half-empty mug. She hadn't thought about that evening in years. She'd learned the game quickly, and she even beat him at one hand while they munched on potato chips and drank organic apple juice because Karen never allowed soft drinks in the house. When Anita woke up she joined them, and they played cards until midnight when the Bedfords returned home and shooed everyone to bed. As they complied and left the kitchen, Kingston had walked beside her.

"You're a worthy opponent," he'd said, grinning. *"I'll teach you how to play spades next."*

That never happened, since any other time she had spent the night with Anita, he wasn't around. She'd never learned how to play spades. Her parents didn't play cards or any other games, and Aunt Bea and Uncle Billy preferred jigsaw puzzles.

Ugh. She jumped up from the love seat and headed to the kitchen. Kingston Bedford was the last person she wanted to think about.

After washing her cup and putting it in the cabinet, then preparing her lunch to take to work tomorrow, she crossed off the day on her refrigerator calendar and went to bed. As she turned off her light, one last thought crossed her mind.

Did he ever remember his promise?

Not that it mattered. He certainly didn't know how to keep one.

Chapter 3

On Wednesday morning Kingston grabbed the chart outside of the exam room in front of him, checked the name, and inwardly groaned. Sylvia Strickland and her twelve-year-old daughter, Sailor. He was already running late—he'd slept through his alarm and rushed into the clinic at ten minutes after eight—but this would definitely put him behind schedule.

He scanned the nurse's notes. Sylvia and Sailor had been here just last week for the same issue—the warts on Sailor's hand. He'd told Sylvia it would take time for those to disappear.

"Dr. Bedford?"

He turned and saw his admin, Janine, approach at the same time his phone buzzed in the pocket of his lab coat. He pulled it out as Janine stood beside him. A familiar number appeared on the screen. He winced. Ray, the head of the biology department at Henderson, had already left five messages about him teaching an evening class, and Kingston hadn't had time to return any of them. The semester was starting next week. He couldn't keep Ray waiting.

"Dr. Bedford," Janine said, more urgently this time. "What are—"

"Just a sec." He slid his thumb over the phone and scooted past her as he walked to the end of the hall for some privacy. "Hey, Ray—"

"About time you picked up."

Kingston cringed at the bite in his friend's tone. "I promise I was planning to call you back. Things have been hectic." *When have they not been?* "But I'm happy to teach anatomy this semester—"

"We found someone else."

"Oh." He looked up to see Janine waving her arms at him. "Okay."

"Sorry, but I had to hire someone when you didn't return my calls."

"Maybe next semester, then." Kingston lifted one finger and nodded at Janine.

"We should probably talk about your future here at Henderson."

The exam room opened, and Sylvia poked her head out. When she spotted Kingston, she glared and marched toward him. "Dr. Bedford," she said, her tone making Ray's sound downright hospitable. "Sailor and I have been waiting for nearly twenty minutes. She's in pain."

Kingston immediately hung up and put his phone into his pocket. He ignored Janine again and went into the exam room. Sailor was sitting on the table gripping her pink phone case, eyes fixated on the screen with no acknowledgment of him or her mother. Kingston smiled at her anyway.

"How are those warts doing, Sailor?" he said as he put down her file on the counter next to the small sink.

"They're gone." She didn't look up.

"Excellent." He walked over to her. "Can I see your palm?"

As Sailor extended her hand without looking up from her phone, Sylvia appeared. "We're not here about the warts, Dr. Bedford."

"Oh?" He examined Sailor's clean palm, the remnants of the warts barely noticeable. His phone was buzzing again. Probably Ray. Uh-oh. He hadn't meant to hang up on him. He'd have to call him later and explain—

"You didn't prescribe medicine for my daughter."

Kingston let go of Sailor's palm and turned to her, puzzled. "For the warts?" He'd frozen them, so there wasn't a need for the prescription.

"No." Sylvia let out a dramatic sigh. "For her *other* issue."

Kingston wracked his brain. What other issue did Sailor have, other than an unhealthy attachment to her cell phone? He'd talked to Sylvia about that problem as he'd applied the liquid nitrogen to the warts. Clearly, she hadn't taken his advice about limiting her child's screen time.

A knock sounded at the door. Now what? "Just a minute, Mrs. Strickland," he said as he stepped toward it.

"But we've been here for over twenty minutes!" Sylvia huffed.

He opened the door partway. Janine was standing there, panic on her face. "I'm with a patient," he said, frowning. She knew better than to interrupt him when he was seeing patients.

"What about your flight to Dallas?"

"My flight?" Oh no. He was scheduled to speak at a four-day symposium, and tonight was the welcome mixer. How could he have forgotten that? Panic coursed through him. "Did I miss it?"

"You will if you don't leave in the next thirty minutes." She shook her head. "I don't suppose you already have a bag packed?"

"I'll buy stuff when I get there." He leaned closer. "Do I have any more patients after this one?"

"No. But you were supposed to be finished two hours ago—"

"Thanks." He shut the door and hurried to Sailor. "Your mother says you're in pain. What's going on?"

Sylvia moved to her daughter's side. "She's—"

"I'm asking Sailor, Mrs. Strickland."

"You don't have to be rude." Sylvia took a step back.

He glanced at the clock. Janine was right. He had only an hour before his flight left. Fortunately, he was flying out of Hot Springs and not Little Rock, or he'd never make it. The symposium organizers had paid him a large honorarium, and they'd be furious if he was late—

"Cramps." Sailor finally lifted her head and looked at the doctor without a speck of embarrassment. "I've got cramps."

That's what all the fuss was about? "Take some ibuprofen," he said, grabbing the file off the counter.

"Where are you going?" Sylvia said.

"Mrs. Strickland, Sailor doesn't need a prescription for cramps. Ibuprofen will help with the pain." He started to open the door.

"Her pain isn't normal."

Kingston counted to ten before turning around. Sailor was Sylvia's only child, and the woman had a penchant for overexaggerating her daughter's symptoms. "Are you having a lot of pain, Sailor?" he asked.

Sailor shrugged. "I guess." She looked back at her phone.

"Ibuprofen twice a day," he said, already halfway out the door. "She'll be fine, Mrs. Strickland."

"But—"

Shutting the door, he quickstepped to Yolanda, one of the clinic's nurses. He handed her the file. "Ibuprofen twice a day for menstrual cramps," he said as he rushed down the hall and into his office, searched for his laptop bag—where had he put it?—and found it underneath a stack of files on the floor near his desk. He shoved his laptop inside, raced out of the office, and was through the door and into his car without another word to anyone.

In minutes he was speeding toward the airport, making a mental list of everything he needed to buy before he went to tonight's mixer. That done, he spent the rest of the drive berating himself. How could he have forgotten about this trip? It had been on his calendar for months.

As he pulled into the parking lot, his phone rang again, and Anita's name popped up on the dash screen. He let it go to voice mail while he grabbed his laptop bag and sprinted toward the terminal. He reminded himself to call her later after the mixer. And Ray. He had to remember to call Ray. He liked teaching at Henderson, even though he was usually wiped out after he got home late on the nights he taught.

Inside, Kingston ran through the airport and fortunately whizzed through security before he snuck on board as the crew was closing the cabin door. He gave the frowning flight attendant a half smile and a shrug and slid into his seat next to an elderly man who was already snoring. He blew out a breath and leaned back, the sound of the flight attendant explaining the rules and features of the aircraft a low hum in his ears.

His eyes closed. The flight to Dallas was only forty-five minutes. That meant nearly an hour of no phone calls, patients, admins, or other responsibilities constantly tugging at his time. He'd have almost an hour of peace before he hit the ground running again, and he was going to savor every minute, because when the wheels touched down, his quick respite would be over.

But for now, he . . . was going to . . .

Zzzzzz.

"Ladies, I'm concerned about my niece."

Erma placed a bottle of water in front of Bea, who had just uttered this statement, and sat down on the only empty chair in the back room of Knots and Tangles. Everyone had settled in for the weekly Thursday-night Bosom Buddies meeting. She glanced at the rest of the BBs seated in a circle on the lime-green couch and a variety of other chairs. Myrtle, her second closest friend, perched next to Bea. Peg, Viola, Gwen, and Madge rounded out the group. The only one missing was Rosa, who was visiting her youngest son at college this week. BFFs for years, the BBs were always there for one another whenever one of them was struggling. Last year it had been Madge, who had nearly divorced her husband. They'd reconciled and were happier than ever. Before that, Erma and Riley had gone through a family crisis, and now their bond was eternally strong. If Bea was worried about Olivia enough to mention it to the BBs, they would rally around her.

"What's going on?" Madge dipped a tea bag into her white mug.

Bea looked down at her ample lap. "She's lonely."

Several women collectively nodded. "We suspected so."

Bea looked up. "You did? How?"

"Her three best friends are married," Peg said.

Viola nodded. "I was the last one of my friends to get married. I felt so left out."

Gwen patted her on the hand. "That had to have been hard."

"Wait a minute." Myrtle straightened in her chair. "Times were different for us back then. We were all expected to get married. Many of us had to. Olivia doesn't."

"But it would be nice if she did, wouldn't it?" Bea said softly. "She needs companionship. Someone to share life with." She picked up a peanut butter cluster and took a huge bite.

"She could get a dog," Myrtle said. "Or a cat. Pets are good companions."

Bea pointed her half-eaten cluster at Myrtle. "You know that's not what I'm talking about."

Erma agreed with Myrtle, but she wasn't about to voice

her opinion out loud, not when Bea was inhaling the rest of the cluster and already reaching for another one, a sure sign she was upset. "Have you talked to her about it?"

"Mff mnn mnff." Bea held up one finger and swallowed. "Sorry. Not in so many words." She picked up her water and took a gulp before continuing. "I pointed out a while back that she was spinnin' her wheels, so to speak. She's stuck doing the same things every day. Work, school, church, meeting with her friends here on Tuesdays. She never goes out on the weekends anymore."

"Are you sure about that?" Myrtle asked. "She doesn't live with you and Bill. How do you know everything she's doing?"

"Because we're very close. She's more than my niece." Bea's lower lip trembled. "She's like a granddaughter."

Erma couldn't argue with that. Bea and Bill didn't have any kids of their own, and therefore no grandkids. Bea had practically raised the girl. Olivia's parents were two of the oddest ducks Erma had ever encountered, not that she would ever tell Bea that. But Olivia was also a grown woman, and Erma was positive that, just like any adult, Olivia didn't share everything about her life. Still, if Bea was this bothered, there had to be some merit to it.

Or maybe her friend was just eager for her niece to get married. Erma could relate to that. She'd tried to force Riley and Hayden together, and thank the good Lord she hadn't messed things up between them, although it had been touch and go for a while. She'd learned her lesson, though. No meddling. Never again.

"I've been praying for years that Olivia would find a nice

young man," Bea said. "But I think she needs a little help. We need to find her a husband."

Madge grinned. "I know Harper would be eager to assist, like she did with Riley and Anita."

"How did she help them with their relationships?" Peg asked.

"Fashion tips. And moral support. She's so devoted to her friends."

True. The Chick Clique—they really needed to come up with a new name—was turning into the younger version of the BBs, and she couldn't be happier about that.

"Oh, this is going to be fun," Viola said while Gwen giggled and Peg grinned.

Myrtle frowned. "I'm not too sure about this."

"Me either." Erma turned to Bea. "Remember what happened with Riley and Hayden?"

Bea beamed. "They got married!"

"Yes, but that was despite my interference, not because of it."

But the rest of the BBs, save Myrtle, were already buzzing among themselves.

"How many single men are in Maple Falls?" Viola asked.

"That are age appropriate? Four," Gwen said.

"Do we have to limit the search to this town?" Madge leaned forward. "I think we should include Malvern and Hot Springs."

Peg shook her head. "Those cities are too big. How are we going to narrow down the suitable suitors?"

"I know!" Gwen held up one finger. "We open an account on Singles, Inc."

"Yes!" Bea said. "We can create a profile for Olivia and find her true love."

Erma looked at Myrtle, who shrugged and said, "We're outnumbered."

"I can see that." Although her friends had good intentions, this scheme portended disaster. "I still think this is a bad idea," she said above the din.

"Me too," Myrtle added, then muttered, "For what it's worth."

Bea clasped her hands together. "This is so exciting! I can't wait for her to start her quest for love."

"We won't let her down." Gwen nodded solemnly.

"I know you won't." Bea smiled, but it soon faded. "By the way, does anyone know how to use Singles, Inc.?"

Peg shook her head. "I don't even have Facebook." The rest of the conspirators stayed silent.

"I can figure it out," Madge offered. "I've never used a dating site, but it can't be that hard."

"I'll take care of it," Erma piped up.

Myrtle's penciled-in brows lifted. "You will?"

"Absolutely. I am the most computer savvy out of all of us, besides Madge."

Madge lifted her hand. "I don't mind doing it—"

"But you're so busy with your new interior-design business," Erma said. "You need to focus on that, sugar."

Madge hesitated, then nodded. "I am working on building up my client list."

"What made you change your mind?" Bea asked Erma.

I'm trying to save y'all from yourselves. But she couldn't say that, not without her friends' noses getting bumped out of shape, not to mention Bea eating the rest of the peanut clusters in response. "I care about Olivia too. And since I have experience in this area"—*unfortunately*—"I'll get the ball rolling."

"Let us know if you need any help," Gwen offered, and everyone else nodded in agreement.

"I will. But I'm sure I can manage."

The rest of the evening they worked on their various crochet and knitting projects and discussed the latest Maple Falls scuttlebutt, which was rather lean this week. Erma wasn't sure whether Riley and Hayden were ready to announce his intention to run for mayor—and hopefully beat the pants off that cretinous Mayor Quickel—so she couldn't mention that. Fortunately, Olivia wasn't brought up again until after everyone except Myrtle had left.

"All right, Erma Jean." Myrtle put her fists on either side of the waistband of her fuchsia pedal pushers. "What are you up to?"

Erma sighed and wiped down the coffee table. "I'm not sure. I just had to do something to save poor Olivia." She straightened. "Can you imagine the men they'd find on Singles, Inc.?"

"I'd rather not." Myrtle dropped her hands and repositioned the easy chair near the couch. "But what about Bea? She really thinks Olivia needs a husband."

"I know. I'll figure something out eventually. If I lollygag long enough, maybe Bea will get that ridiculous notion out of her mind and let Olivia figure out her own dating life."

"Or Bea might go on Singles, Inc., herself."

"She'll never keep track of her password."

Myrtle chuckled. "True. Well, let me know if you need any assistance. Until September, at least."

"Going on another cruise?"

"No. This time I'm meeting Javier in Key West."

Erma paused. "Really? His idea or yours?"

"His." Myrtle sighed. "We're celebrating our three-year anniversary."

"Congratulations. I gotta say, I was skeptical of you dating a man who works on a cruise ship, but you two proved me wrong. And Javier is a nice guy. I'm glad I got to meet him last year when we went to the Bahamas." That had been a fun trip, and Myrtle and Javier had been inseparable whenever he was on break from work. Myrtle had stayed in Miami for three more days after Erma flew back to Arkansas.

"I was skeptical, too, to be honest," Myrtle said. "I was fine with a hot fling—an innocent one, mind you, if you know what I mean."

Erma chuckled. "We might be old, but we ain't dead."

"Exactly. But things have gotten more serious lately. He's calling every day now—when he's not at sea, that is. And now he wants to meet me in the Keys. We've never done that before."

"Do you think he might propose?"

"I don't know." Myrtle folded in her bottom lip. "Maybe?"

"And if he does?" Erma moved closer to her, even though they were the only ones in the shop. Something this important deserved 100 percent attention. "What will you say?"

"I'm not sure. He isn't interested in retiring, not yet. He's eleven years younger than me, after all, and still has a few working years left. But his home base is in Miami, which means I'd have to move."

Erma's heart panged. She didn't like hearing that, but she wanted her friend to follow her bliss. "You love him, don't you?"

Myrtle's expression turned to mush. "Very much. And he's said he loves me. More than once."

"Then I say go for it."

"Really? You don't think it's too crazy at my age?"

"Absolutely not. If you love each other and want to spend the rest of your lives together, then you should." She hugged her friend. "Have Karla and Michael met him yet?" she asked, referring to Myrtle's daughter and son.

She shook her head. "Not yet. Karla knows I have a 'special friend,' but I haven't said a word to Michael. He's been a little protective since the divorce. I need to wait for the right time to tell him."

"When's that going to be?"

"After the wedding." Myrtle chuckled, then grew serious. "This is pie-in-the-sky talk. For all I know we're just going to have a nice dinner and pineapple upside-down cake for dessert. That's his favorite, by the way." She paused. "Don't say anything to the other BBs. Not until I know for sure what his intentions are."

"Lips are zipped." Erma walked over to turn off the lights. "Not a peep about it."

"Thanks." Myrtle picked up her hot-pink handbag. "I feel a little hypocritical talking about this after throwing cold water on everyone's enthusiasm about finding a guy for Olivia."

"Don't." Erma stood. "You're not looking for a man to love. You already have one. Big difference."

"I wasn't looking at all," she said. "Love found me."

"And love will find Olivia too." If that was what the young woman wanted.

Myrtle waited for Erma to lock up the shop, and they both walked into the heavy, muggy air toward their cars. "What about you, Erma?"

She sidestepped a large pebble. "What?"

"Have you ever thought about getting married again?"

"Pishposh, no." Erma opened her car door. "There was only one love of my life. No one's matched up to Gus McAllister."

"Not even Jasper?" Myrtle winked.

"Good gravy, especially not him." She frowned but felt the corners of her mouth lift a little. Jasper Mathis was an amusing man, mostly because he was so curmudgeonly, and it was hard for her to resist yanking his chain from time to time. But romance? With him? Out of the question. Out of the universe too.

"Hmm. Never say never." Myrtle folded into her car. "Love comes when you least expect it. Look at me and Javier."

"Jasper is no Javier."

Myrtle laughed and shut the door. "He could be, if you'd give him a chance," she said through the open window.

Erma waved off her friend's comment and got into her own car. A few moments later she was heading back to her house, where she lived alone. Riley and Hayden had their own home in a rural area of Maple Falls, and more than once they'd suggested she sell her place. "*We can build you a smaller house next to ours*," Riley had said. But Erma refused. She liked living in the house she and Gus had moved into when they married so many years ago. She would never leave.

She had to pass by Jasper's house on the way to hers, and she tried not to look at his modest—and a little run-down—bungalow that sat within walking distance of Main Street. Hard to do since it was on the corner. A short flagpole was planted in his front yard, and every day, except for the rainy ones, he flew the American flag. She'd always admired him for that, especially since patriotism was becoming so passé among the younger generations.

His car, a silver two-door as unpretentious as his home, sat in the driveway. She recalled that he had lived alone in this house since he was in his twenties. The front porch light was still on, and a flashing glow shone underneath the curtains covering the picture window. She could imagine him sitting inside, probably in a shabby recliner, griping at whatever show he was watching on TV. Jasper could complain about anything—and often did.

She must have passed by his house hundreds of times over the years, but this was the first time she'd paused in front of it, musing about what he might be doing.

The curtains suddenly fluttered. Erma looked at her odometer. Not even five miles an hour! She hadn't realized she'd slowed down so much. She slammed on the accelerator, wincing as she heard her tires squeal.

Had he seen her? She doubted it. The curtains hadn't opened. And if he had, so what? He wouldn't have been able to identify her maroon car in the dark. She blew out a relieved breath and sped off.

As she pulled into her driveway, Olivia came to mind again. She'd never thought about her being lonely. Like Erma, she had plenty of activities to keep her occupied—Bea always kept the BBs apprised, and Riley filled in any gaps. When would she find time to be forlorn?

Then again, Bea knew her niece better than anyone, probably better than even Olivia's parents. Maybe she was seeing something Olivia didn't see in herself. But that didn't give Bea or anyone else the right to poke their noses into Olivia's love life—or potential love life, whatever the case may be.

Erma turned off the engine and frowned. She knew Bea wouldn't let this go, not after she'd publicly declared her intentions. Brother. There had to be a way to nip this in the bud.

She got out of her car, fished her mail out of the box, and went inside the house.

Hmm. Maybe if Olivia did go out on a date, Bea would be satisfied and abandon the husband hunting altogether. And who knew, perhaps that someone and Olivia would hit it off. But there was no way they would find him on Singles, Inc. Not in that pool of sharks.

She set her purse on the couch, scurried to the kitchen, flipped on the light, and found some paper and pen in her junk drawer and sat down at the table. She tried to remember every single man under forty whom she knew in Maple Falls. The pickings were slim, but there were a couple of nice young men who were available. Pastor Jared, for one. Bubba Norton too.

She wrote down two more, then stopped.

What am I doing? Resisting the lure of matchmaking was more difficult than she thought.

She crumpled up the paper and tossed it aside. Tomorrow she would sit Bea down and tell her that she needed to let go of the matchmaking idea and let her niece live her life. Like she'd told Myrtle, if it was meant to be, Olivia would find love on her own terms.

She picked up the mail and thumbed through it, stopping at a colorful flyer with a woman and man dancing on the front. She read the print. Ballroom dancing lessons? Interesting. She made a note to call Myrtle and ask her if she was up for learning some moves before she went to the Keys. She had mentioned that Javier liked to dance—

Wait!

Erma stared at the flyer. Smiled. This was perfect. And it didn't involve meddling, interfering, or shenanigans. She fished her cell phone from her purse and went to her Favorites.

"Bea?" she said when her friend answered. She held out the flyer in front of her. "Forget Singles, Inc. I have another idea."

Chapter 4

"Have a seat, Dr. Bedford."

Kingston slowly lowered himself onto one of two comfortable leather chairs in the office of Dr. Lawrence Smith, the chief pediatrician in his practice. As he always did when he came into Lawrence's office, he glanced at the walls. Awards, commendations, and certificates hung everywhere, and several golf trophies lined a shelf behind the elder statesman, as Kingston silently called him. Kingston enjoyed golf, but Lawrence was obsessed with it.

He stifled a yawn. He'd made the symposium mixer at the last minute, and the rest of the event had been a success. But he'd hit the ground running on Monday morning, and even though it was only Tuesday, he was tired. Really tired.

"I guess you're wondering why I wanted to talk to you." From behind his large desk, Lawrence steepled his fingers together, peering at Kingston through square, silver-framed glasses.

"It crossed my mind." He leaned back in the chair, but inside he felt anything but relaxed. Lawrence—not Larry, Lawrence—had invited him for a chat only twice in the five years since Kingston had joined his practice. Once to welcome him to the team, and the other to give him a pin to commemorate his fifth year of employment. That had been a month ago. Kingston hadn't expected to have a personal meeting with him for another five years. And while Lawrence liked formality, he only referred to Kingston as Dr. Bedford in front of staff and patients. Never in private.

Lawrence leveled his gaze at him, unfolding his fingers and sitting upright. "You're going on vacation."

Puzzled, Kingston shook his head. "I don't have one scheduled."

"You do now." Lawrence picked up a small sheet of paper and handed it to him.

Kingston glanced over it. "What is this?"

"A prescription."

Smith Pediatrics was printed at the top of the script, along with Kingston's name and the other docs who worked in the practice. In the center of the paper where scripts were usually written sat one word: *sabbatical.*

"I don't understand."

"You're taking a break. A long one, at least a month."

"From *work*?"

Lawrence nodded. "From both clinics, from the health department, from hospital rounds. All of it."

Kingston shook his head. "I can't do that."

"You can. And you will." Lawrence pointed to the prescription. "Doctor's orders."

Kingston laughed. "Very funny." He dropped the script on the desk. "I know I've been a little harried—"

"'Harried'?" Lawrence's gray eyebrows lifted. "'Harried' doesn't begin to cover it."

"I'll have a talk with Janine about my schedule. It's been pretty full lately. I'm sure I can free up a weekend or two over the next month or so. And I promise, I won't work on those days."

Lawrence shook his head. "That's not good enough." He took the script, scribbled on it, and gave it back to Kingston.

His jaw dropped at the new instructions. "Two months?"

"It's either that or you're fired. Or worse, you lose your license."

Kingston fell back in the chair. "What are you talking about?"

Lawrence turned to the laptop on his desk and tapped on the touchpad. "Have you checked your medical ratings lately?"

"I never look at those."

"You should." Lawrence cleared his throat and started to read. "'I've been taking my two girls to see Dr. Bedford for over three years and have always been satisfied. But the last appointment was disastrous. He didn't listen to what I had to say, he rushed through their checkups, and when my youngest asked for her lollipop, he completely ignored her and rushed out of the room. He also . . .'" Lawrence looked up. "Shall I go on?"

Kingston shrank. "No. Are there more of those?"

"Ten, at the last count. On this site alone." Lawrence sighed. "You're an excellent doctor and a hard worker. Too hard. You've been spreading yourself thin, and we hoped you would realize on your own how it's affecting your patient care. Instead, I hear you've filled up every Saturday with volunteer work at the health department—"

"You know how shorthanded they are."

"And you're only one person. You can't heal everyone, Kingston. The way you're going, the more you try, the more harm you're doing. You need balance." Lawrence pointed to the prescription. "You need time off."

Kingston couldn't respond because Lawrence was right. He was burning the candle at both ends. In addition to extra time at the health department, he had covered for all the other doctors' vacations over the past year, had gone to visit his patients in the hospital on his off-hours, had attended seven medical conferences on his own dime and his own time, and last semester had taken an adjunct teaching gig at Henderson—and then dropped the ball on this fall semester because he was so busy. He was tired, and sometimes he was cranky and short-tempered with his staff, although he always apologized afterward.

But he'd had no idea he was providing subpar care to his patients. And that included their families. Pediatrics wasn't just about the kids.

"Two months?" he said faintly. "What about my patients?"

"Kim will take over for you," Lawrence said, referring to the advanced practice nurse they'd recently hired. "We've also talked about bringing on another PA."

"I didn't know about that."

"We didn't tell you."

How about that? He was being left out of hiring decisions too.

"We've all agreed to cover for you while you're gone." For the first time, Lawrence's features relaxed. "We all think highly of you."

At least there was a little esteem to hold on to. It didn't make him feel any better.

"That's why we're doing this. It will mean some extra work on our parts, but it will be worth it. You've covered enough times for us. Now we're returning the favor. I don't want to see you burn out. The pediatric profession needs you." He stood and held out his hand.

Seeing no room for negotiation, Kingston rose. "Thanks?" he said, shaking Lawrence's hand.

"You'll be sincerely thanking us for this at the end of your sabbatical. I promise."

Kingston wasn't so sure. He'd never heard of any of his peers taking a forced sabbatical. His father sure hadn't.

Oh, great. Now his parents would find out he'd been compelled to take a vacation. He checked his watch. "I've got a patient scheduled in five minutes—"

"Already taken care of." Lawrence went to the door and opened it. "Get what you need out of your office, and we'll see you at the end of October."

Like a chastised child, Kingston dragged himself into the hallway. Two of the clinic's nurses, Yolanda and Brenda, halted a few feet from him. Then Janine poked her head out of the break room. They were all staring at him.

"Guess I'm on vacation!" He fought for a light tone and

somehow managed it, along with a grin that had to be as natural as processed cheese.

The women broke out in smiles. "Have a great time, Dr. Bedford," Janine said.

"Go somewhere tropical," Yolanda added.

Brenda, who stood next to her, nodded. "We went to Hawaii last year. It was beautiful. And *relaxing*."

Kingston nodded, still smiling as he hurried to his office. The grin faded the moment he stepped inside. He leaned against the door and closed his eyes. Unbelievable. Not only had he made mistakes with his patients, but everyone in the practice knew he was burned out.

Everyone but him, apparently.

Kingston opened his eyes and surveyed his office. There was a time when he'd been meticulous about keeping everything tidy. The disaster in front of him was the furthest thing from neat. He couldn't remember when he'd gotten so sloppy. His desk was cluttered, there were files on the floor, and when he'd arrived half an hour late for work that morning because he slept through his alarm, he'd tossed his laptop bag on one of the chairs in front of his desk. Unlike the other doctors, he kept his door closed.

That was a fairly new development, too, just casting things aside because he was always behind. How had things gotten so out of control?

He plopped down on his chair and ran his hand through his longish hair. He'd been meaning to get a haircut, but he hadn't had the time. He glanced at the closed laptop on the left of his desk. His work computer. After debating for a second, he opened it and started googling. When he found one of the numerous doctor-rating sites listed, he clicked on it, typed in his name, and gasped at the two-star rating with . . . whoa. Thirty reviews. He had a few five stars, but those were more than three years old.

There were always more bad reviews than good—it was human nature to focus on the negative more than the positive. But the ratio of bad to good in the last five months was abominable. Not to mention embarrassing.

"I used to like Dr. Bedford, but . . ."

"He seems to have lost his touch . . ."

"My son asked why he was so cranky . . ."

"I wonder if he has a personal problem . . ."

He cradled his head in his hands. This was worse than being humiliated in front of his coworkers. This was public disgrace. Worse, these ratings could affect, and probably had affected, the entire practice.

This is bad. This is so bad.

Somehow he'd have to make amends to his colleagues, his patients, and their parents. He'd call every one of them and apologize. He'd send Janine and the nurses flowers, golf certificates for the doctors. Except for Dr. Parsley. He preferred sailing. If he had to spend the next two months begging for forgiveness, he would do it—

The door opened, and Lawrence stuck his head inside. "I forgot one thing."

"There's more?" he said weakly.

"You are not, under any circumstances, allowed to contact your patients, caregivers, or any of our staff. You are not to step foot inside either clinic, and the health department already knows you're taking a break."

This was micromanaging on steroids. "Is there anything I *can* do?"

"Yes." Lawrence grinned. "Rest and relax." He glanced at Kingston's messy office. "You can tackle this when you get back."

Kingston didn't have a choice. Now that he saw the problem clearly, he was grateful he hadn't been outright fired. "Yes, sir."

As Lawrence closed the door, Kingston moved to shut down the laptop. He spied a familiar name. Sylvia Strickland.

Don't read it . . . Don't read it . . .

He read it.

"Avoid Dr. Bedford at all costs! He's not only rude, he's also incompetent. My daughter had a serious issue, and he blew it off. She ended up in the ER that night."

He froze. Sailor was in the ER? He reached for the phone to call Sylvia, then drew back. Even if she picked up, as of two minutes ago he wasn't supposed to contact any of his patients. But he couldn't go on his sabbatical without knowing how Sailor was doing. He grabbed the phone and called.

"Hello?"

Sailor? Why was she answering her mother's phone? "Hi, Sailor. It's Dr. Bedford."

"Hey, Doc."

She sounded okay. Typical Sailor, actually. "I heard you were in the ER last week."

"Yeah."

Kingston visualized her scanning her phone as she talked into Sylvia's. "Is everything okay?"

"Yeah."

"Then why were you in the ER—"

"Sailor, who are you talking to?" Sylvia's shrill voice blared in the background. "I told you not to answer my phone."

"But you were in the bathroom—"

"Hello?" Sylvia said. "Who is this?"

He grimaced. "Dr. Bedford. I was checking up on Sailor—"

"You have some nerve. I had to take my daughter to the ER because of you."

"I'm sorry, Mrs. Strickland. That's why I'm calling—"

"She was in so much pain." Sylvia sounded like she was choking back tears. "Fortunately, the ER took us seriously. They gave us a list of things to do to help her. They didn't ignore us, like you did."

He tensed. "What was the diagnosis?"

"Menstrual cramps. But that's the last thing I'm telling you about my daughter. We've found another pediatrician." *Click.*

Kingston stared at the receiver, then hung up. Guilt washed over him. Despite knowing Sylvia was exaggerating Sailor's pain, he should have taken time to reassure her when they were in his office. That's what he'd always done before. He'd been Sailor's pediatrician since the child was six, and he knew Sylvia needed extra attention. But he'd bungled his schedule and had indeed blown them off.

His personal phone buzzed in his pocket. He pulled it out and groaned. *Mother.* This was her third call this week, and it was only Tuesday. He hadn't had time to return the other two, even though he'd promised when she'd made an appointment with Janine that he would be more communicative. Well, he had two unscheduled months to communicate with her now. No reason to keep putting her off.

He slid his thumb across the screen and brought the phone to his ear. "Hello, Mom."

"Kingston!"

Her shocked squeal caused him to pull his phone away from his ear. He put it back.

"I wasn't expecting you to answer. You *never* answer my calls."

Now, that wasn't accurate. Before his life had spiraled, he'd talked to her at least once a week, if not more than that. Pointing out that fact wouldn't do him any favors, though. He leaned back in the chair and closed his eyes again, tension sharp in his neck. "Is everything okay?"

"Yes, everything's peachy. I wanted to remind you about Sunday brunch. You seem to have forgotten our monthly tradition."

His eyes flew open. "I haven't forgotten. I've been . . ." Busy. So busy he'd been planning to skip out again this Sunday. Not this time. "I'll be there."

"Splendid!" Her tone shifted from censuring to enthusiastic faster than a racehorse at Oaklawn. "Paisley and Ryan will be here too. They're making a quick weekend trip."

He hadn't seen Paisley in months. He had always intended to make time for a visit to Dallas but never managed to do so. "Do you need me to bring anything?"

"Just your charming self."

Only his mother could say that and sound genuine. "Thanks."

"I just have one request."

"What's that?"

"A haircut, please. You looked like a vagabond the last time I saw you."

He was certain he'd had a haircut since the last time he saw her, which was . . . Oh, wow. He couldn't remember. A trip to the barber was definitely needed now. "Will do."

"Excellent. It will be so wonderful to have all my children under one roof again. I'm flying in Maine lobster for the occasion."

Excessive, but it was her and Dad's money to spend. And he did like lobster. For the first time since he'd been banned from his job, he managed a genuine, yet small, smile. "Sounds delicious."

"It will be. Ta-ta for now."

He put the phone on his desk and blew out a long breath, then glanced around the office. Like Lawrence, he displayed his certificates and diplomas, along with three basketball trophies that he kept on a shelf, hiding the labels so no one knew he'd received them for intramural play in high school. He'd earned those trophies, regardless of where they came from. And he'd been consumed with his studies in college and med school and making sure he graduated at the top of his class in both. There had been no time for extracurriculars then.

Kingston stared at the certificates, his gaze landing on his board certification. What was the point in all this education, all these accolades, if he'd failed his patients and negatively affected his colleagues?

With a sigh, he took his stethoscope from around his

neck and put it in the bottom drawer of his desk. He had a full medical kit in the trunk of his car and one at home, so he didn't need to take the scope.

He picked up his briefcase and started to pack his work laptop, then changed his mind. No doubt, if one of the staff members discovered he'd taken work home, they'd be knocking at his condo door to confiscate the computer. Instead, he gathered up his personal laptop bag and his phone, took one last glance at the office, and walked out.

"Bye, Janine," he said, stopping at her desk. "And thanks for putting up with me. I promise to make things easier for you when I get back."

She gave him a knowing smile. "See you later, Dr. Bedford. A *lot* later."

He left the clinic, the hot August sun beating on his neck, a ball of guilt, shame, and frustration in his gut. He fiddled with the fob in his pocket and remote-started his Audi. The car hadn't cooled down by the time he opened the door, and stifling heat hit him as he sat behind the wheel and shut the door.

Now what?

At a loss, he turned up the air. He couldn't remember a time when he didn't have something to do. Even as a kid his schedule had always been full. Now that he didn't have a schedule, he had no clue how to proceed.

What he couldn't do was sit in the employee parking lot. Not without attracting suspicion. He wouldn't put it past the clinic staff to make sure he left. They were probably spying on him right now.

Giving in, he drove out of the lot to the streetlight at

the busy intersection near the clinic. He glanced to the right as a car pulled to a stop in the lane next to him. For a split second his breath caught. The make and model were the same as Olivia's. But that fleeting moment of panic passed. He hadn't seen or spoken to her in over a year, ever since Anita's wedding. Like the morning after their coffee date, he'd sincerely intended to call her. But he'd forgotten the round of golf he had scheduled for the next day with two of the doctors he worked with at the hospital—something he'd promised to do a month earlier after canceling the month before. Then after that—

Beep!

The light was green, and he quickly turned left onto Center Street. There was no use musing about what he should have done differently with Olivia. He'd gone back on his word—again—and let his job and busy life get in the way. And when the time had passed for him to call and apologize, he'd just let it go. He didn't deserve her forgiveness a second time. He was positive she wouldn't give it to him anyway.

He spent the rest of the afternoon getting a shave and haircut, then went back home to his condo. The cleaning service had stopped by, and unlike his office, the place was spotless. Not that it was hard to clean. He had minimal furniture, he never cooked—the food delivery services knew him by name at this point—and he wasn't home enough to make a big mess. Mostly it was his bedroom and adjoining bathroom that needed attention.

After setting his briefcase on the rectangular kitchen table he never used, he went to the spare bedroom that served as his second office and sat in front of the computer.

He was turning over a new leaf, starting now. He had to decompress from the constant stress and busyness he'd put himself under. The best way to do that would be to get out of Hot Springs. Probably Arkansas too.

Taking Brenda's advice, he searched for vacation packages. Hawaii. Jamaica. Greece and the rest of the Mediterranean. South Korea. Brazil. The world was his playground now. He had the money, and now the time, to go anywhere and do anything. And after Sunday brunch he would hop on a plane and be on his way to somewhere relaxing, where he didn't have to think about work or his calendar. A tall order indeed.

It wouldn't be easy, but he had to rest and recharge. His career and patients depended on it.

Chapter 5

"For the last time, Aunt Bea, I'm not taking dance lessons." Olivia slid a large platter into her aunt's full dishwasher and reached for a detergent tablet. They had just finished eating lunch, something she and her aunt and uncle did after church at least twice a month. She'd barely sat down at a table laden with delicious, fresh summer food—ham-salad sandwiches, tomato-and-cucumber salad, purple hull peas, homemade potato chips, green beans, cracker candy, mini brownies, and fresh-squeezed lemonade—before Aunt Bea had brought up the ballroom lessons. "That's my final answer."

Aunt Bea stuck out her bottom lip and continued to ladle the leftover salad into a storage container. "But it will be so much fun. Your uncle Bill and I are going. So are Erma and Myrtle."

Bad enough she was a seventh wheel with her friends. She didn't need to be a fifth wheel to the Maple Falls elderly set. "I hope y'all have a good time." She dropped the tablet into the compartment, shut the door, and started the washer. There were still several pots and pans that needed handwashing. She turned on the hot water and waited for it to get warm as she rinsed off the Dutch oven Aunt Bea had used to make the purple hull peas with both bacon and a ham hock. The result had been delicious.

Her aunt grabbed a dish towel and stood beside her. "You don't have to do the dishes, sugar."

"I don't mind." She put the stopper into the sink's drain. "You made so much food today, you could have hosted the entire congregation for lunch."

Aunt Bea sighed. "I know. Bill got onto me this morning about it."

Olivia turned to her aunt. "Something's bothering you, isn't it?"

"Don't be silly," the older woman blurted, averting her gaze. She grabbed a brownie from the plate next to the country-blue, owl-shaped utensil holder, the words *Bea's Kitchen* written on its pudgy stomach. She crammed the sweet into her mouth. "Mmf ffmm unf."

Olivia not only understood what her aunt said but also knew she was lying. "Everything is not fine. Not when you make this much food." She squirted detergent into the sink and plunged the Dutch oven into the suds.

Aunt Bea finished chewing. "I just wish you'd go dancing with us."

Olivia gestured with her soapy hand. "You made all of this because you want me to take a lesson?"

"Erm, yes. That's why."

Another fib. Something else was going on here, but she wasn't going to press for more information if Aunt Bea wasn't willing to give it. They did the dishes in silence, Olivia washing and her aunt drying. That was another clue that something was up. Bea was a talker.

By the time the dishes were done, Olivia couldn't stand the silence anymore. She yanked the plug, and the bubbles gurgled down the drain. "If it means that much to you, I'll go."

"You will?" Immediately, Bea hugged Olivia, accidentally slapping her on the backside with her damp towel. "You should wear that bright-pink dress. The one with the flared skirt."

"What's wrong with wearing my work clothes?"

"Nothing." Aunt Bea folded the towel in half, then in quarters. "But you look so attractive in that dress."

"I wore it exactly once, to Viola and Keith's twenty-fifth wedding anniversary eight years ago."

"Do you think it still fits?"

Olivia narrowed her gaze at her aunt. "All right, what's really going on here? Why do you want me to dress up for a dance les— Oh."

Alarm lit up Aunt Bea's round face. Her fingers scrunched the freshly folded towel in her hands. "Oh what?"

"You're setting me up." Olivia crossed her arms. "Who is it? Does Ms. Abernathy have a male assistant?"

"I have no idea. And I'm not setting you up. I promise." The cotton cloth in her hands was now a wrinkled ball.

"Forget it, Aunt Bea." Irritated, she grabbed the damp towel from her aunt, dried her hands, then hung it neatly on the ring next to the sink. "I refuse to engage in whatever plan you've cooked up."

"But, Olivia—"

"What will it take for you to understand that I'm fine being single?" She turned and faced her aunt. "I don't need a boyfriend or a husband to have a fulfilling life."

"Like going to the movies by yourself?" Aunt Bea put her hands on her ample hips.

Olivia shrank back. "I can focus on the movie better."

"How about taking college classes you don't need?"

She glanced at her black flats. "Education is never wasted."

"You spend long hours at the library—"

"It's an all-encompassing job."

Aunt Bea threw up her hands. "You're lonely, Olivia. I can see it. Even your uncle Bill has commented on it."

Olivia stilled. "You're both making assumptions."

"Are we?"

She met Aunt Bea's eyes, surprised at the mix of frustration and concern she saw in them. "This is because all my friends are married, isn't it? You figured I had to be depressed because I'm the odd man—odd woman—out."

"I never said you were depressed." Aunt Bea moved closer and took her hand. "I'll admit that I don't understand why you're not interested in dating. You're nearing thirty years old, and as far as I know, you've never been on a date."

Ouch. Hearing her aunt say the fact so plainly pricked at her ego. "You think there's something wrong with me?"

"No, sugar. Of course I don't. But I do think you might be afraid."

Olivia let go of her hand. "Of what?"

"Taking a risk. Being spontaneous." Compassion filled Aunt Bea's eyes. "Getting hurt."

Too late for that. She'd taken a risk twice and fallen flat on her face—twice. She refused to go through that again. "I like my life the way it is," she said, stepping away. "Uncomplicated."

"And maybe a little boring?" Before Olivia could respond, her aunt continued. "Sweetie, I love you. You are as dear to my heart as if you were my own granddaughter. No, scratch that. My own daughter. And you might be okay with things the way they are right now—"

"I am," she said firmly.

"But when you get older, you might not be. You might wish you'd done things differently. Made different choices. I don't want you to have regrets."

Olivia frowned. "Where is this coming from?"

Aunt Bea sat down at the table. Olivia joined her.

"Genes are a funny thing," her aunt said, touching the blue cap of her mushroom-shaped saltshaker in the middle of the table.

"What do you mean?"

The older woman looked at her. "This may surprise you, but you're a lot like me."

"But you're so bubbly and social," Olivia said. She was nothing like that, and she didn't want to be. Being as outgoing as her aunt was like squeezing herself into a square hole. Uncomfortable, and eventually untenable.

"I didn't used to be. I was very timid when I was young. Scared of everything, believe it or not. During my school dances I stayed at home and read books." Her aunt pushed away the saltshaker. "I convinced myself that reading classic literature was more fun than slow dancing with Bill Farnsworth."

"You had a crush on Uncle Bill when you were in school?"

"Heavens, yes." Aunt Bea smiled. "He was the nicest and best-looking boy in my class. Granted, we had less than fifty students in the whole school back then, but he surpassed all the young men."

Olivia smiled. Aunt Bea enjoyed reminiscing, something her parents never did. They focused on the present, dipping into the past only through their research. But this was the first time her aunt had revealed something so personal.

"After Bill and I married, I heard he'd had a crush on me too. But every time he tried to get my attention, I would avoid him. I thought he'd caught me staring at him, and I was always so embarrassed."

"So how did you two get together?"

"Your grandmother, of all people. She used to tell me I was hiding behind my books, and how when I was little, I used to be so much fun. Junior high was hard on me—I went from a skinny stick to a curvy girl, and I was teased a lot for that. I guess I just folded in on myself. I didn't want to be hurt anymore."

Those words hit a nerve. Olivia didn't know what it was like to be picked on, other than a few wisecracking kids calling her a nerd or a bookworm in school. Some of her classmates had also made fun of her when she was useless in gym class. But when she'd complained after school one day in fourth grade, her mother had told her to look logically at the situation.

"You do enjoy reading and learning," Mom had pointed out. *"And you certainly aren't athletically gifted. Not everyone can be. Your peers are engaging in provocative behavior to*

make themselves feel better about their inadequacies. When they get older, they will reassess their juvenile actions and feel varying levels of guilt. You may even receive an apology at some point. It is a normal pattern among youth and nothing to concern yourself with."

After her mother put it that way, Olivia didn't give the comments much thought or reaction, and that's when the teasing stopped.

But the pain she'd experienced at Kingston's rejection . . . She wished she could have shaken it off that easily.

"I'm sorry you were so hurt, Aunt Bea."

"It's okay," the other woman said, smiling. "The day after we graduated, I found out Bill was going into the army. He'd signed up on his eighteenth birthday, a month before school ended." She shook her head. "That was my turning point. I didn't want him to leave Maple Falls, so I tried talking him out of joining."

"It must have worked," Olivia said. As far as she knew, Uncle Bill hadn't served a day in the military.

"It did." Smiling, Aunt Bea turned to her. "He said he wouldn't join—on one condition."

"Let me guess. He wanted a date."

"Yes sirree. And I said yes, and he didn't sign up. He was a little sneaky about it, though. Later he admitted he'd been rejected because he didn't pass the physical due to a heart murmur. He already knew he wasn't going, but he didn't want to miss out on a chance to go out with me." She sighed, still smiling. "The rest is history."

"Then Uncle Bill is the one who brought you out of your shell."

"He helped. I was never going to be a Skinny Minnie again, and he loves me the way I am. He loves my cooking too. A good thing, since I love to cook."

Olivia grinned. Uncle Bill was, in Aunt Bea's words, "a Slim Jim." Kind of unfair that he could eat large portions of food and not gain an ounce.

"We've been happy for forty-seven years and counting." Aunt Bea took Olivia's hand again. "My point is that if I hadn't listened to my mother and taken a chance, I would have missed out on the best thing in my life. Well, second best, next to you."

Olivia's heart warmed. She could always count on her aunt to make her feel good. "Thanks, Aunt Bea."

"And if I hadn't gained the confidence to approach your uncle, I wouldn't have gotten what I always wanted."

"Marriage," Olivia said.

"Yes. I don't want the same thing to happen to you."

Olivia squeezed her hand and let go. "You're assuming I want to get married."

Her aunt's mouth tugged into a frown. "I reckon I might be wrong to assume that." She paused. "Am I wrong to assume you're lonely too?"

"No," Olivia said softly. "I do get lonely sometimes. But doesn't everyone at one time or another? Even married people?"

Aunt Bea nodded, staring at the plate of brownies in front of her. "They sure do."

"I'm touched that you want to help me, but I'm fine. Really. I'm satisfied with my life, and I have no intention of getting married." Or dating, but she wasn't about to go into that with Aunt Bea now.

Her aunt sighed. "All right. I understand. I need to remember you're an adult, and I'll respect your decision not to go Monday night. I'll also stay out of your personal business from now on."

"Thank you."

Aunt Bea went to the fridge and opened it. She mumbled something about "canceling" and "Singles, Inc.," but Olivia couldn't make out everything she said. Her eyes widened as her aunt placed four plastic containers of food in front of her.

"Are these all for me?"

"You can take what you'd like." Aunt Bea next set a casserole dish covered in plastic wrap and filled with lasagna in front of her. "This is from last night if you want some. The rest will be for Uncle Bill's poker night on Tuesday."

Olivia got up from the table and hugged her aunt, almost knocking a bowl of chocolate pudding out of her hands. "Thank you for caring about me so much."

"Anytime, sugar." The older woman kissed Olivia on the cheek. "All I want is for you to be happy. And healthy too. Don't work too hard, okay?"

"I'll try not to."

An hour later and carrying more food than she needed, Olivia walked into her house and set her bounty on the kitchen counter. She put the food away in her fridge and sat down on the gray love seat in her living room.

In the past she would get together with her friends to have lunch on the Sundays she didn't eat with her aunt and uncle, but that had waned once Harper and Rusty got married. Sometimes those lunches lasted until evening, and

Olivia wouldn't return home until after six or seven o'clock. Then she would prepare a snack, look over her calendar for the week, and either read, study, or watch TV before going to bed. She didn't mind that routine—she loved her friends, but she cherished her alone time.

Tonight was different, though. The hum of appliances mixed with the running air conditioner were the only sounds she heard. And if she was honest with herself, she was spending more evenings and nights alone than ever before. Before Anita married Tanner, she and her friend would get together for lunch in her office at the library, or at least talk on the phone. Now, days passed between conversations. The upside was that she was spending more time with Aunt Bea. The downside? Moments like this when she was acutely aware that she was by herself.

She wondered if her aunt was partly right. Was she hiding? She thought about all the opportunities she'd had to step out of her comfort zone during the past year, and how she had avoided every single one. Refusing to join the church softball team, even though Hayden had asked her twice. Flo continually trying to set her up with her nephew. RaeAnne occasionally inviting her to the lake for the weekend with her family.

And while she was digging deep into her thoughts, she had to acknowledge that even her closest friends had reached out to her when they had time—to go shopping, to come over for supper, or to just hang out at the Sunshine Café. She'd declined all of them.

Aunt Bea was right. It was easier to hide behind the familiar and benign than to face the elephant in the room—

life was changing, and she didn't like it. While her life was staying routinely the same, the relationships she'd depended on had altered.

But there was an even bigger catalyst for hiding out, one she hated to think about: Kingston. She'd been avoiding Anita because of him, and that had led her to avoid her other friends as well. The snowball continued to grow from there.

She popped up from her couch. If she was over him like she continually told herself, then why was she letting him control her life?

The mail from yesterday was still on the counter, and the dance lessons flyer lay on top, ready to go into her recycle bin. A phone number was printed at the bottom right-hand corner. Before she could change her mind, she picked up her cell and dialed the number. She wasn't expecting anyone to answer on a Sunday night and intended to leave a message. But if she was in Ms. Abernathy's shoes, she would prefer to have a head count before the lessons started.

"This is Sunny Abernathy of Ms. Abernathy's School of Dance. I'm sorry I missed your call. Please leave a message."

"Hi, Ms. Abernathy. Olivia Farnsworth. I wanted to let you know I'll be at tomorrow's lesson. See you there." She hung up the phone and set it down on the counter.

There. She was being spontaneous. Well, sort of spontaneous, since Aunt Bea was the one who had brought up the lessons in the first place. But she had changed her mind, a rare occurrence.

She glanced at the calendar. The first lesson was on Vintage Movie Night. Strange. She usually didn't forget a scheduled event, especially a long-standing one. Despite

Kingston ghosting her, she hadn't missed a single Vintage Movie Night, even though she kept looking around the theater to see if he would show up. He didn't, and he hadn't since their first—and last—random meeting there.

Maybe she should cancel and go to the next lesson. *Or I can drop the idea altogether.* She could continue with her usual plans and her schedule, and no one would know that for a split second she'd considered making a change. She could remain in her rut. She could continue to hide.

She pressed her lips together, crossed out Vintage Movie Night on her calendar, and replaced it with Dance Lesson. She wasn't going to hide. Not anymore.

Chapter 6

"Now there's the Kingston I adore."

Kingston cringed as his mother fawned over him, even reaching up on her tiptoes to ruffle his clean-cut hair.

"You look so handsome," she marveled, her smile widening as she touched his freshly shaven chin. "I'm glad you're over your grungy phase."

Wow. He didn't know he'd been looking shabby for so long. And it wasn't a phase, just laziness and being too busy. But he smiled and stayed silent, having decided to keep conversation at a minimum during today's brunch lest he slip and tell everyone about his forced sabbatical. He'd hemmed and hawed about informing his family, but when he had pulled into his parents' driveway a few minutes ago, he'd decided against it. If and when the topic came up, then he'd discuss it. Fielding questions from his mother was the exact opposite of relaxing.

She was wearing an outfit more suited to a country-club event than a meal at home—flowing peach-colored pants with a loose-fitting, off-the-shoulder silk top in a slightly darker shade and neutral high-heeled sandals. She touched the pearl necklace she always wore during the Bedford Brunches with matching pearl earrings. A sleek blond-gray bob and light makeup made her look younger than her mid-sixties. "You look lovely today," he said.

"Thank you, dear." Her gaze dipped in a smoothly practiced, self-effacing gesture. "I just threw this on a few minutes ago."

Sure you did. But he smiled. He loved his mother, quirks and all. Her heart was in the right place. Usually. "Dad in his typical spot?"

"Of course." She led him from the foyer to the entrance of his father's study. "He would have the Golf Channel on twenty-four seven if he could. Go on in. Your sisters and their spouses should be here soon. I need to check on the lobster tails."

Kingston nodded and walked into the study, where his father sat reading a magazine while the TV announcers quietly commented on how the golfer on-screen had blown his drive. "Hey, Dad."

His father looked up, then closed the magazine and stood as Kingston walked toward him. "Hi, son." He shook Kingston's hand heartily. "Glad to see you." He scanned him up and down. "You look good. Life must be treating you well."

"Thanks." He'd gotten a decent amount of sleep since he was put on mandatory sabbatical. Paired with the haircut, he probably did look better than he had in a while. He sat down on the matching recliner next to his father's. "Who's in the lead?"

"Some guy I've never heard of." Dad returned to his seat. "That's the great thing about golf—anyone can win, as long as the drives are accurate and the putts fall in." He turned to Kingston. "How's work going? Keeping busy?"

I wish. Only three days into his "vacation" and he was already at loose ends. He still hadn't pulled the trigger on booking a trip. The idea of packing for three or four weeks sounded daunting, especially after all the business traveling he'd done lately. He wasn't burning every candle down to the base anymore, but he still needed to find something to do that would squelch his restlessness.

"Son?"

At his father's questioning look, he nodded. "Yep. Keeping busy."

Dad frowned. "Hmm."

"What do you mean by 'hmm'?"

His father set the golf magazine down on the coffee table in between the recliners. "You're being vague. Usually you launch into a list of all the things eating up your time."

"I said I was keeping busy."

"Doing what?"

Uh-oh. He'd walked right into that one. He couldn't lie to his father even if he wanted to. And being a doctor, maybe Dad would understand. He sighed and explained what had happened on his last day at the clinic but left out some key details about how long he was off and his online performance reviews.

"Oh boy." Dad crossed his legs, his backless leather slipper dangling from his toes. "Well, I can't say I'm surprised. I had to learn the same lesson back in the day."

"You were forced to take a leave of absence?"

"No, but it would have come to that if your mother hadn't intervened. She rightly pointed out that I spent more time at work than I did at home, and she didn't marry me to become a single mother. She was so organized and in control, I didn't realize she needed my help. That was when y'all were little. I think Paisley had just been born." He sobered. "I wasn't there for the delivery because of work. That was your mother's last straw. I'll admit that even after she set me straight, I wasn't around as much as I wanted to be. That's part and parcel with our occupation, isn't it? I did learn some balance, though. It took some time, but I stopped letting work consume me."

"How?" Kingston asked. "I don't even know where to start."

"I did a lot of soul-searching about what was important to me, and I realized that my job wasn't as high on the list as having solid relationships with my family."

A family. Getting married and having kids had always been in the back of his mind, but he'd never taken the time to ponder if that was what he really wanted or if it was just an expectation. He couldn't even get his act together enough to have a date. How would he handle a family?

His father smiled. "What are you planning to do with all this free time?"

Kingston shrugged. "I don't know. I've never had any free time before."

"I'm sure you'll figure it out. And don't worry, I won't tell your mother that you're on a break—"

"You're on a break?" Mom sailed into the room, arching

one flawlessly groomed eyebrow. "King, why didn't you tell me?"

Dad tossed him a sheepish glance, then exchanged it for a stern one when he turned to Mom. "Now, Karen, he's on vacation. Let him be."

"I wouldn't dream of infringing on his time off." She faced Kingston. "But there is one little, teensy-weensy thing—"

"Just tell her no," Dad muttered.

"If you're free Monday evening, I'd love for you to take a ballroom dancing lesson with me." She pouted and looked at Dad. "Your father refuses to go, and I need a partner."

"I already explained why I can't go," Kingston's father said. "I'm meeting Ron at the driving range that night."

"You could reschedule."

Dad scoffed. "It's hard enough finding a time we're both free. He's just as busy as I am. Besides, this was scheduled three weeks ago. You just brought up the lesson yesterday."

"The flyer had just arrived in the mail." She stepped closer to Kingston's recliner. "Just one lesson. And afterward we can get a late supper somewhere. Call me selfish, but it would be nice to have some time with my son."

"He might already have plans," his father said, but with less verve than before. He turned to Kingston. "It's your call."

Kingston opened his mouth. Closed it. He should tell his mom he was leaving for Hawaii tomorrow morning. That could still happen, if he pulled out his phone when no one was looking and booked the trip. But as he met his mother's pleading gaze, he already knew his answer. He didn't want to disappoint her. She was also right. They hadn't spent any time together in . . . months? Years? He couldn't remember. "I'm all yours."

"Oh, thank you, King!" She clasped her hands together. "This is going to be such fun. I have a committee meeting right before the lesson, so I'll meet you at Abernathy's School of Dance at six fifteen."

Kingston pulled out his phone and entered the activity in his now-empty calendar. "What's the address?"

"The school is across from Anita's café."

His head jerked up. "The lesson is in Maple Falls?"

"Yes. The lovely owner—Sunny is her name, I think—opened her studio a month or so ago."

"Um . . ."

"Is there a problem?" Mom asked, her zeal diminishing slightly. Both of his parents were looking at him with curious expressions.

"No," he said, sliding a little farther down in the recliner. "Not a problem at all."

And there wouldn't be if Olivia Farnsworth wasn't there.

The doorbell rang, and his mother started to leave. "That must be one of your sisters. Or both—wouldn't it be cute if they arrived at the same time?" She swept out of the room.

Kingston stared at the emerald-green rug on the floor in front of the TV. For a year he'd managed to avoid Maple Falls, including skipping church. Pastor Jared had given up leaving voice mails asking Kingston how he was doing and inviting him to lunch whenever he was free. No surprise since Kingston hadn't returned his calls.

"You could have told her no, son."

He glanced at his father, startled by his concerned expression. "I don't mind."

Dad sighed. "That's what you always say."

They heard several voices coming from the foyer. "Sounds like the gang's all here." His father clapped his hands together. "I'm ready to eat."

"Lobster?" Kingston rose from the chair.

"Are you kidding? It's liverwurst time."

Kingston chuckled and followed his father out of the study. Nothing got in the way of that man and a slice of liverwurst. But as he headed for the dining room to join his family, Kingston thought about what Dad had said. He didn't have a reason or an excuse to tell his mother no, and he couldn't avoid Maple Falls forever. More important, his acquiescence had made her happy, and he liked seeing her happy.

Feeling a clap on his back, he turned to see Tanner grinning behind him. "Glad you made it," his brother-in-law said. "Anita's been missing you. We all have."

Kingston smiled. It was nice to be missed, and he was starting to realize how much he missed his family too.

They walked into the room together, and everyone started taking their places around the huge table. As usual, his mother had prepared a feast. In addition to the sliced liverwurst and lobster with clarified butter, there was crisp endive salad, huge cinnamon rolls covered in white frosting, an asparagus and zucchini frittata, fluffy pancakes with whipped butter, plenty of boiled eggs, a variety of fruits, cheeses, and nuts, and olive salad. For drinks, they had a choice of cranberry or orange juice and coffee.

"How does she do that?" Tanner said, surveying the dishes.

"Do what?" Kingston asked.

"Make me look like an amateur." Tanner shook his head. He not only owned and was the head cook at the Sunshine Diner, but he also had a catering service. He was no slouch in the culinary department and could make simple and fancy dishes with ease.

Kingston turned to him. "She's been putting on Sunday brunches ever since we were kids. She's got it down to a science."

"The stranger returns." A familiar voice cut through their conversation. Paisley grinned as she approached Kingston and gave him a big hug. "Good to see you, bro."

"You too, sis. Lawyer life treating you well?"

She pushed her long blond hair over her shoulder. "Now it is. Ryan and I scaled back our workload a bit." She glanced at her husband, who was complimenting his mother-in-law's efforts as she savored every word. "We were barely spending any time together, and we felt more like an old married couple than newlyweds."

Ryan glanced up, and their gazes met. She gave him a little wave and turned back to Kingston. "How are the kids treating you? After all this time, I still can't believe you voluntarily spend your days around rug rats on *purpose*."

"Work is fine." He averted his gaze and glimpsed Anita taking her seat next to Tanner. She looked different for some reason. Or maybe it had been so long since he'd seen her, he'd forgotten how vibrant she was, especially after she married Tanner. It was almost like she had a glow . . .

Ryan was motioning for Paisley to join him. She touched Kingston's arm, then went to take her seat next to her husband. Before going to his own chair on the opposite side, he passed Anita and whispered to her, "Congratulations."

Her eyes grew round. *You know?* she mouthed. When he nodded, she whispered, "How?"

"Tell you later." He walked to the last empty chair in the room beside his father, with Ryan on the other side. He recognized Anita's glow, having seen plenty of expectant mothers bringing their children into his office over the years.

I'm going to be an uncle. Awesome.

Once they were settled and Dad said the blessing, Mom tapped her crystal goblet with the side of a sterling-silver butter knife. "Attention, everyone," she said. When she'd gained the family's attention, tears welled in her eyes. "I just want to say . . . Oh gosh." She grabbed a linen napkin and dabbed at the corners of her eyes. "I told your father I wouldn't cry, but it's just so good to have everyone here today. I know it's not a special occasion, just plain old brunch—"

Kingston glanced at the expensive spread in front of him. He and Tanner exchanged knowing glances.

"But having you here is special to me." His mom pressed her hand against her heart. "Thank you."

"Um . . ." Anita's shy voice tagged the end of their mother's statement. "It is a special occasion." At their mother's confused expression, she grabbed Tanner's hand. "Mom, Dad. You're going to be grandparents."

His sister might as well have thrown a bomb in the middle of the table—a sweet, happy bomb, that is. Their mom shot up from the table, the tears flowing freely, and hugged Anita's neck. Ryan high-fived Tanner over the olive salad, and Paisley joined her sister and mother in a group hug. Dad sat back, beaming, his huge slice of liverwurst forgotten.

"When are you due?" Mom asked after the excitement had somewhat dimmed and everyone returned to their seats. In an uncharacteristically boorish move, she blew her nose into her napkin.

"January. We wanted to wait a little while before we said anything."

"Well, I must say I did notice you had gained a bit of weight." Having regained her composure, Mom took a sip of her water.

"Really, Mom?" Paisley scowled.

"Just a little. And I didn't say anything about it, did I?"

"Until now." Paisley looked at Anita. "Don't let that bother you."

Anita grinned. "I'm not bothered. The doctor said I'm exactly where I should be, and the baby is developing well. We had our first ultrasound last week."

Hurt flashed on Mom's face. "Without me?"

Oops. All their mother's goodwill was on the verge of billowing out the window. Anita took her hand. "You can come to the next one. There'll be more to see then."

Mollified, Mom beamed. "I'll be there with bells on."

"She just might do that," Paisley quipped.

Anita turned to Kingston. "We'd like you to be our pediatrician."

"Naturally," Mom said. "My grandchild will have only the best."

Dad was cutting into the liverwurst. "As long as you have the time," he said, glancing at Kingston.

"Of course I do." He now had the most important reason of all to make sure he was fit to go back to the clinic. He wouldn't miss the chance to take care of his niece or nephew.

"Thanks." Tanner grinned. "All right, now that y'all officially know, please pass the lobster."

As his family filled their plates and celebrated Anita and Tanner's news, Kingston grew quiet, observing everyone. His brothers-in-law fit seamlessly into the family, and it was clear they had all gotten together recently. In the past, he'd taken moments like this for granted because he was able to be here more often. Over the years, though, his attendance had dwindled, and even though he was glad he was finally spending time with them, he also felt a little disconnected. And soon there was going to be a new member among them. Did he really want to spend all his time working and missing out on being a part of their lives?

Then again, he couldn't walk away from his practice or volunteering at the health department. He also enjoyed teaching at Henderson, and being asked to speak around the country increased his credibility and learning opportunities. He couldn't imagine totally giving up any of them.

"Kingston is taking dance lessons with me," Mom announced, bringing him out of his thoughts.

His siblings' heads whipped around in unison.

"*A* dance lesson," he clarified. "One."

"At Ms. Abernathy's?" Anita asked. "She's been working hard to get the word out about her classes."

"Why don't you join us?" their mother said. "It would be such fun!"

Tanner stopped midbite and shot a desperate look at his wife. She patted his hand and said, "I'm sure it would be, but we just don't have the time. With our jobs, church, and now the baby, I don't think it's a good idea to add something else to our schedule."

Relief crossed Tanner's face as he swallowed and nodded. "Anita needs to conserve her energy."

Mom smiled. "I understand."

Kingston sat back, marveling at the ease with which Anita had turned down their mother. He glanced at his dad, who surreptitiously pointed his fork at his sister as if to say, *See? That's how it's done.* But Anita had an advantage he didn't have—her pregnancy. Tanner was right too. Anita didn't need to tire herself out.

Both of his sisters had figured out on their own how to cut back and say no. Impressive.

"Ms. Abernathy is teaching a variety of dance styles," Mom said. "Rumba, waltz, tango—"

"You're going to learn the tango?" Paisley chuckled and looked at Kingston. "Wish I could be there to see it."

"Your brother is an excellent dancer," Mom huffed. "Or did you all forget cotillion, where King won the Best Dancer award?"

Kingston slunk down in his seat.

"How could we forget?" Paisley said.

"You forced us to go," Anita added.

"That's not true," Mom said, sounding a little offended. "Kingston, did I force you?"

"No." It was an honest answer. When he was a kid, whatever she'd wanted him to do, he'd agreed to without argument. That included cotillion.

"Well, you made me," Paisley said. "And as I recall, Anita wasn't too happy about it."

"Hey, don't throw me under the bus." Anita picked up a slice of liverwurst.

"Since when do you eat liverwurst?" Dad asked.

"Since today." She took a bite. "Delicious."

Tanner made a face. "No doubt she's pregnant."

Everyone chuckled, including their mother, whose ruffled feathers were a little smoother now.

"I'm surprised you have the time to do even one lesson, Kingston." Anita spooned mustard over the wurst. "You're always so busy."

"I, uh, took a little time off."

"Good for you." Tanner grinned, skipping over the mustard and the liverwurst to grab a slice of French bread. "We all need a break every once in a while."

He nodded but didn't elaborate, and fortunately the conversation shifted topics. There was no reason for his family to know how long of a break he was taking.

After brunch was over, Paisley and Ryan made a quick exit to start their drive back to Dallas that afternoon. Anita and Tanner lingered a bit longer, and as Tanner listened, Kingston answered Anita's questions about what to do after the baby was born. When they were ready to go, he walked them to the door.

"Thanks, Kingston," Anita said, giving him a hug. "I'm starting to feel more confident about being a mom."

"You can call me anytime," he said.

"Should I go through Janine?"

Kingston paused, judging whether she was serious or not. But Tanner wasn't smiling, and he realized they both thought they had to contact his admin to get his attention. What kind of brother was he? "No. Call me directly. I promise I'll pick up and get you on the schedule."

Anita smiled, and Tanner slipped his arm around her waist as he guided her out the door. Kingston waved and watched them as they got into their car and drove off.

His father appeared at his side, giving the two of them a quick wave even though they were already leaving the neighborhood. "You've never stayed at brunch this long."

He turned to his father and saw his pleased expression. His mom was more outward with her emotions, but he could see his father was just as happy. "Want to watch the rest of the golf match?" Kingston asked, glad for the extra time he had to extend his visit. "Or we could do a little putting practice on the green."

Dad grinned. "I'll get the putters."

Chapter 7

Erma and Myrtle! So happy to see you. Now I know tonight is going to be a blast!"

Erma grinned at Sunny Abernathy's over-the-top greeting as they walked into the dance studio. The woman absolutely lived up to her name. Young, maybe midthirties—although everyone under sixty-five seemed young to Erma these days. Sunny had bright hazel eyes that sparkled and a toothy smile that beamed bright, as if she'd swallowed her namesake sunshine, and she was dressed in a red leotard with a light-pink skirt wrapped around her thin waist. Her dark-brown hair was wrapped into a tight bun.

"Welcome to my studio," Sunny said, her grin widening. "Thank you for coming."

Erma had met Sunny at church, but this was her first time in the studio, even though it was across the street and half a block from Knots and Tangles. She'd had no reason to come here before, although she wished she would have thought to bring Sunny a "Welcome to Main Street" gift.

Maple Falls was improving, particularly the downtown area, but progress was slow, and the last tenant in this space hadn't stayed very long. Hmm. Maybe the town should start its own version of the Welcome Wagon and visit new businesses and people moving into town. She would suggest that to Hayden.

She glanced around. Mirrors covered one wall, and a barre was positioned on the shorter wall next to it. An old upright piano sat in the back corner of the room, and a small table with audio equipment on it was situated next to it. There were several brown folding chairs near the front entrance, and a coat of pale-gray paint covered the exposed walls. One would never know that a musty antique store had recently lived here.

It was six twenty-five, and the only other people there were Pastor Jared and Bubba Norton, who were chatting quietly as they sat on two of the chairs. Jared was dressed in khaki shorts, a powder-blue T-shirt that said *Jesus Loves You*, and plain tennis shoes, a contrast to Bubba's standard uniform of overalls, a white T-shirt, and cowboy boots. For a change, he wasn't wearing a beat-up baseball cap, and his dark-brown hair was combed down and looked neat except for the ever-present cowlick sprouting on the back of his head.

Myrtle checked her watch. "I didn't realize we were so early," she said, glancing around the nearly empty room.

Sunny's toothy smile became a bit strained at the corners. "I only started publicizing this two weeks ago, so it takes time to get the word out. We'll still have fun, even if the group is small."

Erma gave her an encouraging smile, but she was disappointed on Sunny's behalf. And where was Bea, anyway? Her friend had called Sunday night and told her that Olivia refused to attend. "You can cancel the Singles, Inc., account too," Bea had added. "I'm butting out of her business."

While Erma approved of Bea's decision, she'd detected a note of sadness in her tone. She'd encouraged her and Bill to come to the lessons, and Bea had said she'd be here. Oh well. Maybe Bea had changed her mind at the last minute.

She walked over to the two men. "I didn't realize you wanted to learn ballroom dancing, Jared," she said.

The lanky man stood and bent to whisper, "I don't. I'm just here to support Sunny and her new business."

Erma smiled. The man was tirelessly involved in the community, something their previous pastor hadn't been. Youth was on his side, though. That and being single.

Why is he still single? He's a good catch.

She rolled her eyes at her busybody thoughts. *Erma Jean, mind your own business!*

The door opened behind her, and she turned around. *Well, good gravy on a biscuit.* As Jasper Mathis shuffled into the studio, she couldn't help but smile. Now things were getting interesting. She'd never imagined in a million—make that a billion—years that the old coot would take a dance lesson.

Unable to resist, she went to him. "I declare, Jasper. If I wasn't seeing you here myself, I wouldn't believe it. Finally ready to do something about those two left feet of yours?"

He scowled and stared at his grubby old work boots.

"Zip it, Erma. I'm here under duress, thanks to your grandson-in-law."

Hayden had put him up to this? Erma's smile grew.

"He said I needed some exercise," Jasper grumbled. "What does that boy know? I get plenty of exercise walkin' to the diner and workin' at the store."

Her grin faded. Jasper's house was near everything he needed, and not a day passed that she didn't see him walking, even though he was north of eighty years old, so she knew he got plenty of exercise. He was in good shape for his age, having retired from his job in construction over a decade ago. Sure, he spent a lot of time sitting on that old stool behind the counter at the hardware store and ate every meal the Sunshine Diner. Her heart pricked. She hadn't thought about what he ate on Sundays when the diner was closed. And his job at Price's was basically a volunteer position, although Hayden did pay him a small salary. If he didn't have the job, what else would he do with his days?

What she knew for sure was Hayden had a reason for encouraging Jasper to take dance lessons. She was also sure Jasper had put up a good fight not to. The way he was shoving his hands in and out of his pockets was a bit endearing, but she didn't like that he was uncomfortable. Without a thought she threaded her arm through his. "You'll be my partner tonight."

He resisted, but only slightly. "Lord help me," he muttered.

"Lord help us both," she joked and guided him to the center of the room. Myrtle, Jared, and Bubba followed while Sunny fiddled with the audio equipment.

The door opened again, and Senior Jenkins strolled inside, wearing blue jeans and a red polo shirt with *Rusty's Garage* printed on the front right above his heart. He'd been the original owner of the garage before Harper's husband, Rusty III, had taken over the business. Like Erma, Senior was in his late seventies and probably would have kept running the garage if he didn't have issues with his eyesight. He never spoke of it, but Erma had heard through the grapevine that he had macular degeneration. She admired the way he never let it get him down.

When he spotted Erma, Jasper, and Myrtle, he grinned and walked toward them. "If it isn't two of my favorite ladies," he said to Erma and Myrtle, bowing slightly at the waist. "Aren't we blessed to have these fine women here tonight?"

"Yeah. Sure." Jasper moved a few steps away from them and started fidgeting again.

Myrtle giggled. She might be in love with Javier, but she wasn't immune to a little southern charm. "I should have known you'd be here," she said with a smile.

"I wasn't about to miss a chance to brush up on my dance skills. I can't wait to show the ladies at the Swinging Sage my new moves."

"What's that?" Myrtle asked.

"A new senior center in Rockport. Just opened two weeks ago. They have dance night twice a month. This past Friday was the first one. The women outnumber the men, though." Senior turned to Jasper. "You should come to the next one. Personally, I enjoy playin' the field, but you might find a nice lady to keep you company. Myrtle and Erma, you're welcome to join us."

"Erma ain't interested," Jasper blurted, meeting Senior's jovial gaze with a crusty scowl.

"I can speak for myself." She shot him an exasperated glare before looking at Senior again. "Sounds like a good time. What do you think, Myrtle? You want to trip the light fantastic at the Swinging Sage?"

Myrtle moved closer to Erma. "I don't know," she whispered. "I don't want to step out on Javier."

"Gotcha." Wow, Myrtle was more wrapped up in her Latin lover than Erma had thought. *I hope he doesn't disappoint her.*

Sunny clapped her hands and joined everyone in the center of the room. "It's a little after six thirty, so let's begin. How about we start with introductions?"

"We all know each other," Jasper said, his scowl deepening.

Erma elbowed him. "Why do you have to be so grumpy?"

"I ain't grumpy—"

"But I don't know all of you." Sunny smiled, but a note of warning crept into the gaze she was aiming at Jasper and Erma. "I'll start. I'm Sunny Abernathy, and I'm originally from Cumberland, Maryland, a little more than two hours from Washington, DC. I started ballet dancing when I was three, and then I moved to Atlanta after I graduated high school. I danced with Atlanta Ballet for ten years, but I was mostly an understudy. I did a lot of teaching on the side, and I loved it so much I retired from the ballet. I've been a dance teacher for fifteen years, and I moved to Maple Falls a few months ago and opened my studio in July." She grinned and turned to Jared. "Your turn, Pastor Jared—"

"Why here?" Jasper asked.

"I needed a fresh start." She didn't seem offended by the question. "I have some family in Mount Ida, but once I stepped foot in Maple Falls, I knew this was where I wanted to live."

For the next few minutes, everyone introduced themselves to Sunny. When it was Bubba's turn, he could barely speak. He clumsily managed to tell Sunny his first and last name before becoming tongue-tied again.

When the introductions were over, Sunny moved on, letting the group know what to expect from the class and the types of dances they would be learning over the following six weeks. "We'll start with the rumba first, then move to the waltz and cha-cha." After discussing a few more business items, she said, "Time to begin our lesson. First, let's pick our partners."

Jasper immediately grasped Erma's arm. Oddly, he seemed almost desperate to have her as a partner, when a few minutes ago he'd been begging God to help him.

Senior and Myrtle stood next to each other, their partnership claimed. Bubba and Jared exchanged dubious glances.

Sunny laughed. "I'll take turns being your partner," she said. "Which of you wants to go first?"

Jared nudged Bubba forward. The man's cheeks turned scarlet.

"Someone's got a crush on the teacher," Senior whispered, loud enough for Erma to hear. Myrtle shushed him, and he pressed his lips together.

He was right, though. Bubba had puppy love written all over his face. Now Erma knew why the good ol' boy was taking dance lessons, something that was out of character for him.

"All right, Bubba. You and I will go first." Sunny gestured for him to move closer to her, then pointed to a spot on the dance floor. "Stand here, please." She went to Erma and Jasper, led them to Bubba, and directed Jasper to stand next to Bubba with Erma opposite him. "Senior and Myrtle, you're over here."

Once everyone stood in their places, Sunny said, "Now, let's talk position. Face your partner."

Erma looked Jasper in the eye. He did likewise.

Challenge accepted.

"Ladies, put your hands on—"

The door opened, and everyone turned to see Karen Bedford hurry inside, Olivia trailing behind her. Now this was a surprise—both Karen and Olivia. Obviously, the young woman had changed her mind, but Erma never would have guessed Karen would deign to enter Maple Falls unless she was visiting Anita. Even then, she usually stuck to the café, although sometimes she visited the diner. Maple Falls had never been cosmopolitan enough for Karen, and once her youngest child graduated from Maple Falls High—their father's alma mater—she and the doctor had moved to Hot Springs toot sweet.

Karen glanced around the room, a slight frown on her face, while Olivia went to stand by Jared. Her expression wasn't much brighter.

Sunny glided over to them. "Welcome, ladies. I'm Sunny, and I'm so glad you're joining us tonight." She gazed expectantly at Karen.

"Karen Bedford." Karen's frown disappeared as she shook Sunny's hand.

"I'm Olivia." Olivia took a step forward.

Sunny turned to her. "Right. You left a message for me last night. Very thoughtful, thank you. So you and Jared can go stand by Senior and Myrtle. And you—" She gestured for Karen to follow her to the other side of the room. "Bubba needs a partner too."

Karen balked. "But I already have—"

"Ms. Sunny," Bubba said in a slow drawl as horror flashed across his face. "I ain't too sure about this."

But Sunny was already leading Karen to stand in front of Bubba. Once she was in position, Karen sighed. "Hello . . . Bubba."

"Hi, Mrs. Bedford," he said weakly.

Erma would have laughed if Bubba didn't look so forlorn. Karen was clearly disgruntled by something, but it wasn't her dance partner. Bubba would be fine.

I hope.

Sunny started walking around the group of dancers. "As I was saying, face your partner. Ladies, put your hands on your partners' shoulders. Men, put yours on the ladies' waists."

"This is like junior high," Senior said with a laugh as he and Myrtle complied.

Erma glanced at Olivia. Jared's hands were barely touching her, and Erma noticed for the first time that she looked especially cute in her bright-pink dress with a flared skirt. Perfect for dancing. Olivia's hands lightly rested on the front of Jared's shoulders. Both kids looked awkward and uncomfortable.

"Hey," Jasper said, moving closer to Erma. "Get with the program."

"I'm gettin'. I'm gettin'." She put her hands on his shoulders and caught a whiff of a scent that reminded her of those Irish soap commercials. That was one thing she could give Jasper credit for—he might look disheveled, but he was always clean.

Then his hands skimmed her waist. She startled.

"Somethin' wrong?" he said.

"No, just . . ." Just what was that little jolt she'd felt when he touched her? She'd danced with Jasper countless times over the years. But it had always been grudgingly, either on her side or on his side. Mostly both, and it had mostly been for fast numbers when they didn't have to touch each other. Come to think of it, Jasper usually disappeared during slow dances. Surely they'd danced a few of them, though. And she'd never, ever felt a *jolt*.

She lifted her head to see his expression. He was looking past her shoulder, crotchety as usual.

Must have been a gas pain.

"Ladies, take your right hand and hold it up like this." Sunny's palm faced outward. "Men, take your left hand and hold their right one." She paused as everyone situated themselves. "That's great! Now, tonight we're going to practice basic footwork and posture, otherwise known as your dance frame." She checked everyone's stance as she spoke. "Then I'll introduce the rumba."

Erma glanced at Jasper, who was still looking at everyone and everything except for her. He was a short guy, only an inch or three taller than her. His eyes were moss green—why hadn't she noticed that before?—and he had several wayward hairs poking out from his bushy gray eyebrows. They really needed a trim.

He scowled. "What are ya starin' at?"

She jerked her gaze from his face. She did not like feeling this off-center, particularly when it came to Jasper. She forced herself to focus on what Sunny was saying. Jasper could let his eyebrows grow wild for all she cared.

"Everyone looks good," Sunny said. "Now, men, take one step back on your left foot—"

The studio door opened again, and for the first time an annoyed expression appeared on Sunny's face. Everyone relaxed their positions and looked to see who had the nerve to show up well into the class hour. Erma's brow lifted as Kingston Bedford walked in, looking sheepish.

And handsome. *Let's be real.*

"Oh no."

The two words were whispered so softly that Erma almost didn't hear them. She turned to the young woman who'd said them and watched the color drain from Olivia's face.

Chapter 8

Kingston searched the room for his mother, who strangely enough stood in Bubba Norton's arms. He stopped in front of Sunny, who was poised between Erma and Jasper— *huh?*—and Senior and Myrtle. "I'm sorry," he said, not daring to look at Mom. "I lost track of time."

"Better late than never." Sunny smiled, but it wasn't as bright as her name. Not even close.

Kingston heard the familiar clicking sound of his mother's low-heeled pumps approaching. He'd recognize those angry footsteps anywhere. He forced a smile and turned to her just as she reached his side.

"Kingston," she said tightly, then turned to Sunny. "This is my son, *Dr.* Kingston Bedford. He's my dance partner for tonight." Her chin tilted up in triumph, as it usually did whenever she let anyone know she'd birthed a physician. But that didn't fully cover her agitation with him.

He figured he'd be in the doghouse for being late, and for good reason since he didn't have a decent excuse for his tardiness. He'd started searching for vacation destinations after lunch and had become frustrated with his inability to decide. It was a vacation—he could go anywhere. So why couldn't he figure out a plan?

The next thing he knew, he was waking up with his head on his desk in front of a dark computer screen. When he moved it came to life, and he glanced at the time. He'd immediately realized how late he was for the dance lesson, and he'd considered not going at all. But while his mother might forgive him for being late, she wouldn't abide him ducking out altogether.

He cleared his throat. "Nice to meet you . . ."

"You can call me Sunny." The annoyance in the woman's eyes disappeared.

"I'm so glad you're *finally* here," Mom ground out, threading her arm through his and guiding him to the floor.

"I was—"

"You can tell me later." She squeezed his arm. "Right now we're in the middle of our lesson."

He glanced around the room, shifting on his feet as the couples looked at him with varying expressions. Senior Jenkins had his hands on Myrtle Benson's waist, his raised eyebrows questioning. Myrtle smiled and nodded hello. Erma waved, while Jasper . . . Well, the old man looked annoyed as usual. As for Bubba, now that his mother had abandoned him, he stood there awkwardly, dropping his hands to his sides. And Pastor Jared stood with—

Oh no.

"Looks like we're partners again, Bubba." The willowy dance instructor moved in front of Bubba. The man looked like he'd just been given the key to Maple Falls.

Sunny gestured. "Karen, you and Kingston can go over there."

He winced and followed his mother to the empty space on the other side of Jared and Olivia. He couldn't recall a time when he'd seen Olivia enjoy dancing. This had to be out of her comfort zone. Yet here she was looking stunning in a hot-pink dress with a flared skirt that reached the top of her knees, making his own knees turn weak.

When he and his mother were in position, Jared grinned at him. "Never would have guessed you'd show up here, Kingston. But I'm glad you did. Things going well with you?"

How was he supposed to answer that question? He was late, and he'd brought unwanted attention to himself. His mother was putting on her best social smile, but he could see she was simmering underneath the ruse. The woman considered punctuality the eleventh commandment.

And Olivia wouldn't even look in his general direction. Add that to his sabbatical and the fact that he couldn't do something as simple as book a vacation or be on time to a dance lesson, and he was doing great. Peachy. "Things are good," he mumbled.

Sunny was instructing the students to go back to their initial position. His mother put his hand on her waist and held up her right hand. "We're getting ready to learn the rumba, dear. You remember that dance, don't you?"

He nodded, although it had been a long time since he'd done any ballroom dancing. He figured it would come back to him. Unlike his sisters, he hadn't minded cotillion, and he hadn't just learned how to dance. He'd learned manners and etiquette—two things that had helped him in his career. At least until lately. The bad reviews came to mind. He shoved them off and clasped his mother's hand and smiled. She finally gave him a sincere one in return. Hopefully all was forgiven.

He couldn't help but glance at Olivia, who was looking straight ahead at Jared. She wouldn't pardon him so easily. *If ever.*

Sunny commenced instruction on position and footwork. He and his mother fell into a natural rhythm as they practiced the rudimentary rumba steps over the next fifteen minutes. That gave Kingston the opportunity to watch Olivia and Jared.

"Sorry." Jared regained his balance after nearly tripping Olivia for the third time. "I've never done this before, and I can't seem to get the footwork right."

"Me either," she said, her hand slipping from his.

Her sweet voice tickled Kingston's ears, and he tried to keep his attention on his mother's face. They had danced on and off over the years, starting with his first cotillion party when he was in third grade. He and the other students had practiced their new skills and then danced with their parents. Tonight, he could tell his mom was getting a little bored with the basics. She wasn't a dancing maven, but she did know the fundamentals.

"All right, one more time," Jared was saying. "Step forward. Then back."

Olivia let out a little yelp.

Jared looked down at their feet. "Are you okay?"

Kingston was also checking out her foot. She tapped the toe of her simple, low-heeled black pump. "I'm fine."

"I'm hopeless at this." Jared's shoulders slumped.

Their predicament had finally gained his mother's notice. "No one's hopeless at dancing." She let go of Kingston's hand and reached for Jared's. "I'll show you what you're doing wrong. King, dance with Olivia."

Kingston met Olivia's petrified gaze.

"Thank you, Mrs. Bedford." Jared turned to Olivia. "Do you mind? I'm afraid I'll break one of your toes if I keep going this way."

She nodded but didn't say anything.

Jared and Kingston changed places, and Kingston stood across from Olivia. There was nothing he could do but hold out his arms. She hesitated, then moved closer to him and slipped her hand into his, barely holding it.

Having Olivia this close should be bliss—if she wasn't as stiff as a brand-new pencil.

Sunny passed by them, unfazed by the partner switch. "Relax, Olivia," she said, lightly touching her shoulder. "This is supposed to be fun."

"Yeah," Olivia mumbled. "Fun."

"Now that you all have the basics down, I'll put on the music," Sunny called out, walking over to a small table that held a Bluetooth speaker. "Remember to count. One, two, three, four." She clicked a thin silver remote, and the room filled with a slow, romantic number that Kingston remembered from an old Tom Cruise movie.

"One, two, three, four," Senior counted above the music.

"Perfect, Senior!" Sunny took her position in front of a very pleased-looking Bubba.

"Kingston," his mother hissed, already dancing a decent rumba with Jared. "The music's started."

He looked down at Olivia, who was staring straight at his chest. As the male, he was supposed to lead. "Ready?"

She barely nodded, and he started to move. Somehow, she managed to follow him without bending an inch. It was like dancing with a broom handle.

After a few minutes of this, he bent down. "Sunny's right—you need to relax," he whispered.

Her head jerked up. "Don't tell me what to do," she shot back.

"I'm not. I'm trying to be helpful."

She glared at him. "I don't need your help." She pressed her foot firmly on his toe.

Pain shot through his shoe. He bit his bottom lip. "Feel better now?" he snipped.

"No." She moved to stomp on his foot again, but he jumped out of the way.

"This is pretty fun," he heard Jared saying to his mom. "Thanks for helping me."

His mother was now in her element. "See? Anyone can dance."

At Olivia's third attempt to take her anger out on his feet, Kingston tugged her close to him so she couldn't see her target. She squirmed, but he held firm.

"Let me go," she said.

"Not until you promise to keep your feet to yourself."

"What do you know about promises?"

Ouch. She had him there.

And he had her in his arms. Whatever strange movements they were making weren't anything close to a rumba, but his pulse started ramping up anyway. He was sure it was unintentional, but she had somewhat eased her stiff stance, and he detected the familiar scent of clothes fresh off the line. But it was the angry fire in her eyes and the way her cute nostrils flared that had him going. Wow, had he missed her.

"Olivia," Sunny said, appearing out of nowhere. "You need to let your partner lead."

She nodded, sending Kingston another hot glare.

Sunny put her hand on Olivia's shoulder. "Let me show you what I mean."

He had no choice but to let Olivia go. Sunny slid easily into his arms. He was educated enough in this type of dancing to know the partners needed to be close, sometimes waist to waist, depending on the dance. That had been an excruciating lesson during cotillion classes. He and Sunny weren't that close, but only inches separated them.

"You seem to know what you're doing," she said as she placed her hand in his. "Have you done the rumba before?"

"A long time ago," he acknowledged.

"So you know how to lead." She took a step forward.

Like he'd figured, the rhythms came back to him. And unlike Olivia, Sunny not only was relaxed but fully allowed him to guide the dance. On instinct he moved them away from the other couples, and the two of them danced until the song finished. When they stopped, he heard applause, his mother leading the way.

"Bravo, King!" she said, grinning. "Bravo!"

Sunny dropped out of her dance frame, nodding approvingly.

He glanced at everyone in the room. They were all smiling. Even Jasper held a half-pleased expression, although he wasn't applauding. Thank goodness. This was embarrassing enough.

Then he glanced at Olivia. The scorching anger in her eyes was gone. Instead she stood stone-faced, her hands at her sides.

"That's all for tonight," Sunny said as she turned to the rest of the class. "Time certainly does fly when you're having fun."

"You call this fun?" Jasper mumbled.

Erma smirked. "You had fun, and you know it."

He lifted his chin. "I would have if you hadn't been yakking the whole time."

"I was correcting your mistakes, you old codger."

"More like bossing me around, Ms. High and Mighty."

"Now, now." Sunny rushed to the couple and continued speaking in a tone reserved for two-year-olds fighting over a toy. "I think we can all agree we have a lot to learn."

"Kingston don't." Bubba's round cheeks lifted as he smiled. "Bet he could teach the class."

"No," Kingston said, holding up his hands, his palms facing outward. "I took classes when I was younger. That's all."

"Don't be so modest." His mother moved to stand next to him. "You executed a perfect rumba."

He grimaced. "Mother. Stop."

The rest of the class started milling around as Sunny walked over to Kingston and his mother. "Both of you are very good," she said. "I'm sure you're familiar with the other dances I'll be teaching in this course."

"Yes," Mom said.

Kingston was less confident. "I could use a refresher."

Sunny shook her head. "I think these lessons will be too basic for you two. I don't want you to be bored."

Kingston started to nod. He doubted he'd be bored, and he really did need to bone up on the dances. But he'd only agreed to come to this class, and now that his obligation was fulfilled, he didn't intend to come back. Olivia wouldn't have to worry about seeing him again. And he could save his feet from punishment.

Mom snapped her fingers. "I have a splendid idea," she said, turning to Kingston. "You can be Sunny's assistant."

"What?" they both said.

"I can help out too." She smiled.

He gaped. "But I'm only doing one lesson—"

"What a perfect way to relax while you're on break," his mother continued as if he hadn't said a word. "What do you think, Sunny?"

Their instructor tapped a thin finger against her chin. "I could use some help. I'm hoping that once the word spreads about the lessons we'll have more students. But I don't want to impose—"

"It's no imposition, is it, King?" Mom looked at him expectantly, clasping her hands together. "Just think, we'll get to spend more time together!"

The conversation around them was a low murmur as Kingston scrambled for an answer, trying to come up with reasons to say no. He was supposed to be resting, not working. But dancing wasn't work, and he did like teaching. And it was only once a week for six weeks—

Nuts, why was he thinking of positive reasons to be Sunny's assistant?

There was one reason he had to say no. He glanced around the studio, looking for Olivia. The senior-citizen crowd was still there, and Bubba and Jared were talking near the front door. But Olivia was gone.

"You can think about it and let me know." Sunny gave him a wide smile.

"We don't need to think about it, do we, King?" Mom looked up at him.

He met her gaze, withering a little inside. How many times over the years had he seen that look directed at him? Expectation mixed with confidence that he wouldn't dare say no.

Then he glanced at Sunny. Even though she had told him to think about it, he could see the hope in her eyes. If he turned her down, he'd disappoint two people. He'd already upset Olivia tonight.

"Okay," he said, digging deep for enthusiasm he didn't feel. "I'll help."

"Wonderful!" Sunny exclaimed.

"Splendid!" Mom added. "You've more than made up for being late, dear."

He should have known she wouldn't let that faux pas go.

"See everyone next week!" Sunny moved away from him and Mom and told everyone goodbye. "And please, if you had a good time tonight, bring a friend with you next time. The more the merrier!"

"Thanks, Sunny," Senior said. "I just might do that." He winked at her and escorted Erma and Myrtle out the door, Jasper lagging behind them.

Jared came up to them, Bubba following. "I appreciate your help, Mrs. Bedford."

"Please, call me Karen."

Kingston had to smile. At least his mother was having a good time.

Jared continued, "I was intending to do just one lesson to support Sunny, but I'll be back next Monday. I really enjoyed learning something new."

If his mother's smile had been any brighter, she would have lit up Neptune. This was what she lived for—helping others and basking in appreciation. "You're so welcome. You're an excellent student."

As she and Jared continued their mutual-adoration conversation, Kingston scanned the studio again. Still no Olivia, so his fleeting thought that she'd gone to the restroom was moot. He wasn't surprised she'd left. Or that she was so mad at him that she'd smashed his toes. He deserved it, and he was ashamed he'd avoided her for so long. Would she be back next week? Hopefully she'd enjoyed the parts of the lesson he wasn't involved with. Maybe by next Monday she'd have cooled down and he could apologize to her.

"Ready to go?" Mom said, still glowing from Jared's praise.

"Sure." He turned to Sunny, who was taking her phone out of the dock next to a Bluetooth speaker. "See you next Monday."

"See you then."

"Wait here." Mom scurried to Sunny. "You'll need his phone number. You know, in case anything changes."

Naturally his mother would give out his number without consulting him. *Unbelievable.*

"Thanks again." Mom hurried back to him. "Now we're ready to go."

As they walked out of the studio, she pouted. "It's too bad the café is closed. I'd love a cup of Anita's chai right now." She stopped on the sidewalk in front of her car and pulled out her phone.

"What are you doing?" he asked as she ran her thumb over her screen.

"Calling her."

"You're not going to ask her to come down here and make you tea, are you?"

She scoffed and pressed the phone to her ear. "Anita. Hello. Your brother and I are here at the dance studio . . . Yes, we both took a lesson, and guess what? Kingston and I are going to be assistant teachers!"

Kingston rolled his eyes and looked around Main Street. It had been over a year since he'd last been here, and not much had changed, other than the dance studio opening. However, in the past three years there had been some developments to the main drag in Maple Falls. All the facades were painted and refreshed, including the last empty building on the street. Then there were the two new businesses—Anita's café and Sunny's dance studio. Progress was happening here, and he was glad to see it.

"So you don't mind if we stop by for a little while?"

Mom said. "Wonderful. We'll see you soon. Ta-ta for now."
She put her phone in her purse. "Anita invited us for a visit."

More like Mom invited herself. It was up to Anita to
decide whether she wanted company or not. "Okay. I'll meet
you at her house."

"Splendid!" She hugged him. "I'm so excited we'll be
working at the studio together, Kingston." She pulled back,
her expression turning serious. "It means a lot to me that
you said yes."

And with that, any doubt about accepting the assistant
position disappeared. "I'm happy, too, Mom. Let's get to
Anita's before it gets late."

"See you in a few." She waved to him, then got in her car.

He had parked a few feet in front of his sister's café. As
he opened the driver-side door, he glanced at the intersection
at the end of the block. If he took a left at the light, he would
be near the Maple Falls Library. And if he continued driving
a few more minutes, he would be at Olivia's house. He'd
been there exactly once, years ago, when Anita had thrown
her a housewarming party. He'd put in only a scant appearance, dropping off a bottle of white wine he'd bought at the
last minute, not knowing if she preferred red, or even if she
drank wine. He still didn't know.

Kingston got into his car and started the engine. What he
did know was that he had unfinished business with Olivia,
and one way or another, he was going to talk to her next
week.

"I'm sorry about your ankle, Aunt Bea." Olivia plopped down on the couch, fighting for a measured tone, still infuriated not only that Kingston had been at the studio tonight but also that she'd been forced to dance with him.

"It'll be fine, sugar." Aunt Bea's tired voice sounded over the speaker. "I should have paid more attention to that last step on the staircase. I've had ice on it most of the day, and the swelling's gone down. Your uncle Bill has been taking good care of me."

Olivia didn't doubt that. Her uncle doted on Aunt Bea, and that was always sweet to witness. "Do you need me to bring you anything?"

"No. I'm just glad you called. Now, how was your dance lesson? Who was there? Did you have fun?"

Olivia dug her bare toes into the gray rug in front of her couch. When she hadn't seen Aunt Bea and Uncle Bill at the studio tonight, she'd gotten a little worried, since she knew they had intended to come. Her plan had been to take the lesson, then find out what was going on. But then Kingston had shown up, twisting her stomach into knots. When his mother had made her switch partners, she'd been furious. It was bad enough dancing next to him. Worse to be in his arms again.

His strong arms.

"Olivia? Are you still there?"

"Yes." She scowled at her wayward thoughts and answered the rest of her aunt's questions.

"Oh, I wish I could have been there," Aunt Bea said with a chuckle. "If only to see Erma and Jasper fancy dancing together. How'd they do?"

Olivia couldn't tell her because she didn't know. She'd been so focused on her anger that she hadn't paid attention to anyone else. So much for Kingston being too busy with work to go out with her. Or even call. He had plenty of time to dance, though, and even give lessons.

Just no time for me.

She wasn't upset with him only—she was even more furious with herself. Because the moment he'd put his hand on her waist, she'd known she was in trouble. He smelled so good, like he'd just finished a shower and put on subtle cologne, and his light-blue polo shirt and black cargo shorts fit him perfectly.

Why was she noticing his smell or his clothes? How could she still be attracted to him after what he'd done?

Even worse was the fact that there was more than pure physical attraction going on. Despite her anger and her embarrassment that she'd fallen for him not once but twice and then spent more than an entire year trying to get him out of her mind . . . she missed him. It didn't make any sense. She'd never missed Kingston when they were growing up. Either he was there or he wasn't.

But she'd never kissed him back then. Or felt his arms around her, or—

She jumped up from the couch and started to pace. Once she realized she'd missed him—and hated herself for it—she stomped on his foot.

Not one of my best moments. But as childish as that had been, it had felt good. *Let him feel some pain for once.*

"Olivia?"

She startled, forgetting that she was still on the phone. "Sorry, Aunt Bea."

"You seem a little distracted. Is everything all right?"

"Yes." She perched on the edge of the couch, her posture straight. "Erma and Jasper had a good time." That's what she'd heard as she slipped out of the studio without anyone noticing. Erma had been smiling, but it was hard to tell with Jasper. He was always a sourpuss.

"I'll have to give her a call and find out all the details. I still want to take lessons, and I'm sure I'll be better next week. Uncle Bill and I will meet you there."

Olivia ran her hands over her pajama pants. As soon as she arrived home, she'd thrown off the dress and put on her most comfortable pj's. She felt foolish for being so dressed up when everyone else was casual. She'd even outdressed Karen, who had worn slim jeans and a three-quarter-sleeved pink shirt. How could she go back there, knowing Kingston would return?

Or would he? It wasn't as if he needed any lessons. Once he and Sunny had started dancing together, she could see he was way out of everyone else's league. The two of them looked good together. Very good.

Something ugly twisted in her stomach. "I'll have to check my schedule," she said.

"You and that schedule of yours." Aunt Bea chuckled. "All right. I think I'm going to turn in. Spraining my ankle was enough excitement for me today."

"I'll call and check on you in the morning on my way to the library," Olivia said. She was concerned, even though her aunt was downplaying the incident. "Or I can stop by—"

"That's not necessary, sweetie. I'm fine."

"Are you sure?"

"Positive. I'm just clumsy."

"Okay." Olivia stood up again. "But I'm still going to call you."

"Please do. I love hearing from you. Have a good night, sugar."

Olivia hung up and pinched the bridge of her nose. She didn't want to go back to the dance studio. Tonight had been a disaster even before she'd been forced to dance with Kingston. Jared wasn't the bad dancer—she was. He'd been covering for her mistakes by overplaying his.

She shouldn't be surprised. She wasn't graceful or athletic. She was a bookworm who liked vintage movies and got smacked down every time she tried to do something different.

She went to her bedroom, pulled out her laptop, and brought up her Eighteenth-Century English Literature class notes—the course schedule, procedures, and syllabus. Class started on Friday, but she didn't have anything due for the next few weeks. She frowned. She couldn't even use her classwork as an excuse not to continue the lessons—not honestly, anyway. Then again, she could say that she was busy with school, and just do the assignments ahead of time. That was what she typically did anyway, but she'd always had several classes to juggle along with work, so staying ahead was crucial or she'd fall behind.

She could tell everyone she had too much to do to take a stupid dance class. She didn't have to go back to the dance studio, ever. She would never be in Kingston's arms again or experience the same thrill she had when, during their dance, his hand had moved from the side of her waist to the back. He'd taken control of the dance.

And I liked it.

She shut the laptop and scrambled off the bed, then did a little shimmy as if shaking him off. She could come up with all the excuses in the world not to go back to Sunny's studio, but there was only one real reason: Kingston would be there. Maybe. He might decide the lessons were too easy and skip the whole thing. But if he did show up, there were several other men she could dance with. She'd even pick Jasper if it came down to him and Kingston. She could handle the old man's bad disposition.

It was clear she couldn't handle her feelings for Kingston at all.

What she could do was avoid him. Pretending he didn't exist would be even better. Whatever it took for her to completely rid herself of him to the point where he didn't elicit any emotion from her, positive or negative. She was breaking his hold on her tonight. That was a promise she was determined to keep.

Chapter 9

The following afternoon, Kingston began preparing for his first night as an assistant ballroom dance teacher. Now that he'd made the commitment, he needed to practice the different dance steps. The rumba had always been easy for him, so he didn't practice that one much, but he found some online videos and refreshed his memory of the cha-cha, the waltz, and the tango. It was almost impossible to practice the tango by himself, and out of the four dances he was the least proficient at that one. He decided to call his mother and see if she was available to practice.

"I'm sorry, Kingston, but this week is completely booked," she said above the *click* of her turn signal. "I have my garden club meeting today, Wednesday is church potluck before the evening service, Thursday I'm going shopping with my friends from the country club—"

"It's okay." He didn't need a litany of her activities, and she would have happily given him one if he hadn't interrupted.

"I'm sure you'll do a fine job as a dance instructor," she said.

"Assistant instructor," he corrected. And he probably wouldn't be doing much instructing, only helping Sunny as needed. Still, he liked to be prepared.

"And you'll be the best assistant instructor she's ever had," Mom continued.

He rubbed his neck. He was helping Sunny, that's all. But his mother's expectation was clear. Being good wasn't enough. He had to be the best.

"Why don't you call Sunny and see if she can tutor you? You two made a lovely couple on the dance floor. She's so lithe and graceful. I wonder if she's single—"

"Mother—"

"I'm just wondering, that's all. I didn't say you should ask her out on a date. Unless you want to."

He padded in bare feet to his kitchen and took a glass out of the cabinet. He didn't want to ask Sunny out. She was pretty, but she wasn't his type.

She's not Olivia. He winced.

"I know—I'll give Sunny a call," his mother said. "I can let her know that you're looking for a practice partner."

Kingston gripped his phone. "Please don't do that—"

"I needed to talk to her anyway and make sure we're on the same page with our lessons."

He didn't miss the word "our," and in Karen Bedford-speak that usually meant her taking over. "You're an assistant, remember? Not the actual teacher."

"I just want to run a few ideas past her. Then I'll let her know you need some practice."

"Mother—"

"Ta-ta for now!" *Click.*

Kingston almost slammed the glass down on the quartz countertop. Now what was he supposed to do? He was a grown man, and he didn't need his mother making plans for him.

But hadn't she done that most of his life? Except for the past few years, when he had filled his own schedule so full that there was no opportunity for her to add anything else in, she'd micromanaged his free time.

His only option was to call Sunny and head things off at the pass. He made a quick online search for the number of her studio and tapped the digits into his phone. When he got her voice mail, he left a quick message asking her to call him back and hung up.

He then filled the glass with water and gulped it down. He couldn't spend the next two months asking his mother to stop interfering in his life only to have her ignore him. But he'd had conversations with her about respecting his boundaries before, and it never seemed to stick. He wondered if it ever would.

Then there was the troubling fact that she was almost always right. Everything she'd signed him up for or volunteered him for were things he was not only decently good at but most of the time excelled at. He also enjoyed the activities, almost without fail. But that didn't mean she could continue to be so intrusive. He just didn't know how to stop her.

His frustration rising, he went to his bedroom and changed into an old rock concert T-shirt from his collection that only he and Anita knew about, then put on some athletic shorts. He grabbed his phone and earbuds and headed outside for a run. Jogging always helped him clear his head.

When he returned home an hour later, sweaty and less disgruntled, he took a quick shower. During his jog he'd realized he needed to talk to Anita and ask her how she'd figured out how to handle Mom. He wasn't the only one who had a challenging relationship with her or who had been held to high standards. After he got dressed, he left his condo and drove to the Sunshine Café.

As he walked into the café, the rich scent of coffee hit him head-on. *Aah.* He'd been here only a few times since Anita had opened the café, and zero times this past year. Guilt nagged at him. He loved coffee, and he should be patronizing her and Tanner's businesses more often. Today was a good day to start.

He scanned the seating area. Business was slow this afternoon, and other than him and the unfamiliar barista behind the counter, only two other people were there—an older gentleman he didn't recognize and . . .

Oh boy.

Olivia was tucked into the far corner of the café, near a short hallway that led to the restroom. A laptop sat open on the table before her, and her dark eyebrows furrowed into a flat line of concentration as she tapped on the touchpad. She looked cute today, her emerald-green short-sleeved shirt and black skirt highlighting her olive skin. Although a small silver barrette held back her thick black bangs, the sides of her blunt-cut hair rested against her cheeks, almost obscuring her face from his view. Yes, definitely cute. But he liked her better in that pink dress she'd worn at last night's lesson.

Oh yes.

His palms grew damp. Thank goodness she hadn't noticed him yet. He could grab a coffee and leave, since it didn't look like Anita was there. Or he could spin on his heel and exit right now.

Coward.

He inwardly flinched. Even his conscience was giving him a dose of truth. He was a coward. He'd been a coward for months, although he'd avoided acknowledging that fact by burying himself in work. Now he didn't have a choice. Well, he had one. *Make things right.* Or at least attempt to.

Clearing his throat, he walked over to her table, remembering the last time he'd had coffee with her. Or more accurately, what happened *after* coffee. His pulse surged.

"Hi, Kingston." Sunny appeared at the end of the hallway. A huge grin spread across her face as she stepped between him and Olivia. "Nice to see you. I just got off the phone with your mom."

He plastered a tight grin on his face and braced himself. "What a coincidence."

"I know, right? She said you wanted a private dance lesson?"

Obviously, she hadn't gotten the voice mail he'd left. He peered around her slim shoulders. Olivia was typing now, either oblivious to him and Sunny or ignoring them. He looked at Sunny again. "About that—"

"I have some free time now. My next class doesn't start for"—she glanced at the smart watch on her thin wrist—"another hour and a half. That's plenty of time to teach you the tango."

"I, uh . . ." He glanced at Olivia again. Still typing. Still ignoring. "Sure," he said to Sunny. "I've got nothing going on this afternoon."

"Great." Her grin widened. "Did you get your coffee yet?"

"No."

"Me either. We can grab them and then head to the studio. How does that sound?"

"Fine." He gave Olivia one last look. There was no doubt she could hear their conversation. So that's how it was going to be. He shifted his gaze to Sunny. "Just fine."

He and Sunny went to the counter to put in their orders. "Karen gave me some great suggestions about future dance lessons," she said.

"I'm sure she did," he mumbled.

"Can I help you?" the barista asked.

"I'll have a caramel coconut latte, please." Sunny fished for her wallet inside the large purple bag slung over her shoulder, *Ms. Abernathy's School of Dance* emblazoned on the side in black letters.

Kingston took out his wallet. "My treat."

"You don't have to do that."

"You're right. But I'm happy to."

She smiled. "Maybe I should have gotten a large, then."

He grinned. "You still can. I haven't paid yet."

"I'm joking," she said, chuckling. "A small is all I need."

After he placed his order for a plain black decaf, Anita appeared behind the counter. "Hey, Kingston," she said. "I didn't know you were here."

"I just arrived a few minutes ago."

Anita looked at him, then at Sunny. Was she wondering if they were together? She reached for an apron and put it over her head. "How are the dance lessons going, Sunny?"

"Our first one was a success." Sunny adjusted the bag on her shoulder. "I'm hoping we'll have more students as the course progresses. Why don't you and Tanner join us next Monday?"

"I wish we could. But . . ."

Although she'd revealed her pregnancy to the family, obviously Anita wasn't ready to spread the news to everyone else. And even though she was as hospitable as she always was with her customers, going back to the days when she was a waitress at the Sunshine Diner, he could see lines of fatigue around her eyes. The first trimester was exhausting for most women.

"Are those cookies new?" He pointed to a display of large oatmeal-type cookies in the glass case, attempting to change the subject.

"The Cowboy Cookies? We've had them for a while. Harper started making those six months ago. Or was it seven? They're always a big hit."

"I'll take one." He glanced at Sunny, who was also looking at the cookies. "Make it two."

Anita slid two cookies into a waxed-paper holder as the barista set the drinks on the counter. "One black decaf, one caramel coconut," the young woman said and started tapping on the register screen.

"These are on the house." Anita handed him the cookies. "The drinks are too."

He set the cookies down and opened his wallet. "Can't let you do that, little sis."

"It's my business." She lifted her chin, but her amber eyes were filled with mirth. "I can do whatever I want to. And that includes treating my brother when he makes a rare appearance in my café."

Guilt hit him again. "Fine. You win." He slid his wallet into the back pocket of his shorts and picked up the drinks, then handed Sunny hers.

"Did you see Olivia?" Anita asked.

He froze. "Um, yeah. She looked busy."

"She comes here to work sometimes. She could use a break, though, and we're slow right now. We were going to chat for a bit. Y'all want to join us?"

"I've got a dance lesson," he said quickly. "I'll take a rain check."

"Me too," Sunny said. "But I'd love to have coffee with you both sometime."

"Rain check it is." Anita smiled and walked around the counter. After giving Kingston a playful punch on his shoulder, she walked over to Olivia's table.

"Ready to go?" Sunny asked.

He nodded and, resisting the urge to look at Olivia again, followed Sunny. They stepped outside into the late-August heat, one of the hottest times of the year.

"I don't know if I'll ever get used to the humidity here." Sunny fanned herself as they looked out for traffic. Two cars whizzed by, then they crossed Main Street. "We have a few muggy days in Maryland, but nothing like this."

"I don't think anyone gets used to it, including us natives."

They reached the dance studio, and she took out her key and opened the door. Cool air welcomed them, and she turned on the lights.

"Make yourself at home." She smiled.

She was the cheeriest person he'd ever met, and her smile was contagious. "Thanks. I have to tell you, though. I already know how to do the tango. I just need a little practice."

"All right. Practice it is." She walked to the picture window and pulled the metal chain on the side of a large shade. Several chairs were lined up nearby, presumably for parents and kids to sit on during lessons. "Do you mind if I open this? The sun isn't as harsh in the afternoon."

"Go ahead." He sipped his coffee.

She tugged on the chain. The shade didn't move. "Huh. I thought I fixed this the other day."

"Here." He set down the coffee on a nearby chair and went to the window. Standing behind her, he reached up to check the mechanism. "It's stuck."

"Again?" She looked up. "I'm going to return this thing. It's given me nothing but trouble since I bought it."

"I think I can fix it." He fiddled with the pulley and yanked out a bit of tangled thread. "Here's your culprit. Probably happened during manufacturing." He pulled on the shade, and it easily went up.

"Thank you!" She turned around as he finished opening the shade. "It must be nice to be tall."

"It comes in handy sometimes."

As he lowered his arms, she started to move away, only to stumble. He put his hands on her shoulders to steady her.

"Sorry. Caught my toe on the corner of the rug." She

laughed. "I'm not always as graceful as I look." As he dropped his hands, she added, "Ready to dance?"

"As ready as I'll ever be."

Olivia bit the inside of her cheek and stared at her steaming cup of Earl Grey, forcing herself to stop looking out the front window of the Sunshine Café. It figured she'd manage to choose a table in the almost-empty café with a clear view of the opposite side of Main Street—and Ms. Abernathy's School of Dance.

Against her will she glanced up to see Sunny stumble straight into Kingston's arms. An ugly thread of jealousy wound around her heart, and it didn't disappear after he and Sunny moved apart.

"I wonder what's up with them?" Anita said, turning and following Olivia's gaze. She'd sat down at Olivia's table right after Kingston and Sunny left.

Olivia jerked her eyes from the window and looked at her tea again, as if it held all the answers to her confusion. This was the first time in months she'd spent an afternoon working in the café, telling Flo and RaeAnne that she was going to do some work outside the office. And that had been fine. She was missing Anita, and the two women had talked a bit when she arrived. Anita had said she would join her after she made a few phone calls in the office.

But then Kingston had shown up. She'd seen him the moment he walked into the café. It had been hard enough to pretend that she didn't know he was there or that she'd heard every word of his conversation with Sunny. He seemed to have a lot of free time lately. So much for his *busy* schedule.

"Earth to Olivia."

Her gaze jerked up. Anita sipped her glass of water—she was giving up caffeine during her pregnancy—and said, "Is everything okay?"

She nodded and glanced at the window again. Fortunately, Sunny and Kingston had disappeared, presumably to practice the tango during their *private* lesson. She bit her cheek again, this time hard enough to wince.

"You don't seem okay."

She wasn't, and she couldn't tell her best friend that her brother was the reason why. Settling herself, she remembered her vow not to let him affect her. "I really am fine. I just have a lot of things on my mind with work and my class." She waved her hand. "Never mind about me. How are you feeling? Is the baby kicking yet?"

Anita laughed and then launched into almost unbearable detail about her pregnancy so far, including the morning sickness. "Sorry," she said, when Olivia finally put her fingertips over her mouth. "Guess I was a little too descriptive."

"Hopefully all that will pass soon. I'd hate to think of you being sick the whole time."

"Me too. But it will be worth it." Anita glanced at the window again. "Do you think there might be something going on with Sunny and King?"

Olivia shoved down the sudden stab of jealousy attacking her heart. "She's giving him a dance lesson. That's her job."

"I know. But you have to admit they look good together."

No, I don't. She nodded anyway, because confound it, Anita was right. With her honey-colored hair and willowy frame, Sunny looked like she'd stepped off the cover of a fairy-tale book. Even worse, she was so *nice*. And a talented dancer, and a good teacher. On paper, she was perfect for Kingston, who was basically a prince. Or pretended to be.

"I kind of hope there is a spark," Anita said. "He's been so focused on work for so long. I'm surprised he had time to come to the café, much less take another dance lesson. But Mom mentioned he was taking some vacation time, so I guess that's why."

Olivia squeezed her teacup so hard her knuckles hurt. "Seems he makes time for what he wants to."

"Well, maybe if something happens with Sunny, he won't work so hard. I know Mom would be over the moon if he ever found someone. I think she might be giving up hope. She's determined for all of us to get married. 'Two down, one more to go,' she likes to say. I thought Kingston would be the first one of us to tie the knot."

Olivia drained the tea. "Oh?" she said, holding back a sudden burst of curiosity.

Anita nodded. "I was in love with Tanner for so long, I'd given up on him."

"He was quite clueless," Olivia said.

"Even so, I could never imagine falling for anyone else. And Paisley was always so single-minded about law school. I couldn't believe it when she said she and Ryan were getting married before she finished her degree. I always thought she'd wait until she was established in her practice. That left Kingston. He dated around some, and you know how much he loves kids. I figured he'd be eager to get married and start a family after he finished med school." She laughed. "Wow, I was wrong about everything."

Cassidy, the café's barista, came over to the table. "Do you mind if I take my break a little early, Anita?"

"Sure. We're not busy, so take an extra five. If I need you, I'll let you know."

Cassidy nodded, pulling her phone out of her apron and texting as she walked into the back room.

Before Olivia and Anita could resume their conversation, however, the front door opened and three customers walked in. Anita stood. "It never fails. As soon as I say out loud that we're slow, we get busy again. I've got to man the counter until Cassidy gets back. Will you still be here in twenty minutes or so?"

"Probably not. I need to get back to the library." Olivia didn't, but she wasn't about to sit here at the table torturing herself.

"Okay." Anita leaned over and hugged Olivia's shoulders. "I'm so glad you came by. I miss you."

"Me too." She squeezed Anita's shoulders.

As her friend walked way, she packed up her laptop and headed out of the café.

Don't look. Don't look.

But she slowed her steps and did exactly that, and all she saw was the empty front window of the dance studio. Not Kingston and Sunny dancing beautifully for Maple Falls to see. Her imagination took over anyway. She visualized him dipping Sunny, their eyes locking as he cradled her slim waist. She'd seen enough old movies to know that classic move, which was usually followed by a kiss. Or, in comedies, a drop to the floor.

She shook her head at her own ridiculousness. So what if Kingston and Sunny were dancing, or embracing, or even became an item? Good for them. It wouldn't affect her one way or another.

She started to walk again. She would just ignore—

"Oof!"

Olivia felt a hand on the side of her shoulder. She looked up and found herself inches from Pastor Jared. "Sorry about that." He gave her a sheepish grin. "I was trying to dodge you, but I guess you didn't see me."

"No, it's my fault. I wasn't paying attention."

"Well, it's nice bumping into you." He smiled. "Just came from the diner. Tanner's got a new special this week— grits and shrimp. Have you tried them?"

"Not yet."

"I highly recommend them." He glanced across the street. "Oh, hey, there's Kingston. He's leaving the dance studio."

Against her will she turned and looked at him. This time, their eyes met. Locked. And for a moment, she couldn't breathe.

"Will you be there on Monday?"

Jared's question buzzed in her ear like a pesky fly. "What?" she asked.

Kingston turned and walked toward Price's Hardware. As if he hadn't even seen her.

"The dance studio. Are you going to continue taking lessons?"

She turned back to Jared. For a split second she thought about going back on her word to herself to be more adventurous. It would be easier than seeing Kingston every week. But she remembered her vow not to let Kingston affect her life. "Yes," she said, giving Jared a smile. "I'll be there."

"Great. If we're partnered up again, I promise I won't step on your feet." He grinned and moved past her. "I've got a meeting at the café in a few minutes. See you Sunday."

"See you then."

She watched him walk away. He was a nice guy. Always friendly. Good-looking too. If she was interested in dating, Jared would be a good choice.

And risk getting hurt again? No thank you.

She got into her car and drove back to the library, putting both Kingston and Jared out of her mind.

"Whatcha lookin' at?"

Kingston glanced at Jasper as the old man sidled up to him near the glass door of the hardware store. Ducking into Price's had been an impulsive decision after he'd seen Olivia standing outside the café . . . talking to Jared. When she'd turned away from the pastor and looked straight at him, he'd almost dashed across the street to talk to her. But she'd made it clear she didn't want to have anything to do with him, so he chickened out. Now he was watching her smile at Jared. He felt a muscle jerk in his jaw.

"Cat got your tongue?"

He looked at Jasper and moved away from the door. "Where do you keep your wrenches?" He couldn't come up with a good excuse for staring out the door, but at least he could pretend he needed a tool or something.

"Depends." Jasper ran his stubby thumb over the edge of the counter where an old-fashioned register sat, a smaller modern one next to it.

"On what?"

"What size you need. And the brand. And the job."

"Any size, any brand."

"What are you tryin' to fix?"

My life. At least the part that couldn't stop being attracted to Olivia. "A faucet."

"Okay, now we're gettin' somewhere. Follow me, Doc."

He trailed Jasper and listened to the old man wax ineloquently but with knowledge and enthusiasm about wrenches. By the time he left, he'd purchased an entire wrench set he hadn't known he needed. The old man possessed excellent sales skills. Kingston thanked him and went to his car. It was getting close to suppertime. He thought about stopping at the diner to grab a bite to eat and fulfill his promise to himself to support his family's businesses. But he wasn't hungry. He was unsettled.

He got into his car and turned on the engine. Instead of leaving, he sat lost in thought. The dance practice with Sunny had gone well. She was not only an excellent teacher but also an excellent partner, and he'd enjoyed himself. But he couldn't get Olivia off his mind. And he knew the reason why. The guilt and shame over how he'd treated her, and was still treating her, would stick around unless he did something about it. And it was past time he did.

Kingston put his car in Drive and headed to the library.

Chapter 10

Olivia turned the Open sign on the front of the library door to Closed and walked back to the circulation desk, where she spied a stack of young-adult books on the return cart. She could wait until tomorrow for Flo or RaeAnne to put them back. It was closing time, after all. But working within the stated library hours was the one area of her life where she didn't follow a firm schedule. And while returning books to the shelves wasn't technically on her duty list, it wouldn't take long to put a few back. Then she would visit Aunt Bea and check on her ankle. According to her aunt's text, she was feeling "just fine," but Olivia wanted to see for herself.

She pushed the cart to the YA section and started shelving the books. *The Belle of the Ball* had a princess on the cover. *Hall of Snow and Sky* had a female warrior decked out in a shimmering ice-blue cloak and armed with a bow and arrow. *The Girl You Loved* had a cartoon drawing of a teenager in a flowery dress holding a puppy. Cute. It had been a long time since Olivia had read any YA fiction, and she set *Hall of Snow and Sky* to the side. It was the only book that didn't appear to be a romance. She was staying away from those for a long while.

As she pushed the last novel on the cart, *Forever Sophia*—great, another romance—into its slot on the shelf, she heard knocking on the front doors. She stood and pushed the cart to the front desk, walked over to the entrance . . . and froze.

Kingston waved. Grinned. Pointed at the locked door.

She drew in a deep breath and took measured steps toward him, stopping a few feet from the door. "We're closed."

"I know." His voice was slightly muffled, his grin less bright. "I wanted to talk to you. Can you let me in? Or I can wait until you're ready to go."

Olivia didn't move.

"I won't take up much of your time. Promise."

Her gaze met his, and she saw the entreaty in his alluring blue eyes. But she'd been here before and fallen for his pleas. She wouldn't be fooled this time. "I don't want to talk to you." She turned on her heel and walked away.

"Olivia . . ."

Ignore him. She walked back to her office, sat at her desk, and opened her laptop. The first assignment for her lit class popped up. She was almost finished, and she had a week before it was due, so there was no urgency to work on it. The last thing she wanted to think about was how the Industrial Revolution had influenced romanticism and classicism and how both literary movements affected current contemporary works. Blech.

She began typing anyway, glancing at the clock every so often. After half an hour she looked over her progress and groaned. Four pages of nonsense. Her professor would think she'd had a stroke. She erased her work, stared at the blank screen, and tapped her fingers against her desk. *Tap . . . tap . . . tap.*

Forty minutes later she closed her laptop and turned off the office light. Surely Kingston was gone by now. After making her usual rounds to secure the library, she opened the back door and walked out, locking the door behind her. She glanced around the parking lot and was relieved that Kingston's car wasn't there. But when she approached her coupe, she saw a note tucked under one of the windshield wipers, the words written on a small square sheet of paper with the nonsensical name of a prescription medicine at the top.

Olivia,

I don't blame you for not wanting to talk to me, but I hope you reconsider. I'm sorry for what I did to you. An apology note isn't enough, though. I want to explain why. I also hope you'll continue to take dance lessons. Don't let me stand in the way of your fun.

When Anita opened her café, she gave me a key. If you change your mind about hearing me out, I'll be waiting for you inside. Like I said, I won't take up much of your time.

K

She crumpled the note in her hand. The Sunshine Café closed at six thirty every night except Sunday, when it was closed all day. She glanced at her watch. Six fifty-three.

Forget it. I'm not talking to him. He can sit there all night for all I care.

But as she started her car, she hesitated. He was offering her closure. She wasn't interested in what he had to say, but she had plenty to tell him. And hopefully, if she got her anger off her chest, she could move on. She could be around Anita and not think twice about Kingston, the way she had most of her life. It would be easier to avoid him. And a little delicious to let him stew in his guilt—if he even had any.

A knot formed in her stomach. She stared at the back of the library as her car engine hummed. Finally she picked up her phone and texted her aunt.

Working late tonight. How are you feeling?

Aunt Bea was always near her phone, and on cue she replied right away.

Right as rain. Doesn't feel like I did anything to it. Do you
    want to stop by on your way home for some pie?
No, thank you. It will be late when I finish here.

She had no intention of staying at the café any longer than necessary, but she also didn't want her aunt waiting on her.

All right, sugar. If you change your mind, me and the
    peach pie will be here.

Olivia replied with a heart emoji and put her phone back into her purse. She took a deep breath, put the car in Drive, and drove off.

Kingston gulped down his second demitasse of espresso and stared out the Sunshine Café's window. He glanced at his watch. Almost seven o'clock. He'd been here since five forty-five and had helped Anita close up at six thirty. He'd been restricted to washing dishes, since he knew little about the coffee machines or anything else concerning the running of the café. The espresso he was drinking had been left over, and Anita had given it to him to take home rather than waste it. His plan had been to drink it in the morning, but as the minutes ticked away and Olivia didn't show up, he caved.

The ultra-hit of caffeine wasn't helpful, and he'd regret it later on tonight, but right now he had to have something to do while he waited for Olivia. He'd even tried to read some research abstracts on his phone—surely he wasn't prohibited from even reading about medicine—but he couldn't concentrate. And as seven o'clock came and went, he became positive she wasn't going to show.

He took the small cup to the kitchen in the back, washed it by hand, and set it on the rack to dry. When he'd told Anita he would lock up tonight, she'd been surprised but relieved. Business had been slow, but she was ready to go home and rest. Something he needed to be doing too. Even though he had gotten more sleep in the past two weeks than he had in years, he still had catching up to do. Sleep would be elusive tonight, though, and not only because of the caffeine.

He shut off the light in the kitchen and headed to the dining area to put his chair up on the table, like the rest of them were when the floor was mopped. He took one last look at the door. Main Street was quiet this time of day, as almost all the businesses were closed, and the Sunshine Diner would be locking up in an hour or so. He should have known Olivia wouldn't come. Her shocked expression at seeing him at the library, followed by an arrow-sharp look and her refusal to let him in, had put an exclamation point on her words.

"I don't want to talk to you."

He didn't blame her. But persistence was his middle name, and he'd decided at the last minute to put that note on her car and hope she changed her mind.

He walked over to the light switch on the opposite side of the room and was about to turn it off when he heard a soft tap at the door. He whirled around. Olivia.

Kingston rushed to the door, unlocked it, and let her inside. He stepped back to give her space, but he couldn't resist visually taking her in. She was downright adorable. He still marveled that he hadn't noticed her beauty before that fateful night at the Sunset Cinema. How could he have been so blind all these years?

Olivia crossed her arms over her chest, her small handbag hanging from one arm. "I'm here. Speak."

"Why don't we have a seat? I can get you—"

"I'm not here for pleasantries, Kingston. You said you wanted to talk. So talk."

He pressed his lips together at her curt tone. She wasn't so adorable now. "Can we at least move away from the door and windows? I don't want anyone to see us—"

"Together?"

"No." Good grief, where did that come from? "I don't want anyone to see us fighting."

"Is it going to come to that?"

"I didn't think so. Now I'm not so sure."

She glared at him and walked to the center of the dining room between two tables and turned around. "Far enough?"

"It's fine." He moved toward her. "All right. No pleasantries. Olivia, I'm—"

"Sorry. I know. You're sorry, you lost track of time, you should have called but you didn't, you were busy, you're a very important doctor, blah blah blah."

Her vitriol caught him off guard. He'd planned to say all those things, except for being an important doctor and the blah-blah part.

"Look, I'll save you the trouble," she said. "You're forgiven."

"Doesn't sound like it," he mumbled.

"You can leave me alone now."

Something in her eyes made him pause. A good portion of his job required being in tune with his patients' body language. Kids didn't always know how to express their symptoms, discomfort, or pain. Sometimes they lied about it for various reasons—they didn't want to miss a Little League game or they were injured while at a place their parents had forbidden them to be. Or, in more tragic cases, they didn't want to get their parents in trouble. While he'd become an expert at figuring out children's unspoken words, he was pretty good at assessing adults too. He wasn't perfect with either group, but right now he was pretty sure Olivia wasn't just angry with him. She was hurt. Deeply hurt, and that was a shot to his heart.

"I'm a jerk," he said, to both her and himself. "A class A bona fide jerk. You're right. I was going to tell you all those excuses, and a few more. And I did put work before you, and I lost track of time and my schedule. I didn't have any time for one date, much less anything else."

"But you have time to be a dance teacher."

"There's a reason for that—"

"I don't care."

He sighed. "Right again. It doesn't matter. What does is that I didn't call you to apologize and explain why I blew you off. I'm not only a jerk; I'm a coward too."

Her arms, still crossed, relaxed slightly, and for just a moment he noted a little less fire in her eyes. Immediately she tensed again.

"Do you feel better now?" she snapped.

"I hurt you. So no, I don't feel better."

"You didn't hurt me." She averted her gaze. "We kissed a few times. Big deal."

"It was a big deal to me."

Olivia's gaze shot back to him. "Obviously not."

He ran a jittery hand through his hair. Espresso regret, right on cue. "I don't go around kissing women all the time, if that's what you're thinking."

"I wouldn't care if you did."

That made him smirk. "Oh really."

She took a step toward him. "Really. You could kiss every woman in Maple Falls if you're so inclined, and I wouldn't bat an eyelash."

Now he was amused. "Even your aunt Bea?"

"Keep your hands off my aunt Bea." Her lips twitched. Then she moved away from him, her expression hardening. "I've said my piece. You've said yours. Let's move on." She started to leave.

He put his hand on her arm. "Please. Don't go."

Olivia glanced down. Kingston's hand was so large that it almost covered her entire forearm. Then she met his gaze. Pleading again, but this time there was something else. Not the heat that had been between them in the past but something different. This was openness. And up until this moment, she hadn't realized that he'd always had a facade, a distance, about him. He was charming and affable and perpetually willing to help. But he always held himself back too. Even when they were kids.

This time he wasn't.

"Olivia." His voice was gruff and shaded with emotion. "I'm a mess." He dropped his hand from her and backed away, almost knocking down one of the chairs behind him. His hand was shaking.

She moved toward him, forgetting she was supposed to be furious and on her guard. "Are you okay? You're not sick, are you?"

"What? No." He glanced at his hands and let out a flat

chuckle. "Too much espresso while I was waiting for you." He put his hands behind him. "The truth is I really wanted to go out with you. I like you, Olivia. I still do. But for years I've been pretending to have things under control, and I really don't. I'm lucky I didn't get fired, just put on sabbatical."

"Sabbatical? What are you talking about?"

She listened as he told her about overscheduling himself to the detriment of his patients and his reputation. "Every time someone asked me to do something, I'd do it. 'No' isn't in my vocabulary. It all caught up with me. So that's why I have time to take dance lessons. I didn't intend to, but my mother asked me."

"And you couldn't say no."

"Bingo. Same thing with helping out Sunny. I don't really mind, to be honest. I like to dance, and I learned the steps in cotillion, so I do have some experience. It's good exercise, and it's something to do. I've been at loose ends lately, and I have two months to fill up."

"That sounds horrible," she said seriously. "I couldn't imagine taking two weeks off, much less two months."

"Trust me, it is." He laughed, this time sounding more relaxed. "Wow. It felt good to admit all that. Sorry to dump it on you."

"It's all right." And it was. She felt like she was seeing the real Kingston for once, and she was surprised that the golden boy had a little tarnish on his crown. It made him seem more . . . human.

"Anita doesn't know about the sabbatical," he said. "I just told her I was taking some time off. Other than my clinic and my dad, you're the only one who knows why."

"I won't tell anyone. Promise."

He grinned. "Good."

Miracle of miracles, she was able to smile back. Amazingly, she wasn't angry anymore. She'd listened to his apology, said a few harsh things herself, and now found out that his ghosting her wasn't even about her. It was because he'd taken on too much. "You should have just told me you were swamped," she said. "I would have understood."

"I know. It was stupid. But I didn't want to admit that I don't have everything under control."

She knew a little bit about control. *More than a little.* "It can be hard to let your guard down," she said, surprising herself with the words.

"Very true. And I can't say that I'm going to tell everyone 'no' right away, but I'm going to work on getting some balance." He shoved his hands into his pockets and looked down at her. "Truce?"

She mulled over the word. She'd trusted him twice, and he'd let her down. Even though his reasons made sense, it didn't mean she could completely trust him. But she didn't want to be at odds with him anymore either. "Truce," she finally said.

He grinned, his relief clear in his eyes. "Thanks for understanding. And forgiving me." His smile faded a bit. "We're still friends, right?"

"Yes." And for her own self-preservation, she added, "Only friends."

"Agreed. The ship has sailed on anything else."

A twinge of sadness hit her, but she shoved it away. They were on different paths right now. He was figuring out his life and how he could return to work with better habits, and she was still in her rut.

"Are you still going to Sunset on Monday nights?" he asked.

"Yes, but I put that on hold until dance lessons are over."

"You're still planning to take them?" When she nodded, he said, "That's a relief. I didn't want to chase you away."

"I'm not the most graceful person, but it was pleasant for the most part."

He rocked back on his heels. "I know the part that wasn't. I've got a little pull with the teacher, by the way. I'll make sure we don't get paired up again. I can tell Sunny to get you another partner, and we won't have to dance together again."

"What about Jared?"

"Uh, sure. Jared it is."

Olivia nodded. Her arms were at her sides now—she didn't remember when she'd unfolded them—and she was less edgy than she'd been in a long time. Kingston had cleared the air for both of them, and she was glad she'd changed her mind about talking to him.

"Guess I'd better get back home and do something about this caffeine buzz." He paused. "Thanks, Olivia."

"For what?"

"For being a friend. I could use one right now. That's another thing I neglected because I was so busy—friendships."

She smiled, appreciating his frankness. "You're welcome." Then she had a thought. "Do you like peach pie? Aunt Bea made a fresh one today."

He thought for a moment. "Sure, why not. Supercharged caffeine and a sugar rush is a great way to end the day."

Olivia chuckled. "Could you look at her ankle too? She twisted it the other day and says she's fine, but I'd feel better if a doctor checked it out."

"Be glad to."

"You won't get into trouble with your boss?"

"Not for looking at an ankle. But just to be safe, let's keep it between us."

"Of course. Let me give you her address." She told it to him, and he nodded.

"I know where that is. I just need to lock up here." He walked her to the door. "See you in a few . . . friend."

She grinned. "See you there."

Erma opened her eyes to a buzzing sound. She blinked, then let her eyes flutter shut. When the buzzing continued, they flew open again. She sat up and reached for her phone. It was past eleven o'clock. Who was calling her this late at night? A spark of panic lit in her chest. Was Riley in trouble? Hayden? Both?

She picked up the phone and glanced at the screen. Bea? The woman was never up this late. She slid her finger across the bottom of the screen. "Are you okay?" she said as she turned on the small lamp next to her bed.

"I'm sorry I'm calling so late, but this can't wait until morning. We need another emergency meeting of the BBs."

Erma blinked again, pushing the last remnants of sleep out of her eyes. "Bea, did you hit your head when you fell the other day? Because that totally could have waited until the morning. I'm not going to call everyone at this ungodly hour—"

"You're right." The excitement in Bea's voice wavered. "I shouldn't have disturbed you, but they didn't leave until five minutes ago, and I had to talk to someone."

"Who left?"

"Olivia and Kingston," she gushed. "Oh, Erma, I think he's the *one* for my sweet niece."

Erma pushed herself up until her back was resting against the headboard of her bed. "Bea, we talked about this. You said yourself that you were giving up on finding someone for Olivia."

"I know, I know. But that was before tonight." Bea sighed. "They're so perfect together."

After seeing Olivia and Kingston spar with each other at Sunny's dance lesson, that was the last thing she'd expected to hear. And now she had to tell Bea to curb her enthusiasm. "Sweetie, I know how much you love Olivia—"

"You should have seen them tonight. I invited her over for peach pie, and she turned me down, and then half an hour later she arrived with Kingston by her side. Talk about surprised. They're really a striking couple—he's so tall and blond; she's petite and dark. Their children will be beautiful, mark my words."

"Bea, slow your roll. Just because they came over for pie doesn't mean it's time to send them on a honeymoon."

"But you didn't see them—"

"Yes, I did. They were at the dance lesson last night. And they weren't chummy, if you get my drift."

"Well, whatever that was, they made up for it tonight. I couldn't get a word in edgewise, they were talking so much. About their jobs, books, movies, things that happened during their childhoods. Olivia spent a lot of time with the Bedfords when they were all growing up."

"It sounds like old friends reminiscing." Erma shifted position on her bed to accommodate her leg. It still flared up sometimes, even though two years had passed since she injured it sliding into third base at a church softball game. "I am glad to hear they're not at odds anymore." She'd never tell Bea this, but it had been uncomfortable watching their kerfuffle. Erma had no idea Olivia could be so belligerent, and Kingston had looked more than guilty about whatever it was he'd done.

"Oh, they're more than friends," Bea continued, "and they're definitely not at odds."

"Bea—"

"You didn't see the way they looked at each other." Bea paused, and Erma was sure her friend was going to let out another sigh. "They had the moon *and* stars in their eyes. Which is why we need to nudge them along. They might not realize it now, but they're completely smitten. Oh, who'd have thought I'd have a doctor for a nephew-in-law? Erma, I'm simply giddy over this."

"No kidding," Erma mumbled. But she should at least hear Bea out. "Do you have a plan of some sort?"

"The dance lessons. Kingston's an assistant teacher, and Olivia said she wants to continue taking them. We need to make sure they always dance together. That's step one."

"There are steps to this?"

"Step two is getting Karen involved."

Oh no. Erma grimaced. "Karen Bedford?"

"Yes. We need her full support."

"And what if she doesn't give it?"

"She will," Bea insisted, sounding a little offended. "Who wouldn't want my niece as their daughter-in-law?"

Erma pinched the bridge of her nose. "Have you given any thought to what might happen if you're wrong about this?"

"Erma Jean, I'm surprised at you. I've never been so sure of anything in my life, other than Bill, and here you are, doubting me."

"I'm sorry." Egad, this could end up exploding in their faces. But when Bea was resolute, she was resolute. "All right. Call Karen tomorrow, and I'll set up the meeting."

"I was hoping you would call her."

"Me?"

"To be honest, she's a little intimidating. And she's always saying, 'Ta-ta for now.' Like Tigger from Winnie-the-Pooh. It's weird."

Erma blew out a resigned breath. "Okay, I'll call Karen, and you set up the meeting."

"Perfect. Thank you, Erma. You're a gem."

"And you're a peach," she said, somehow able to chuckle a little. But when she hung up the phone, she wasn't smiling. She'd thought the matchmaking shenanigans were over. Now they were worse than before, because of who was involved. Kingston certainly was a catch, and at one time she'd thought he and Harper would end up together. She'd called that one wrong—Harper and Rusty were meant for each other. If

Kingston was really interested in Olivia, she could see how they would work well together. But getting Karen involved? Egad . . . again.

She set her phone down and turned off the light. Maybe divine intervention would happen twice, and Bea would give up on interfering with Olivia's life again. But as she started to fall back asleep, another thought came to her mind.

What if this time . . . she's right?

Chapter 11

Wednesday morning, daylight streaked through the white blinds in Kingston's bedroom. He opened his eyes and glanced at his phone on the side table next to his bed. Almost eight o'clock. He hadn't bothered to set his alarm during the past week. Not a good habit to get into. But while he was on his forced sabbatical, there wasn't a reason to get up at 4:30 a.m. like he used to. Sleeping until eight, though? He'd wasted half his morning.

He rolled out of bed and padded to his kitchen. Intent on getting his morning coffee, he opened the cabinet and started reaching for the bag of beans, then changed his mind. He didn't need any coffee right now. It had taken forever for him to fall asleep, thanks to the espresso overload and Olivia. But instead of stressing over making things right with her, he'd had a fun night with her at Bea's, and he found himself mentally replaying the highlights.

What surprised him most was how relaxed he'd felt with her and Bea. The pie was delicious, Bea's ankle was fine, and the conversation flowed between him and Olivia. She also seemed completely at ease, more so than when they'd gone out for coffee after *The Quiet Man*. Her eyes lit up when she was talking about old movies, and they'd gotten into a bit of a lively debate over whether *The Quiet Man* was a superior film to *Gone with the Wind*. As a history buff, he was more partial to Leigh and Gable than Wayne and O'Hara, but both films were excellent.

He hadn't anticipated staying at Bea's until after eleven, but the time flew by. Hopefully Olivia had gotten more sleep than he did and wasn't too tired at work today.

Shuffling back to his room, he began undressing to take a shower when his phone buzzed. He glanced at the screen and immediately answered it. "Hi, Lawrence."

"Good morning, Dr. Bedford. I'm following up to see if you're enjoying your time off."

He sat on the edge of the bed. "Surprisingly, I am." A pause. "Thanks. This was the right thing for me. I feel rested and balanced, so I don't think I need the whole two months off. Another week and I'll be fine to go back to work."

"Continue to follow doctor's orders, and we'll see you in October."

"But—"

Click.

Kingston stared at the phone. Then he smiled. Lawrence was doing what any good doctor would do—checking on his patient. Next time he called, though, Kingston was going to keep his mouth shut about coming back to work early.

Lesson learned.

Just as he set down the phone, it buzzed again. He winced

at the name on the display. *Mother.* He was tempted to ignore her call and return it later, but that was just postponing the inevitable—he was 99 percent sure she was calling to ask him to do something he probably didn't want to do.

"Hello, Mom." He leaned forward, bracing himself for whatever plans she had for him.

"Good morning, dear. How are you?"

She was in the car again, off to who knew where. "I'm fine. Just fixin' to jump in the shower. What's up?"

"I have an appointment in Maple Falls today, and I thought you might like to have lunch."

"Sure—" He stopped, remembering what he'd admitted to Olivia last night about always saying yes. But this was his mother, and she was impossible to say no to. And lunch wouldn't derail his plans for the day. He'd decided he was going to call a travel agent and book his vacation today. The idea of flying somewhere tropical still hadn't left his mind. He couldn't go now since he was committed to dance lessons, but afterward he'd have two more weeks to fill. He might take off to Hawaii. Or maybe do something completely different and go to Europe. Or Japan.

Once his trip was booked, he'd intended to do some research on a few of the movies Olivia had mentioned last night that he was unfamiliar with. All that could wait until after lunch, though. "Sure, Mom. How about the diner?"

"Perfect. I'll see you at noon. Ta-ta for now!"

Kingston chuckled and dropped the phone on his bed. Well, lunch with his mother was one way to pass the time. And Tanner and his crew always made good food. He hurried to the shower before he was interrupted again.

"The BBs are meeting here this morning?"

Erma nodded at Riley as they worked in the back room of Knots and Tangles. Her granddaughter was unpackaging blank hanks of yarn and setting them near the vats she used to dye the fibers. "For about an hour. Maybe less." She still had a smidge of hope that Bea would change her mind about meddling with Olivia and Kingston. When Erma had woken up this morning, she'd seen the situation more clearly. Nothing had changed as far as she was concerned, and Olivia and Kingston surely didn't need a bunch of nosy women getting in the way of whatever there was between them.

Riley frowned. "I've got a ton of yarn to dye, and I need to finish it all today."

"Oh." That put a pinhole in her planning.

"Can you meet at the café? Or maybe the library?"

"Not the library," she said quickly. At Riley's curious look she added, "You know how noisy we can be."

"That's true. Olivia would spend all her time shushing y'all."

Erma nodded. Besides, that girl didn't need to know she was half of the topic of conversation.

Riley selected three bottles of dye from the shelves bolted into the cinder-block wall above the vats. "This is the first time I've heard of the BBs having an emergency meeting. What's going on?"

"Nothing important."

"Then why is it an emergency?"

"Oh, you know." Erma faux chuckled, trying to come up with a viable reason. She should probably tell Riley what was going on since Olivia was one of her BFFs, but Erma hoped today's conversation would end up in nowheresville and never be spoken of again. If Kingston and Olivia were meant to be, it would happen naturally.

Riley lifted an eyebrow. "No. I don't. You're acting a little suspicious, Mimi."

"Me?" She fiddled with the piping on the lime-green couch Riley had picked up two years ago. "Suspicious? Never!"

"Thanks for proving my point."

"All we're doing is shaking things up a little. We've been meeting on Thursday nights for forever. It's getting stale. I thought we could try a morning meeting this time. I should have checked with you first, though. My bad."

"Well, it's my fault I'm dyeing this batch at the last minute. I've been so busy helping Hayden plan out his campaign. I didn't realize there was so much involved in running for office. He filed the papers already, so there's no turning back now. He starts his campaign in January."

Erma walked over to her granddaughter. "Are you having second thoughts?"

"I always have second thoughts. That's my MO." Riley sighed. "Hayden's so excited, and he has great plans for Maple Falls. I'm thrilled to be a part of all the positive changes he wants to implement. But . . ."

"But what?" Erma asked gently.

"I don't like being in the spotlight. Or the center of

attention. Hayden's not an attention seeker either, but he's used to pressure. He had a lot of it when he played pro ball. Even before then. He thrives on this. I don't."

"Oh, honey. It will be okay. You've got mine and the BBs' support, and your friends' support too. In fact, I'd be surprised if anyone votes for that slimeball Quickel. And I love attention, so if I can take the heat off you, let me know."

Riley's shoulders relaxed. "Thanks, Mimi. I'm so grateful you're always in my corner."

"Forever and ever." She hugged her granddaughter.

"By the way," Riley said as she went back to setting up her dyeing station. "How did your dance lesson go on Monday?"

"Um, it was okay."

"Just 'okay'?" Riley lifted a surprised eyebrow. "You love to dance."

That was true. She did like to shake a leg when she had the opportunity. Truth be told, she'd had fun Monday night, even though she found the rumba a dull dance. And she did plan to visit the Swinging Sage at the earliest opportunity. But she was still stunned by her reaction to Jasper when he first put his hands on her waist, which was a little thicker now than it was back in the day. He hadn't seemed to notice or care, but when he finally stopped scowling enough to focus on the dance steps, she'd experienced the *jolt* again, and it definitely didn't have anything to do with the chili she'd had for lunch that day.

"Did you see Jasper there?" Riley asked. "Hayden mentioned he might be there."

"He was."

Riley faced her. "And?"

She shrugged. "He was his usual killjoy self." *Mostly.*

"Did you dance together?"

"What's with the twenty questions?" Erma fluttered her hands at her. "Get back to work. I need to figure out a new meeting place for the BBs."

Her granddaughter chuckled as Erma left the back room and went to the front of the store. She had no idea what Riley thought was so funny about their short discussion. There was nothing humorous about the weird reaction she'd had to Jasper Monday night. Perplexing, maybe, but not chuckle worthy.

No customers were in the store yet, so Erma focused on figuring out where they could hold their emergency meeting this morning. Maybe she should cancel it. But Bea would be upset and probably show up at the shop with four casseroles and six desserts to ease her stress, so Erma started texting the group.

Change of venue. We're meeting at

She paused. The café wasn't a good idea because Anita worked there, and she didn't want anyone overhearing their conversation. They really needed somewhere private. She snapped her fingers.

my house. Riley is dyeing yarn this morning.

Myrtle: Great! See you there.
Madge: I might be late. I have my first client meeting
today.

Erma: Focus on that. We'll fill you in later.

Madge: Thanks

Bea: I'm bringing a hummingbird cake. Made it this morning.

Erma, Peg, Myrtle, Gwen, Viola: 👍

Karen: I'm gluten free. What is your address, Erma?

Erma typed it in. No surprise Karen was gluten free. But when Erma had called her last night at Bea's behest, she'd been excited at the prospect of an Olivia-and-Kingston pairing. *"I never thought about the two of them together,"* she'd said. *"Naturally, we adore Olivia. And my Kingston is such a catch. I'm open to discussing the possibility."*

The bell above the door rang, and four women walked in at the same time. Erma smiled. They were from Hot Springs Village, and they usually carpooled to visit Knots and Tangles once a month.

"Hello, ladies!" She sailed to them. "What can I help you find today?"

She could work for an hour before heading back to her house for the meeting, and even though Riley was dyeing yarn, she could take care of any customers while Erma was gone. God willing, the meeting would be short and sweet, with everyone coming to their senses.

🦢

"How's the vacation going?"

"Pretty good." Kingston took a swig of sweet tea as Tanner slid into the seat across from him. The Sunshine

Diner was almost packed with the lunch crowd, and he'd had to wait a few minutes for the table to be cleared.

His brother-in-law leaned back, a beat-up baseball cap backward on his head, a ponytail tucked underneath. Not long ago, Tanner's hair had been past his shoulders, and he'd cut it short. Now he was growing it out again, much to Anita's delight. "I figured you'd go somewhere exotic, not Maple Falls."

Kingston grinned. "I still might."

"How much time do you have off?" Tanner asked.

"Too much," he muttered. "How's Anita feeling today?"

"She's tired. I told her this morning she needed to cut down to part time at the café."

"Is she going to?'

"She's still thinking about it. She sure is stubborn when she wants to be." Tanner shifted in his seat. "Is it normal to be this nervous about having a baby?"

"Yes, especially new mothers."

"I'm talking about me, dude." Tanner lowered his voice. "What do I know about being a father? My dad died when I was young."

"But you helped raise your brother. You have some experience."

"Yeah, but not with *babies*." His friend's tone bordered on terrified.

Kingston would have laughed if Tanner hadn't been so serious. "Honestly, you can read all the books and learn everything you can about parenting, but it won't be enough."

Tanner grimaced. "That's reassuring."

"It is. Every child is unique, and the way you approach

parenting them will be different. The best advice I have is to go with your gut. You and Anita are good people. You have ethics and boundaries and are responsible. You're going to be a great dad. A dad that makes mistakes, but you'll still be great."

"Thanks. It's good to have an expert in the family." Tanner grinned. "When you have kids, you'll be all set."

"Hey, Tanner." Bailey, one of the waitresses, headed to the table. "Jasper's complaining about his turkey sandwich again. Says he wants to speak to management."

Tanner slid out of the booth. "The old man does this every day. Sometimes at lunch, sometimes dinner." His smile faded. "I think he's lonely and likes the attention. Better go find out what I did wrong. Maybe I added an extra lettuce leaf or something." He clapped Kingston on the shoulder and headed across the dining room to Jasper, who had his arms crossed and the dish pushed away from him.

Kingston watched as Tanner sat across from Jasper and nudged the sandwich closer. He couldn't hear what either of them was saying, but as they talked the old man's scowl evaporated, and he picked up the sandwich and started eating. Tanner stayed and talked for a minute or two, then went to the kitchen.

His brother-in-law was right. Jasper was lonely. Kingston was glad the guy was taking dance lessons. Despite having a reputation for being a wet blanket, he clearly liked being around people. And watching how Tanner instinctively knew how to handle him just proved Kingston right—his brother-in-law was going to be an excellent father.

He glanced at his watch. Two minutes after twelve. Hmm. His mother was never late.

Just as the thought cleared his mind, she breezed into the diner. He waved his hand, and she spotted him.

"Hello, darling!" She sat across from him, the soft scent of her perfume cutting through the fried-food aroma filling the diner. "Sorry I'm late."

"No problem. Tanner and I were chatting for a bit."

"I hope he's taking good care of Anita. She needs as much TLC as possible during this delicate time." She set her purse down on the bench seat and frowned. "She's being stubborn, though."

"So I've heard."

"Every time I try to give her advice, she ignores me."

"She seemed fine with our visit on Monday."

"That's because I held my tongue. Last week she almost snapped my head off."

"You remember what it's like, Mother." He opened the menu. "Her hormones are all over the place."

"Yes, but she should want me by her side." Hurt crossed her features. "I'm going to miss out on so much when Paisley gets pregnant since she's so far away. I'd hoped to have a better experience with Anita."

He squeezed her hand. "She's tired, hormonal, and a little scared."

"Then she needs me more than ever—"

"Or she's getting what she needs from her husband. Give her some space, Mother. I'm sure she'll come around when she's feeling better."

She sighed. "You're right. I have been a little stifling."

Kingston's eyebrow arched. His mother rarely had moments of self-awareness.

"Anyway, I'm not here to discuss Anita. I'm here to spend time with my wonderful son. Did you get a chance to practice with Sunny?"

"Yep." He waited for her to say how pretty Sunny was and point out how *splendid* or *marvelous* they looked together. Or worse.

Silence.

Alarmed, he said, "You didn't call her again, did you?"

"No. Why would I do that?"

He relaxed. He wouldn't put it past his mother to set the two of them up on a date.

"However, I was hoping you could give Olivia more help."

"Olivia? Why?"

"She seemed to struggle with the steps."

She didn't struggle to stomp on his foot several times, though. But that was before they had gotten back on the friendship track. He was more than ready to let bygones be bygones.

"I remember when she was young, bless her heart," his mother continued. "She was never the most graceful child."

Kingston didn't remember that. Then again, he couldn't remember ever seeing Olivia do anything physical. Wait, there had been one time. He'd managed to catch one of the church softball games. She played right field, and he couldn't gauge her fielding ability because no one had hit any balls in her direction. But he'd seen her up at bat. She wasn't horrible, but she wasn't good either. He'd admired her for trying.

"If you could give her some basic pointers, I think it would really help."

Kingston nodded. "That's what Sunny's teaching. The basics."

Mother scoffed. "I mean the basic basics."

Bailey came over to the table. "Hi, Mrs. Bedford. Haven't seen you here in a long time. Tanner said lunch was on the house. What can I get for you?"

"Unsweet tea and a chef salad, minus the turkey, ham, cheese, and egg. No dressing."

Bailey smirked as she scribbled on her pad and turned to Kingston. "What can I get for you?"

"Chicken-fried steak, mashed potatoes, corn, a roll, and pecan pie for dessert." He closed the menu and spied his mother's disapproving look.

"Coming right up."

After Bailey left, his mother said, "That's a lot of saturated fat, King. It's never too early to take care of your arteries."

He almost laughed, considering that his father, the cardiologist, wouldn't have hesitated to order the same thing if he were with them. He and his dad didn't eat like this all the time, but a few saturated fats here and there wouldn't hurt. "I'll work it off dancing," he said.

"On Saturday," she said.

"No, on Monday." Weird. She never mixed up days.

His mother's smile resembled that of a cat who lived on a dairy farm. "I stopped by the library and invited Olivia for supper Saturday night. She agreed to come."

"Let me guess—you told her Anita would be there."

"I didn't tell her she wouldn't."

"Did you tell her I would be?"

She paused. "No. But you will be. I'll have a lovely supper prepared, and afterward you can practice dancing with her."

He sank back against the seat. "Is this a setup?"

"Heavens, no." But she was furiously polishing her spoon with a paper napkin. "Why would I do something like that?"

"I don't know. You tell me."

"I'm trying to help Olivia. I would think you'd want to help her too. She's Anita's best friend, after all. And . . ."

"And what?"

"Oh, here's my tea."

Bailey set the tea in front of Mother, and she took a huge drink. "That hit the spot. Now, supper will be at six sharp, so arrive a little beforehand."

He didn't answer.

"Did you hear me? Six sharp. And wear something blue. It brings out the color of your eyes."

His gut clenched. He had no idea why she was setting him up with Olivia, and she was as subtle as a truck plowing through a glass wall. And when Olivia discovered the real reason for his mother's supper invitation, it would ruin their truce, especially if she thought he had something to do with it.

Tanner delivered the food himself, and Kingston stared at his steak while Mother dropped several anvil-size hints that he and Anita should be more open to accepting her help. Tanner nodded at the appropriate times, and once gave Kingston a "help me" look, but all Kingston could do was shrug. He had his own problems with her that he needed to figure out.

During the rest of lunch, he half listened as his mother picked through her salad and talked about her social calendar while he tried to figure out what to do about Saturday. He could tell her no, but her nose would bend so far out of joint that he'd have to get his medical bag. One thing he didn't want to happen in public was her getting upset. She wouldn't make a scene, but she had a way of side-eyeing him that made him want to crawl under a rock. And even then, there was no guarantee she wouldn't try some other matchmaking scheme.

"King. King." She snapped her fingers in front of him. "You're not listening to me, are you?"

"Sorry," he said, starting on his pecan pie. He'd eaten only half his food, even though everything was delicious. "I was distracted."

"As I was saying . . ."

She kept talking, and he fell back into his thoughts again, and— Wait. He could just tell Olivia what was going on. Then she would decline the invitation, and that would take care of that. He grinned.

"Why are you smiling?" Mother said. "I just told you Bernice's second cousin died. They were very close."

He flinched. "I'm sorry for her loss."

"You've been acting strange this entire lunch. Are you okay?" She leaned forward, worry creasing her brow. "You're not sick, are you? Or having financial trouble? Please don't tell me you've been gambling, Kingston."

He'd laugh except she'd probably take it the wrong way.

"I'm not sick. I don't gamble—where did that even come from? My finances are fine."

"Then why do you have so much time off work? I asked your father if it was normal for doctors to take monthslong vacations, because he never did."

"What did he say?"

"That some doctors do, if they want to."

Good. Dad had kept his secret—

"Or need to."

Or not.

"Which one is it for you?" she asked.

I should have stayed home.

"Hi, Karen." Sunny appeared at their table with her usual wide grin. "Kingston. Nice to see you both."

His mother immediately launched into a description of how she was doing. All the words ultimately equaled "fine," but he took the chance to stare out the window and figure out how to answer her earlier question, because his mother would circle around to it again. Maybe he should just tell her the truth. She'd once been a counselor, so there was a chance she'd understand. More likely she'd be disappointed. She'd hide it behind platitudes and *helpful* advice. But he would know, and he couldn't blame her. He was disappointed in himself for not having better control over his life—

"That's a wonderful idea!"

He startled at his mom's exclamation and turned to see her hands clasped together and Sunny's smile wider than usual—something he hadn't thought was possible.

"Don't you think so, King?" Mom looked at him expectantly.

He froze. He had no idea what they were talking about. Should he just nod and pretend he'd heard their conversation? That would be risky. "Sorry, got lost in my thoughts again."

Mom's smile became strained at the edges. "Sunny said she'd like to have a recital at the end of the dance course."

"More like a showcase," Sunny said.

His mother motioned for her to sit down. When she moved to sit next to Kingston—she was closer to his seat— Mom held up her hand. "Have a seat right here," she said, scooting over to give Sunny some room.

So now she didn't want Sunny sitting next to him? Confirmation he and Olivia were being set up.

Sunny complied and folded her thin hands together on the table. "It would be fun to make it an event," she said, her eyes full of excitement. "An evening showcase, with sparkly dresses and suits. Tuxedos, even. We can serve finger foods and put up twinkling lights. A big spotlight is a must. I plan on reserving the community center. My hope is to drum up enough interest that more people will want to take lessons in the future."

It was a great idea and an imaginative marketing concept. It also sounded like a lot of work.

"I can help you plan everything." Mom pulled out her cell phone and started tapping on the screen. "We'll need decorations in addition to the lights. Also some round tables. That will lend glamour to the ambience. Tanner can cater."

"You should probably ask him first," Kingston pointed out.

But she was off and running. "You'll need a bigger sound system than what you have. Oh, and programs. There must be programs." Her fingers flew. "And a little favor for everyone to take home."

Sunny's smile wobbled. "That sounds, um, great."

"What dates did you have in mind?" Mom set her phone between them with the calendar app open. They quickly decided on a date six weeks from this Saturday, and his mother marked it and put her phone back in her purse. "Excuse me," she said, motioning for Sunny to move. "There's so much to do! I'll talk to Tanner about the catering right now." She scooted out of the booth and turned to Kingston. "Thanks for lunch, dear. Ta-ta for now!"

"Bye, Mother."

Mom blew him a kiss before heading for the kitchen. Tanner had a strict rule about only employees being in his inner sanctum, but apparently that was suspended for his mother-in-law, who disappeared through the door.

Kingston turned to Sunny, who looked a little dazed. "This is her whirling-dervish mode. Feel free to tell her no," he said, then paused as his hypocrisy hit him square in the face. No one felt free to tell his mother no, least of all him.

"I'm thrilled with her ideas. I was thinking much smaller. I'd even thought about having it at the dance studio, but there wouldn't be enough room for anyone to sit, much less to have an audience."

"If you're okay with her taking over, I can assure you she'll make the evening special. Planning events is her specialty."

Sunny smiled. "That's good, because it isn't mine."

"Me either."

"Traditionally, during a showcase the instructors also dance. I thought maybe you and I could do a spotlight if you're okay with that."

He shifted in his seat. "I don't know. I'm not much for spotlights."

"It would be short, probably a minute or two. Just to show the audience what the dances look like. You can choose which one you'd like to do. Think about it, at least."

"Sure."

Bailey walked over to their table. "Do you two need anything else?"

Sunny shook her head and slid out of the booth. "I'm fine, thank you." She looked at Kingston. "Let me know what you decide. I'll see you on Monday." She gave him a smile and a wave and walked away.

He fished in his pocket for his wallet. Bailey shook her head. "Tanner's buying."

"I know." He opened his wallet and handed her a twenty. "Thanks for the great service."

She grinned as she took the money. "Thank you. I really appreciate it."

He got up and headed for the door. Time to tell Olivia about his mother's machinations. He wasn't looking forward to that conversation, but he was anticipating seeing her. As a friend. Nothing more. He had to keep telling himself that.

As he headed for the door, he bumped into an older lady with square glasses and large red earrings seated at the table near the door. "Sorry," he said. He really did need to start paying more attention today.

"That's all right," she said. Her dinner companion—another senior citizen with a cloud of white hair—nodded. "It's nice to see you in town again."

Hoo-boy. He didn't recognize them, but they knew who he was, so he faked it. "Thanks. I've missed being here too." That was true, he realized. Maple Falls had a charm of its own.

"Don't be a stranger," the cloud lady said in a singsong tone.

He nodded, then zipped out of the diner and went to his car. Their names would probably come to him later, like at 2:00 a.m. or something. He got in the Audi, blasted the AC, and headed to the library to warn Olivia about his mother's nonsensical plan.

Chapter 12

The bell above the door at Knots and Tangles clanged as Viola and Peg bustled inside. "Erma Jean!" Viola said, hurrying toward her. Peg, who'd had a hip replacement last year, moved at a slower pace.

"What's wrong?" she asked as her friend came to a breathless halt at the counter. She'd been sitting by the cash register thumbing through baby crochet patterns—a mimi could dream—and enjoying a little peace and quiet. Riley was at Price's Hardware having lunch with Hayden. "What happened?"

"We've got a problem." Peg finally sidled up to Viola, who was nodding. Both women were perspiring.

"Have you two been running?"

"Yes, and I'm never doing it again." Peg leaned against the counter and pushed up her glasses. "But desperate times call for speed. Or at least a little more pep in the step."

Erma closed the pattern book. "All right, spill. What's got you two in a tizzy?"

"After this morning's meeting, we went to lunch at Sunshine," Viola said.

"Tanner makes the best chicken salad," Peg added.

"And who did we see eating lunch together?" Viola looked at Peg, and they both said, "Kingston and Sunny!"

"So?" Erma relaxed.

"How can you be so blasé about this? He's supposed to be with Olivia."

"He's helping Sunny teach ballroom dancing lessons. By the way, you two should come. You'll enjoy it."

"Really? Who did you dance with?" Viola asked as Peg found a tissue in her purse.

Uh-oh. She'd walked into that one. "Jasper. Now, before you jump to conclusions—"

"You and Jasper, huh." Peg grinned as she dabbed her forehead.

"The only other people to dance with were Bubba, Senior, and Pastor Jared."

"But you chose Jasper." Viola's eyes shone.

Good gravy on a biscuit, everyone had the romance bug. "We've danced before, dozens of times over the years."

"Yes, but not ballroom dancing. Did you do the tango?"

"We could barely keep from tripping each other." That wasn't true. Once they'd gotten the hang of the steps, they were in sync, but she didn't need Peg and Viola to latch on to any more matchmaking ideas. "Back to Kingston and Sunny. I'm sure they were just talking about dancing."

"Maybe. But when we sat down, they looked kind of cozy." Viola fanned her face with her hand.

"They also looked nice together." Peg frowned, her chest still heaving.

Viola stilled, looking only a smidgen better than her counterpart. "What if Olivia has competition? How are we going to break it to Bea?"

Erma came out from behind the counter and headed for the back room.

"Where are you going?" Peg asked.

"To get you two some water before you pass out. Peg, you take the man chair." She gestured to the small seating area in the store where visitors could sit and knit or crochet. A large, comfortable chair sat close by where an indulgent husband or boyfriend could take a nap while his significant other shopped. "Be right back."

"Thanks, Erma," Peg called out as she flopped into the chair.

As she walked to the fridge, Erma pondered the news. If what Peg and Viola said was true, then they had an unanticipated complication. If Sunny and Kingston were dating, they were keeping it from Karen. That seemed extremely foolish in Erma's opinion, since she wouldn't want to be on the receiving end of the woman's ire, and there would definitely be ire if one of her children was keeping a secret.

But what if Sunny and Kingston were an item, or on the way to becoming one? And now his mother was trying to fix him up with Olivia when he already had a girlfriend, or at the very least a love interest.

Never mind telling Bea. She had to call Karen. She grabbed two bottles of water, hurried to the front of the store, shoved them at Viola and Peg, and rushed off again.

Viola opened hers. "Now where are you going?"

"To call Karen." Erma went behind the counter and snatched up her cell phone. "You're right. We might have a problem, and we need to nip it now."

🖋

Olivia sat down in her office chair and glanced at the clock. One twenty-five. Normally she had her lunch at one sharp, but there were times like today when she was too busy to stick to her schedule. She'd spent the morning setting up for toddler story time and sat in for a little while as RaeAnne, who was excellent with the younger children, entertained them and their parents for thirty minutes. Afterward, she assisted the parents with selecting books and checking them out, and after that she'd had a surprise visitor—a librarian from southeast Arkansas.

"I've heard about all of the wonderful programs you've implemented here," she said after introducing herself. "I wanted to see for myself. Do you have some time to talk?"

Olivia had shown her around, discussing the ideas that worked and the ones that had failed. When she'd been hired as an assistant librarian five years ago, the library, like much of Maple Falls, had been on the decline. She'd turned that around when she became the head librarian after less than a year. It was nice to be recognized by her peers for her hard work. The Maple Falls community had expressed their appreciation as well by patronizing the library in greater numbers than they had in a decade.

She relaxed in her chair, opened a small package of

unsalted almonds, flipped up the cover of her laptop, and frowned at the unfinished assignment staring back at her. Ugh. She'd never been stuck on a paper like this before. But she had to plow through it, or she would end up behind for the first time in her life. She had precisely twenty-eight minutes to get some of it done.

She popped an almond into her mouth and started typing. Only three words in, there was a rap on her door. Lifting her fingers and clenching them, she saw Flo's head poke inside her office. "Yes?" she said, trying to hide her irritation at being disturbed when she'd specifically asked not to be.

"Sorry for bugging you, but you have a visitor." Flo grinned. "A tall, blond, handsome visitor. He said it was urgent."

Kingston immediately came to mind, but he didn't have any reason to see her in the middle of the day at work. It could be another librarian, but that wouldn't be urgent. And if it was Aunt Bea, either she or Uncle Bill would have called her directly. For whatever reason, it must be Kingston.

She glanced at her laptop again. So much for getting the assignment off her plate. "Send him in."

"Happy to," Flo said, still smiling. "Although I wouldn't mind looking at him a little while longer."

"Flo—"

She slipped out of the office. Olivia shook her head and smiled. Flo lived in Malvern and wasn't acquainted with the Bedford family other than Anita, who sometimes had lunch with Olivia at work.

She stared at her screen, fingers poised above the

keyboard. She could eke out a sentence or two before he got here. She started to type.

"Hey," Kingston said as he rushed into the room. "Sorry to bother you at work. Mind if I shut the door?"

"Go ahead." She finished writing the sentence as he closed the door and turned around. When she faced him again, her breath hitched. Oh no. Not this again. They'd spent almost three hours talking at Aunt Bea's last night, and she'd had nary a tingle. Now she was tingling all over. Somehow he managed to make a basic white T-shirt, olive-green shorts, and wheat-colored canvas slip-ons look like high fashion. And he smelled good, like leather and lime and . . . french fries?

He sat down in the chair in front of her desk. "We have a problem."

Her nerves jumped. "We do?"

"Yes." He rubbed his palms over his thighs.

Don't do that. Olivia tightly clasped her hands underneath her desk, forcing herself to look at his face and not his body. Unfortunately for her, that was perfect too.

"My mother is setting us up," he blurted.

That was the last thing she expected him to say. "What do you mean?"

"She's matchmaking. She hasn't come right out and said so, but I'm sure that's her plan."

Olivia shut her laptop. "I'm confused."

"Me too. I don't know when or why she got it into her head that we should be a couple, but she has. You know how dogged she can be about something once she sets her mind to it."

"You're probably mistaken," she said.

"Did she tell you I was going to be at supper on Saturday night?"

"No."

He sighed. "That was intentional. She wants me to teach you 'basic dance steps' before supper," he said, using air quotes.

"That's what the ballroom lessons are for."

"Doesn't matter. It's just an excuse for us to spend time together. Alone."

Olivia let his words sink in. She'd thought it strange when Karen stopped by midmorning and invited her over, something she hadn't done since she and Anita were school-age. "I thought she was talking about a family dinner."

"She was. I'm the family."

"You explained that we're just friends, right?"

He fidgeted in his chair. "I didn't get the chance. Sunny showed up, and next thing I knew she and Mom were planning for a showcase at the end of the dance course."

"What's that?"

"A recital of sorts. She asked me to be her partner for the spotlight dance."

Something pinched inside Olivia's chest. "Are you going to?"

"I'm mulling it over. I probably will, though."

There was no reason for him not to, and zero cause for her to feel . . . whatever that painful pinch was. "Good. You two dance well together."

"Thank you." He leaned forward. "What are we going to do about Saturday night, though? Telling Mom no won't work, because she'll find another way to get us together."

The word *no* was exactly what Olivia was going to

suggest, but Kingston had a point. She'd spent enough time with the Bedfords that she knew he was right—Karen wouldn't give up, at least not easily. "We have to convince her we're not couple material," she said.

"Exactly."

He didn't have to be so blunt about it. "What if we pretend to—"

"Hate each other?"

"'Hate' is a strong word," she said.

Kingston sat back and nodded. "I couldn't fake that anyway. Not with you."

Her face heated. She grabbed the almond packet and dumped half of it in her hand, needing the diversion from the teeny-tiny fluttering sensation in her stomach. She shoved them into her mouth. Good grief, she was acting like Aunt Bea, and over a simple passing comment. "Almond?" she said, holding out the bag to him.

"No, thanks. Just had lunch at Sunshine."

That explained the slight scent of fried food. She chomped and tried to refocus so they could solve the Karen problem. She wasn't one for subterfuge, but since his mother was engaging in it, she wondered if they didn't have much of a choice but to reciprocate.

"I think I have an idea," Kingston said, frowning. "I don't think you'll like it, though."

Kingston wasn't sure he liked his idea either. It would require some restraint on his part. Okay, a lot of restraint, because even though he and Olivia were firmly in the friend zone with each other, he couldn't deny the jolt of attraction that had shot through him when he entered her office. He hadn't felt it last night when they were together, which was odd. Then again, Bea had been present the whole time, plying them with delicious peach pie. Now they were here alone, and he couldn't get over how adorable she looked today in a light-red top with a large, rounded collar, a darker red bow in the center, and the sides of her sleek hair tucked behind her unpierced ears. He really liked her style.

He pulled his gaze away from her. He knew that turning off chemical attraction wasn't going to happen overnight. He was also a man who prided himself on self-control, although he'd been lacking that lately. But if they did decide to go with his plan, he'd handle himself appropriately.

"What's your idea?" She took a sip from her water bottle. "I might like it after all."

Drawing in a deep breath, he said, "We pretend to be a couple." At her shocked expression, he quickly added, "If we're already dating, she has no reason to try to get us together. She'll give up. Once that's accomplished, we'll break up."

She stilled, the water bottle hovering over her desk for a second until she slowly set it down. She snatched the nut packet again, this time folding the small top edge over and over until it hit the remaining almonds.

"Yeah," he said, seeing she was having the same off-kilter reaction he had. Well, not the same. He was sure she wasn't fighting any attraction to him. He'd killed that with his prior behavior.

As she stared at the packet and remained silent, he

wished he'd kept his big mouth shut. Faking a relationship was something out of a basic rom-com movie. Totally unbelievable. When she continued her silence, he reckoned she was pondering what method she'd use to throw him out of her office.

"The other option is to pretend we're dating other people," he said quickly, although he didn't like that notion. Not one bit.

She paused for a few moments, then set the packet aside. "That would open Pandora's box. Aunt Bea would want to meet him, for starters."

"Yeah. Mom would want to meet the imaginary her too. All right, that's off the list." *Thank God.*

Olivia nodded. "Any other options?"

He rubbed his chin. "Nothing is coming to mind."

"Me either." She folded her hands on her tidy desk, her expression serious. "If we did pretend to date, we'd need some parameters."

"Of course."

She picked up a small blank pad of paper. "When do we break up?"

He grimaced at the hit to his pride. They hadn't even had their first fake date, and she was already planning the end of the relationship. "A month?"

"That long?"

If he'd wondered whether she had a fragment of feelings for him, he didn't anymore. Again, his own fault. "Two weeks?"

She tapped the pencil point on the paper. "How long is your sabbatical?"

"Seven more weeks." Seven long weeks.

"How are you planning to spend that time?"

Kingston frowned. "I don't exactly have a plan." He chuckled at her horrified reaction. "It wasn't like I had any warning I was going to be put on leave." His good humor disintegrated. "Other than the dance lessons and a possible trip, I'm a free agent."

"When is your trip?" She was writing on the pad now. When she finished, she pulled her phone out of her desk and tapped on the screen. "Where are you going?"

"I don't know, and I'm not sure." He scooted his chair closer to her desk and saw a calendar appear on the screen.

She looked at him with a baffled expression. "Your calendar isn't full?"

"Nope. Not for the next seven weeks. Other than our dance class."

Suddenly, it hit home to him that this might be the first time he could oversee his own schedule. His entire life had always been mapped out for him. He'd followed school schedules, sports schedules, clinic schedules, organization and symposium schedules, his *mother's* schedule . . . but he'd never made his own before. No wonder he was floundering.

"Does it bother you?" She tilted her head. "I can't imagine not knowing what I was doing for almost two months."

"I think that's the point," he said. "I'm not supposed to be bound to work responsibilities."

She straightened in her chair. "If we're going to be a couple, we need to schedule some activities."

He noticed she didn't say "pretend" couple. An unintentional slip, obviously. But a part of him wished it wasn't. "Or we could play it by ear."

She glanced at her calendar, then at him again. "How about a compromise? We can plan a few things, and we can also be . . ."

"Spontaneous?" he offered.

Nodding, she set down her pencil. "Yes. Spontaneous."

He smiled. But he still wasn't sure if she was on board with a temporary fake relationship. "Are you saying that you want to go through with this?"

Her emphatic nod caused a lock of hair to fall against her cheek, reminding him how soft it had felt between his fingers. He shifted in his chair, something he'd been doing a lot of since he'd arrived.

"Being in a pseudo relationship might solve a few problems. Aunt Bea is concerned about me. She thinks because I'm single, I'm lonely. Which I'm not," she promptly added.

"Mom thinks the same about me. That, and she's worried I'll never have a family."

"Is that something you want?"

"Sure. Eventually." *When time permits.* "What about you?"

"I never really thought about it much before." She glanced down at the pad.

"You've never considered if you want children?"

"I've always been focused on other things. Getting my degrees, finding employment, improving the library."

"You've done a terrific job," he said. "I haven't been in here in years, and I can see the difference. Same building, but it's not a dusty tomb anymore. Remember Ms. Periwinkle?"

"Who could forget her?" Olivia smiled. "She was always fussing at the after-school kids."

"'There'll be no laughing in my library, you whipper-snappers.'"

She started giggling. "You sound just like her. I still have a copy of her Library Ten Commandments."

"Really?"

She got up from her chair and went to a three-drawer file cabinet in the corner of the office, opened the second drawer, and pulled out a folded sheet of manila paper. She opened it. "'Thou shalt not write, draw, or color in any library book.'"

He jumped up and went to her, reading the commandments over her shoulder. "'Thou shalt not drink or eat in the library.'"

"'Thou shalt not chew gum in the library,'" she said.

"'Thou shalt not talk, giggle, or laugh in the library.'" He chuckled. "I can't believe this still exists."

"I kept it when we did a little remodeling right after I was hired." She folded up the paper and put it back in the file. "I thought about keeping it up for posterity. Her rules really weren't outlandish." She shut the drawer and turned to him. "But I didn't want kids coming in here and seeing a bunch of 'shalt nots.' I have the rules posted, but they're written in a positive framework."

He approved of her decision. "Did you ever get in trouble with Periwinkle?" he asked.

"No. Did you?"

"Are you kidding? I always follow the rules."

"So do I." She looked up at him.

His pulse started to race, and he took a step back. Being this close was too dangerous, even though they were only reading Ms. Periwinkle's antiquated rules. "What other changes have you made?"

"I'm especially excited about our children's program."

Kingston sat back down. It was best to keep his distance. "I'd like to hear about that."

She sat back down at her desk, and he listened as she explained the different events and programs she'd developed for children and young adults, her brown eyes warm and sparkling as she talked. "Sounds like you have a soft spot for kids," he said when she finished.

"I have a passion for literacy. The younger a child learns and develops a love for reading, the more literate they will be. They'll also pass that love on to others, even the adults in their family who might not enjoy reading or aren't able to read." She glanced down at her desk. "I'm not good with kids, though," she said, her voice low. "I don't have the patience."

"That's what a lot of people say, until they spend time with them. Patience is a process. Even the most patient person can lose it when a kid presses the right buttons."

"I can't see you losing patience with anyone."

"Oh, it's happened, trust me." He thought about Sylvia and Sailor. From the online reviews, they weren't the only ones he'd been impatient with.

"RaeAnne's doing a great job reading to the toddlers and preschoolers. I'd like to start a book club for the older students on the weekends this winter. That's still in the planning phase. I have an upper-elementary-school reading group on Tuesday afternoons, and it's been a success."

"Could you use any volunteers?" he asked. "I wouldn't mind doing that occasionally. It would be fun reading to the kids."

"I don't know." She smirked. "Can you fit it into your *busy* schedule?"

He laughed. "Very funny."

She picked up her pen and wrote on a pink sticky note. "You could be a special guest. This month's theme is weather. I'll have the book ready to go. All you need to do is read it to the kids and field questions."

"Perfect. Just let me know the time and date, and I'll be here." At the doubt emerging in her eyes, he said, "I promise."

She paused, then nodded. "Thank you."

He grinned, excited about the opportunity. But they still hadn't defined their new bogus relationship. "Are you sure you're okay with this relationship thing?"

Her smile dissolved into a frown. "I don't like being deceptive. But I don't see that we have much choice." She glanced at the clock on her wall. "My lunch is almost over. I have to go back up front."

The time with her had flown by. He stood. "I hope I didn't mess up your lunch schedule."

"It was already off before you got here." She looked up at him. "How should we proceed on Saturday?"

Taking her businesslike cue, he said, "We show up for supper. Dance a little. By the end, we're a couple."

"Okay. We can talk about specifics then."

She was being so clinical about this now. He knew that was for the best. But it didn't mean they couldn't have a little fun. "How about we throw Mom for a loop, and I pick you up?"

When she hesitated, he realized this was an opportunity to restore some trust with her. "I promise I'll show up."

"All right," she said, her voice barely discernible.

Good enough. "I'll see you around five, then."

She wasn't quite smiling, but there was a little softness in her eyes. "See you then." She tapped on her phone and entered the date on her calendar.

He gave her a little wave and headed out of her office. He took the time to stop at the front desk. The older woman who had brought him to Olivia's office wasn't there, but he checked out the brochures advertising the toddler and preschool story time, plus a few other programs the library was offering. Next he went and read the calendar of events posted near the front door, then left the building. When he returned to work in October, he could recommend the children's programs to the parents of his patients. He also thought of a few of them who could benefit from the adult literacy program the library offered. He would talk to them privately about it, knowing it was a sensitive subject.

As he walked to his car, the hot summer sun beating down on his back, he thought about his and Olivia's scheme. He wasn't exactly having second thoughts, but he wasn't too keen about the dishonesty part. It was only for a little while, though, and he'd get to spend time with Olivia. *As friends.* Only friends. And he had three days to convince himself that was all they ever would be.

At six thirty that evening, Karen's number showed up on Erma's phone. "You finally called me back," Erma said, settling in her recliner, her finger poised over the remote to turn on *Wheel of Fortune*. She hated to miss Pat and Vanna.

"I've had a busy, busy day, Erma."

Karen's voice had an edge, but Erma ignored it. "I won't take up much of your time. Kingston was spotted at the Sunshine Diner with Sunny Abernathy today. According to my sources, they looked pretty intimate."

"You have spies?"

Erma grimaced. "No—"

"I approve. But you don't need to worry about Sunny and Kingston. First of all, Kingston and I were at lunch when Sunny showed up, and she is—I should say she and I are—planning a ballroom showcase at the end of our dance course. I was probably talking to Tanner in the kitchen about catering the event when your *sources* spotted her and my son together."

"Oh." Doggone Viola and Peg. They shouldn't have jumped to conclusions.

"Second, my son would *never* keep a secret from me. If he and Sunny were interested in each other, I would know. Trust me."

"Gotcha. Thanks for calling me back, and sorry for the false alarm. Let us know how Saturday goes."

"It will go perfectly. Ta-ta for now."

Erma shook her head and set her phone on the end table by her comfy recliner. Karen was delusional if she thought Kingston told her everything about his life. No grown man would do that—not a healthy-minded one, anyway. But now that Erma knew the full story behind Sunny and Kingston talking at the diner, it made sense.

She blew out a breath. This was getting too complicated, and she was ready to excise herself from these antics ASAP. Hopefully after Saturday night, she and the rest of the BBs would do just that.

She had picked up the remote and turned on the TV when she heard a knock on the door. Confound it, someone was just about to solve the puzzle.

With a sigh, she muted the TV and went to answer the door. Her jaw dropped. Jasper stood there, the waning sun behind him. There was still plenty of daylight left, and not a cloud in the sky. Sweat pooled on his neck, and he wiped the perspiration off his forehead.

"Did you walk here?" At his nod, she opened the door wider. "Well, come on in and cool off."

He complied but didn't go more than a few steps into her living room. She shut the door and moved to stand in front of him. "What are you doing here? And why didn't you drive?"

"Car's been actin' funny." He still had his hands in his pockets. "It's not that far a walk, neither."

"When it's hot as blazes out, it is." She motioned for him to follow her. "I've got some sweet tea, fresh made this morning."

They settled in the kitchen with the ceiling fan whirring above them. Jasper downed half the glass of tea she poured him. Erma topped him off. "Now, tell me why you're here."

He looked her straight in the eye. "Why'd you stop in front of my house the other night?"

The other night? When had she— Oh. *Oh no.* He'd seen her? "I, uh . . ." Poppycock, he was catching her flat-footed.

"I was gonna bring it up at the dance lesson," he said. "But I didn't think you'd want anyone knowin' you're a Peepin' Tom."

"Excuse me?" How dare he say that after she'd shared her fresh sweet tea with him? "I am not a Peepin' Tom."

"Then why were you lookin'?"

She opened her mouth to speak and saw something she hadn't seen before—or hadn't noticed. His mouth, surrounded by short gray whiskers, barely lifted at the corners.

He's enjoying this.

She crossed her arms, finding herself tempted to smile too. "I don't have to tell you anything, Jasper Eugene Mathis."

The smile disappeared. "Now, don't go invoking my middle name, Erma Jean McAllister."

"When it comes to you, I'll invoke anything I want." She lifted her chin, a rush going through her. Sparring with Jasper was always fun. "What's wrong with your car?"

"Needs new spark plugs." He gulped down more tea. "Also new struts, brakes, and an oil change."

"Goodness." She uncrossed her arms. "Why don't you get it fixed?"

"Don't wanna spend a fortune on a car I don't use much. I don't go anywhere other than Maple Falls. Ain't got a hankerin' to, neither."

"I'm sure Rusty would work with you on the price," she said.

"Don't want no handouts."

Erma frowned as she got up from the chair. "You're the most stubborn old coot I've ever met." She went to the counter and removed the foil from the pan of leftover hummingbird cake Bea had shoved at her at their emergency meeting this morning when everyone refused to take it home. "It's not a handout. It's called being helpful. That's what neighbors do—help each other."

She cut two pieces, put them on glass plates, and grabbed two forks out of the drawer. Truth was she wasn't too mad that she'd been stuck with the rest of the cake. It was scrumptious. She set Jasper's plate in front of him. "It's a hummingbird—"

"I seen a hummingbird cake before." He eyed it. "Bea Farnsworth's recipe?"

"Yes." She sat across from him, which wasn't that far away due to her table being on the small side.

"Real cream-cheese frosting?"

"You know Bea doesn't mess with that canned stuff." Erma took a bite, and pineapple-coconutty sweetness exploded in her mouth. *Bea sure can bake.*

He picked up a forkful. "When you gonna tell me why you stopped in front of my house?"

Rats. Back to that again. She'd hoped plying him with a quality baked good would sidetrack his brain. Well, nothing left but to tell him the truth. "I was wondering how you were doing. That's all."

He stopped midchew and gaped at her. "You were?"

"Yes. And don't talk with your mouth full." She pressed the side of her fork into the cake, refusing to look at him and hoping he wasn't looking at her, because right now her cheeks were flaming.

They ate their cake in silence, Erma for once not knowing what to say. As for Jasper, he was enjoying his cake. She had to admit it was kind of nice to have a surprise guest, even though it was Jasper. Usually only Riley and Hayden stopped by unannounced, as they were always welcome to do.

Jasper scraped the last bit of crumbs and frosting from his plate and shoved the fork into his mouth. Then he drank the rest of his tea. When he set the empty glass down, Erma noticed he had crumbs on the front of his shirt. "Here," she said, holding out a napkin.

"What's that for?"

"You really are a caveman, aren't you?" She leaned forward and brushed off the crumbs. There were some on the corner of his mouth, and she moved to wipe them off too.

"Erma," he said, his voice softer than she'd ever heard it. Gently, he took the napkin from her. "I'll do it."

She sat back, dazed at the fluttering in her stomach as she watched him dab at his lips. She had plumb lost her mind. She hadn't had that feeling since she'd first met Gus, her late husband and love of her life. This was Jasper, the exact opposite of her darling Gus. Although she liked to joke and say, *"I ain't dead yet,"* she didn't exactly have a young libido. And how could she possibly be thinking about her libido with her archnemesis right in front of her?

"Well, guess I'd better be gettin' along." Jasper stood, obviously oblivious to Erma's reaction.

"I can take you home," she said weakly. Land's sake, perspiration was forming on her brow. She grabbed one of the napkins and quickly wiped it off. Hot flashes? *Really?*

"Nah. I'll walk." He left the kitchen.

She trailed behind him. "Are you sure? It's still hot and muggy outside."

He turned to her. "I'll be fine, Erma." He walked to the door.

"Wait!" She scurried back to the kitchen, opened the fridge, and snatched a water bottle off the shelf. "You'll need this." She handed it to him, almost smiling at the surprise on his face.

Jasper took the bottle, tipped it at her, then opened the door and left.

Erma collapsed into the chair, fanning herself. This was ridiculous. This was *Jasper*. And she was too old to be having hot flashes and a fluttering stomach.

She rushed to the bathroom where she kept her thermometer. When she took her temperature, it was normal. Drat.

She stared at her face in the mirror. Took in her short gray hair, numerous wrinkles, and still-pink cheeks. "You do not like Jasper Mathis," she said to her reflection. "Got that? You do *not* like him!"

Flutter. Flutter.

Chapter 13

Last chance to change our minds."

Olivia looked at Kingston. They were parked in the Bedfords' circular driveway, a huge Mediterranean-style home in front of them. He was rubbing his palm back and forth on the leather steering wheel. Since they'd made their decision to pretend to be a couple, they had texted each other over the past few days, both offering the other one an out. Neither one had accepted. Despite the ball of anxiety forming in her stomach, she had to go through with their plan. Karen wasn't amenable like Aunt Bea, who had stuck to her promise not to interfere with Olivia's love life. Aunt Bea listened. Karen never did.

There was something else keeping her from backing out. She'd spent the last three days and sixteen hours expecting Kingston not to show up. Not only had he kept his word, but he'd also texted her before he left his condo and even arrived a few minutes early and escorted her to his car. She avoided looking at the hood, remembering their after-coffee make-out session. Even now she had a hard time pushing the memory out of her mind—

"We can always walk in there and tell her we're just friends." He continued to stare at the massive front door to his parents' house. "We just sit her down and insist that's all we will ever be."

"We both know that won't work." She placed her hands on her knees, the soft fabric of her gray houndstooth skirt shifting underneath her palms.

He turned to her, regret in his eyes. "I'm sorry about this."

"Don't be." She smiled. "Let's try to have fun with it."

"Will do." He grinned.

Tingle. Tingle.

Kingston got out of the car and opened the passenger door for her. He held out his hand.

She stared at it for a second. This was the moment of truth. Once she slipped her hand into his, she was Kingston's girlfriend—for the time being. They still had to discuss the timeline of their "relationship." She intended to nail that down tonight. He might be okay with a few weeks of unscheduled time, but she wasn't.

She lifted her gaze to his. He was still smiling, a playful twinkle in his eye.

Have fun.

She took his hand, and he helped her out of the car. After giving her fingers a quick squeeze, he let go, and they made their way to the front door. Kingston pressed the doorbell, and before it finished ringing, the door flew open, revealing his mother and her stunned—no, shocked—expression. She had to have been peeking out through one of the small arched windows on the door to have opened it so fast.

"Hello, Mother." He leaned forward and kissed her on the cheek.

"Um, hi." Her gaze darted to him, then Olivia, then back to him. "You two came together?"

"Yes." Olivia stepped forward. "It didn't make any sense to take two cars."

"And I didn't mind driving to Maple Falls," he added. "Aren't you going to let us in?"

Karen composed her expression and smiled. "Welcome."

They walked inside, and as usual, Olivia was impressed with the house. High ceilings, bright and airy, and filled with expensive décor and details. She felt like she was walking through a mansion. The structure wasn't quite at that level, but close.

"Supper is almost ready," Karen said, the hem of her ankle-length lavender sheath dress fluttering around her silver-sandaled feet as she closed the door behind them. Several strands of lavender crystals twinkled around her neck. "Kingston, why don't you go to the bar and fix Olivia a drink?"

"She doesn't drink alcohol, remember?" Kingston glanced at Olivia, and she nodded, surprised he'd remembered that detail, which she'd mentioned during their talk at Bea's when they were listing their favorite beverages. Kingston did like an occasional glass of wine, she'd found out.

"There's plenty of other options." Karen shooed them both toward the den. "I'll let you know when it's time to dine." She smiled, a satisfied glimmer in blue eyes that matched Kingston's. She turned to Olivia. "You look lovely tonight. Doesn't she, King?"

The ball of anxiety rolled around in her gut. Karen wasn't even trying to be discreet.

"She absolutely does."

She turned and saw him gazing at her, awestruck. Wow, just like a gorgeous actor staring at his beautiful costar. The tingles amplified.

He's acting . . . only acting.

But the smile she gave him wasn't an act. It felt good to hear his words and take in his appreciation, even if it wasn't real.

"Ah, yes." Karen clasped her hands together. "Tonight is going to be wonderful."

"Shall we?" Kingston offered Olivia his arm, and she took it. He guided her to the Bedfords' expansive den. A pristine white couch with gold and burnt-orange throw pillows sat in the center of the room, along with a wrought-iron, glass-topped coffee table, rust-colored easy chairs, and a cream shag rug on the floor. Suspended from a white ceiling with oak beams was a black iron chandelier. One wall was covered with tall windows, the gold, forest-green, and rust-colored drapes pulled to the side of each one, revealing a stunning backyard complete with a mosaic-tiled pool.

He dropped her arm as soon as they were in the room. "Wow, she's laying it on thick, isn't she?" he whispered. "I'm not surprised, but I don't want you to feel uncomfortable."

"I won't. I'm used to her, remember?" She walked over to the couch. She hadn't spent much time at this house compared to the one in Maple Falls where the Bedfords had lived until all three of their children graduated high school. "I always loved this room," she said, sitting down on the sofa. So comfy.

"It is nice. Mom's always had good taste." He walked over to the bar in the corner of the room and stood behind it. "What would you like?"

"Ginger ale, if it's available."

"I'm sure it is. Mom keeps this well stocked." He pulled out two glasses and set them on the marble countertop.

Olivia settled into the couch and looked outside. Although she didn't swim, the pool looked inviting. Her body relaxed. She and Anita had spent a lot of evenings here when they were both less busy, and before Anita had married Tanner. The Bedfords were Olivia's second family.

And I'm lying to them.

"Here." Kingston handed her the drink and sat next to her, keeping a gentlemanly space between them. "Uh-oh." He peered at her. "Something's wrong."

"I'm feeling a little guilty. Your parents have always been so good to me." She stared at the bubbles floating in the amber ginger ale.

"Hey." He set his own ginger ale down on the coffee table and moved closer to her, lowering his voice. "I'll take full responsibility, okay? It was my idea, after all. I don't think we have to worry about any fallout, though. We're breaking up, remember? They'll never know it's a ruse."

She took a sip of her drink. The ginger started soothing her nerves. "Thanks. I hope you're right."

"I am." He smiled. "We're the ones who should be

annoyed, by the way, for being set up like this. Just remember that."

True. She took another sip. Now would be the time to get out her calendar and discuss when their inevitable breakup was going to happen. Instead, she leaned her head back on the sofa cushions. There would be time for that discussion later.

She glanced at the pool again. "Do you swim here often? I remember you were a fish when we were kids."

He shook his head. "I think I've used the pool twice since they moved here. I never have the time. I should have thought about that, though. We could have brought our suits and taken a dip."

"I don't swim."

"You don't like to swim, or you don't know how?"

"Both. I'll dip my toes in, but that's it."

"Are you afraid of the water?"

She looked at him. "I'm so unathletic I'd probably drown in an instant."

"No," he said, his voice soothing. "You wouldn't. You don't have to be athletic to learn how to swim. I can teach you sometime."

Her eyebrow rose at the thought of Kingston in a swimsuit. She reined in that emotion, and it was replaced with a new one: embarrassment. She didn't want him to see her in one. She wasn't overweight, but her body was disproportionate, and her thighs were thick, which was why she wore skirts all the time. The only time she'd worn shorts in the recent past was when she was playing softball.

"Olivia?"

She hadn't realized she'd been staring at her drink again. She looked at him, seeing his puzzled look.

"I wouldn't let anything happen to you," he said. "I was a lifeguard in high school for two summers at a public pool."

She already knew that. Then there was the fact that he was a doctor. Performing CPR would be second nature to him. She couldn't be safer with anyone else than she would be with him. Learning to swim was also an important life skill, although she'd done just fine avoiding water for most of her life.

"It would be fun," he continued. "I'm sure Mom wouldn't mind us borrowing the pool for an afternoon or evening."

"That sounds marvelous!" Karen entered the den, beaming. "You and Kingston can use the pool anytime you want to. How about tomorrow after church?"

"Uh," Olivia said.

"I'm sure she's busy, Mother." He turned to her. "Right, Olivia?"

For the first time in her life, her brain went dead. Somewhere in the recesses, she sensed she should agree with Kingston and take the escape he was offering her. But Karen was incandescent with glee at the thought of the two of them swimming together.

"Surely you can spare an hour or two," Karen said, her anticipation-filled eyes latching onto Olivia. "All work and no play is no fun, after all."

Nuts. Now she fully understood why Kingston had a hard time telling his mom no. She'd witnessed Karen eliciting a positive response from others, but she'd never been on the receiving end. Not like this. There was something about her expression, her tone of voice, and the way she literally would not quit staring at Olivia until she acquiesced. "Sure," she squeaked, just to make Karen stop looking at her. "I'm, uh, free."

"Splendid!" Karen's grin was dazzling, and she clapped softly. "And on that note, dinner is served."

As she walked away, Kingston turned to Olivia. "I'll talk to her and tell her you've got other plans—"

"No." If she was committed to their scheme, she needed to be 100 percent on board. "It's fine. I'll meet you here around two, if that works for you."

His expression uncertain, he nodded. "All right. As long as you're sure."

"I am."

He stood and held out his hand. She hesitated, still trying to get her bearings. Oh, right. He was helping her off the couch. She didn't need help, but Karen was probably lurking around the corner watching them, so she took his hand and tried to ignore how warm and strong it was.

Surprising her, he bent down. "If at any time you want to cancel tomorrow, you let me know."

She nodded and smiled. "Thank you."

He straightened and looked at their hands together, then at her. His eyebrow lifted, questioning.

She got the message. Showtime. She linked her fingers with his and headed for the door, making a mental note to text Harper later to help her find a swimsuit. She didn't even own one.

Not only had his mother outdone herself with the meal, but Kingston was also blown away by how much he was enjoying the evening. Naturally, his mom had made a romantic meal, with lobster tail—she was on a lobster kick, apparently—and steak with all the trimmings and chocolate-covered strawberries for dessert. She'd also set the stage for romance in the large dining room by removing the leaves in the table. Now it seated four people, but she'd placed only two chairs on opposite sides. "*I tasted the food so many times while I was preparing it,*" Mom had said when he asked where her chair was. "*I'm stuffed. Your father is on call at the hospital tonight, so you two enjoy. Let me know if you need anything.*"

Over a candlelight dinner, he and Olivia talked with the same relaxed affability they had over at Bea's. He'd even offered to cancel tomorrow's swimming *date* again, but she refused. And he was glad she did. The thought of Olivia in a swimsuit . . . he cleared his throat.

"The lobster is delicious." Olivia dipped a small piece into clarified butter. "I feel so spoiled."

"Me too. Mom goes over the top, but she does love to make an elaborate meal. Most people think she caters in food. She probably could, but I don't think she'll ever give up cooking. It's the only domestic activity she does anymore."

"I'm not big on cooking," Olivia said. "Aunt Bea taught me how to, and I can make a decent meal if I set my mind to it, but I'm out of practice."

"It's hard cooking for one. I find it easier to order in or make a sandwich." He scooped a forkful of golden baked sweet potato. Fancy meal or not, it was fairly healthy.

"My aunt keeps me well stocked too."

He nodded and was about to take another bite of the sweet potato when he heard soft jazz music filter through the sound system in the house.

Olivia smiled. "Guess dance lessons are up next."

"We're not even finished with our meal." He frowned. He'd expected his mother to do a full-court press, but she was being ridiculous. He started to say that to Olivia, but he saw her swaying slightly to the music as she enjoyed the lobster. If she was bothered by Mom's preposterousness, she didn't show it. He had noticed her discomfort about swimming, though, and her shock when his mother had suggested using the pool tomorrow. Now he was glad she had. He was eager to teach Olivia how to swim.

His phone buzzed in his pocket. He pulled it out and glanced at the screen. Sunny. He started to answer it, then stopped. He was supposed to be turning over a new leaf, and part of that was not allowing interruptions. With a mental shrug, he slipped the phone back into his pocket. She'd leave a message if she wanted him to call her back.

He picked up a strawberry and grinned. "My mother is as subtle as an iceberg."

Olivia laughed. "More like a dozen of them."

"You two enjoying yourselves?" Mom entered the room with another effervescent smile.

"Yes," Olivia said. "Supper is delicious. Thank you."

"You're so welcome." She turned to Kingston. "After you're finished, why don't you go back to the den? You can show Olivia some of the dance steps you've been practicing."

He inwardly groaned as Olivia hid a smile behind her napkin. This was more embarrassing than the time in high school when his mother had tried to fix him up with the daughter of one of her country-club friends. The excuse then had been calculus tutoring, and after she'd plied the two of them with after-school snacks, she'd suggested that Kingston show the young woman his science-fair project. He'd forgotten the girl's name, but he hadn't forgotten the way she rolled her eyes and told his mother she had to go home because supper was in two hours.

"I'd love to see that." Olivia's soft-brown eyes twinkled in the candlelight.

"Superb!"

Was there a superlative his mother didn't abuse?

"You could show her some tango steps," Mom continued, slyly pushing the plate of strawberries in Olivia's direction.

So much for her idea of practicing the basics with Olivia. "Sure," he said, gesturing to his mother with a jerk of his head for her to leave.

Her brows shot up and she nodded, floating on a cloud of satisfaction as she exited the room. He rubbed the bridge of his nose. "Well, that wasn't embarrassing at all."

Olivia moved the strawberries to the center of the table. He'd noticed she hadn't touched them. "Sunny's teaching you the tango?"

"Yes. We were practicing that the other day at her studio. The tango will come up later in the course, so I wanted to be prepared for assisting in class."

"Do you like dancing with her?" Olivia sipped on her

ginger ale, which his mother had kindly refreshed for her. The woman was an exceptional hostess.

"I do. She's easy to dance with, obviously." He glanced at her empty plate. "We should dance a few steps to make Mom happy," he said. "No rush, though."

"I'm finished." She dabbed at her mouth with her napkin and stood, picking up her drink. "I'd like to learn the tango."

He rose, grabbing his drink too. "Don't expect much," he said as they made their way to the den. "I need another lesson or two." He walked over to an oak cabinet, set his drink on the coaster on top, and opened the doors to reveal command central for the sound system. He used an app on his phone to change the music to a tango beat, and after a second, the song played. "Sometimes the system is glitchy," he said, closing the doors. "I think it will behave tonight." He turned to face her.

She was standing in front of the row of windows, staring out at the backyard. He went to stand next to her. "Still okay with swimming tomorrow?"

After a pause, she nodded. "It's about time I learned."

Suddenly the lights dimmed in the room. Kingston shook his head. "Mom—"

"—Karen," Olivia said at the same time. They grinned.

"I'm sure she's spying on us somewhere." He put his hand lightly on her waist and led her to an open space in the den. "We should have enough room here."

"What do I do?"

The music changed from a tango to a slow jam. "I guess it's going to glitch after all. I can change it—"

"Or we can dance to this." She stepped toward him. "Once she sees us dancing, she can go relax."

He took her hand. "This isn't exactly ballroom music," he pointed out, resting his hands on either side of her waist.

"It doesn't matter." She put her hands on his shoulders.

His breath caught. He'd known it was going to be difficult to ignore her allure, and he'd spent the entire afternoon and evening preparing himself for this moment. But similar to how he felt before their make-out session after *The Quiet Man*, it wasn't just a physical attraction. Even though Olivia was used to his mother's quirks, Mom had pushed things to the limit tonight, but Olivia had been gracious throughout the evening. She was also the most interesting woman he'd ever met—he doubted they could ever run out of topics to talk about. And even though he'd blown his chance with her, and they both agreed to seeing this stunt through, he couldn't stop wishing that the enticing way she was looking at him was *real*.

"I'm going to pull you closer," he said, not wanting her to feel a second of discomfort. He'd made her feel that way long enough. "Is that all right?"

She nodded, her hands moving closer to his neck. She was too short to entwine her hands behind it, but this was close enough. He drew her as close to him as he dared, and they swayed to the music. On instinct he closed his eyes as the smooth R&B singer crooned about love and . . . other things.

"Kingston?" she said, breaking into his trance.

"Yes?" He opened his eyes, prepared to put space between them if she wanted him to.

"Is it okay to do this?" She leaned her cheek against his chest.

He smiled. "Absolutely." After a few seconds he said, "We talked about going public at Monday's lesson, but I forgot about church tomorrow. Should we do that instead?"

"No. Too many people will be there. If we do it on Monday, there's only a handful. We'll be broken up before the grapevine is in full swing."

"Yeah. That makes sense. The fewer people that know, the better. Plus we're just trying to stop my mother."

"And Aunt Bea."

He wondered if she knew she was nuzzling her cheek against him. He wasn't going to point it out to her.

She pulled away and looked up at him. "The last thing we need is to be the topic of Maple Falls' gossip."

"Yes. That would be awful."

His feet stopped moving. So did hers. He couldn't take his eyes off her, and she wasn't shifting her gaze away. He already knew the bliss of kissing Olivia, and more than anything he wanted to experience it again. Unable to stop himself, he leaned down. By some sort of miracle, she was tilting her head toward him.

"Oh. My. Gosh."

Kingston jumped as the lights brightened to full strength. Olivia jumped out of his arms. He jerked his head to the doorway . . . and saw Anita's and Tanner's jaws hit the floor.

Chapter 14

"Y ou and my brother?" Anita clapped her hands in an eerie imitation of her mother. "I can't believe it! Why didn't you tell me?"

Olivia blinked. Somehow she'd managed to follow Anita to one of the spare bedrooms, and now, behind a closed door, her best friend's giddiness was almost on par with Karen's. How had this happened? One second she'd been about to kiss Kingston—or thought she was. She was ready to, despite every logical brain cell in her head screaming no, no, a thousand times no. But pure physical drive had won, or almost had. Anita had no idea she'd just saved Olivia from making a horrible mistake.

Another one.

Anita plopped on the edge of the queen-size bed, her cheeks aglow from pregnancy and excitement. She patted the empty space. "I want every detail."

Olivia tried to gather her thoughts as she perched on the bed. Now what? And what was Kingston telling Tanner? In the back of her mind, she recalled Tanner saying they had shown up to surprise Karen, who had been bugging them to spend time with her. Nice for Karen, but their timing was horrible.

"I have to go to the bathroom." She popped up from the bed. Before Anita could answer, she shot out of the room. She entered the hallway just in time to see Kingston duck into the powder room. She hurried and knocked on the door. "Hey," she whispered. "It's me."

He opened the door, grabbed her hand, and pulled her inside. "Where's my sister?"

"Spare bedroom. Tanner?"

"The den." He glanced at the toilet. "Guess you and I had the same escape plan."

She clutched her hands together and looked up at him. "What are we going to do? I don't want to lie to them."

"Me either." He shoved his hands through his hair. "We don't have a choice, though. And in the end, nothing changes—we're breaking up, regardless of who finds out we're together. No one needs to know the truth, though. We'll let Mom take the credit for our romance. She certainly worked hard enough." He put his hands on her shoulders. "It's going to be okay, Olivia. I promise."

She'd heard his promises before, and she hoped this time he was right. She drew in a deep breath. "Yes. It's going to be okay—"

"Kingston?" Tanner's voice sounded on the other side of the door.

"Be out in a minute!" he hollered, then walked to the toilet and flushed it. He turned on the tap, then quietly opened the frosted shower-stall door and waved her to go inside. When she was hidden, he left the bathroom.

"What's the dessert you brought again?" Kingston said.

"Apple fritters." Tanner's voice sounded more distant.

"I could sure go for one of those."

Olivia exited the shower and put her ear against the door. Nothing. She stood back, ready to leave, then changed her mind and used the bathroom. After washing her hands, she opened the door. Anita stood there, poised to knock.

"Are you okay?" Her brow furrowed. "You were gone so long I was worried about you."

"I'm fine." Olivia forced a smile. She hated deceiving Anita. Fortunately, it was only temporary. *Very* temporary. "How about we try some of the apple fritters Tanner brought?"

Anita frowned. "How did you know he brought those?"

Olivia froze. Anita hadn't mentioned the dessert, and Olivia hadn't spoken to Tanner. "I, uh, heard you two talking in the hallway. Let's go get some. I'm sure you're hungry, eating for two." Olivia headed down the hall, Anita behind her.

"I am hungry. Again." Anita caught up with Olivia as they entered the kitchen. "I hope Mom still has some leftover liverwurst."

Olivia's stomach turned as Anita went straight to the fridge. She saw Kingston and Tanner sitting at the kitchen bar, Kingston shoving a fritter into his mouth. Karen stood behind the counter, a mix of happiness and horror on her face.

"Have you ever considered making a *light* dessert,

Tanner?" Karen eyed the pile of fritters. Olivia thought she saw her shudder.

"Nah." Tanner grabbed one and took a bite. "My reputation would take a hit."

"Mom, do you have any liverwurst? Oh, and cream cheese. And olives. The green ones, not the black. Ooh, strawberry jelly sounds good. Where's the bread?" Anita looked away from the fridge at the apple fritters. "Save me one of those too."

Karen turned green-gilled. "Dear, how about we make you a healthy snack?" She went to the fridge and gently drew Anita away.

Olivia paused, surveying the room. Anita was tied up with her mother, while Tanner and Kingston were feasting on fritters. There was an empty chair on either side of the men. She walked over and sat next to Kingston. To her surprise, he put his arm around her shoulders and offered her a bite of his fritter. She met his gaze. *One hundred percent commitment, right?* She bit into the sweet pastry.

"Well, aren't y'all cute," Tanner drawled, then laughed. "Seriously, I'm surprised. I wouldn't have put you two together."

"Me either," Anita said, popping a green olive into her mouth. Apparently, that was on Karen Bedford's approved-snack list.

"I did," Karen gushed.

"I've been interested in Olivia for a while now." Kingston looked at her, a surprising mix of fascination and apology in his eyes. "Since last year."

Well, that was the truth. Maybe. He'd at least pretended

to be interested in her on two occasions, but it hadn't lasted long enough to go any further. Still, she was relieved her friends were hearing some honesty. "Me too."

"Wait, what?" Anita dropped an olive. Karen quickly scooped it off the floor and threw it into the sink. "Neither one of you ever said anything."

Still focused on Kingston, Olivia said, "I didn't think we'd ever get together." She turned to Anita. "So I kept it to myself."

Her friend nodded and put her hand on her stomach. "I understand."

"And now you're a couple," Karen said, going over to Olivia. "Welcome to the family."

"Mother," Kingston said.

"Oh, I know I'm putting the cart before the horse." Karen stood back and smiled. "But I can't help it. I'm thrilled beyond belief, and I wish I would have thought of bringing you two together sooner. Thank goodness Erma called me and, um, told me about the dance lessons. If she hadn't, I wouldn't have noticed your *chemistry*."

"I thought you saw the lessons advertised on a flyer." Kingston put his half-eaten fritter on one of the plates on the bar counter.

"No, it was Erma who told me about them." Karen grabbed a towel off the counter and began wiping it. If she moved the towel any faster, she'd take the shine right off the granite.

"I didn't realize you two were friends," Anita said, heading for the fridge again. "Are you joining the BBs?"

Karen's eyes widened. "We're acquaintances," she said.

237

"And no, I'm not joining the BBs. I don't have a single free moment in my schedule. Speaking of, you and Tanner need to come to the showcase."

"What's a showcase?" Tanner asked as Anita pulled out the liverwurst.

Olivia listened as Karen described her plans for the ballroom recital. She put her hands on her knees, and a second later she felt Kingston's hand cover hers. She immediately relaxed.

Half an hour and one liverwurst, cream-cheese, green-olive, and strawberry-jelly sandwich later—Karen had given up on policing Anita's pregnancy cravings—Kingston spoke. "I need to get Olivia home," he said.

"It is getting late." Karen came over and gave each of them a hug. "See you tomorrow," she said, smiling.

Kingston glanced at Olivia. She nodded, and he said to his mom, "See you then."

They walked outside and headed to the car in silence. He opened the passenger door for her, and she started to step inside but hesitated. "Wait. I forgot my purse."

"We've both been a little distracted. Want me to get it for you?"

"No, I know exactly where it is. Go ahead and start the car." She hurried to the house and lifted her hand to knock, only to stop herself. Her purse was on the couch in the den. Maybe she could sneak in and get it without the other three knowing, avoiding any inevitable fawning over her and Kingston. She slowly opened the door and shut it quietly behind her, scurried to the empty den—thank the

Lord—grabbed her purse, and hurried back to the car. She got inside, shut the door, and fell back against the seat.

Kingston's phone was pressed to his ear. "Are you sure that's the only time you have available? Yeah, I want to have plenty of time to practice too. All right. I'll meet you there. Bye." He slid his thumb across the screen and looked at Olivia. "Mission accomplished?"

"Yes." She could finally go home and process what had happened tonight, including their almost kiss. Now that she was away from his mother and their friends' excitement, she could think clearly. Well, almost clearly. Her brain was still foggy, another rare occurrence.

Kingston set aside the phone, put the car in Drive, and exited the circular driveway. "That was Sunny. She's the one who called earlier, so I called her back while you were inside. She wants to meet at the studio tomorrow after church to plan our spotlight dance. She says her schedule is completely booked for the next three weeks, and we do need the practice time." He shifted in his seat and glanced at her. "Rain check on the swim lessons?"

"Yes." A small thread of relief wound through her. Now she wouldn't have to make a mad dash to the store to find a swimsuit that camouflaged her thighs—if she could even find one this late in the season. Although with Harper's help, she was sure she could have managed something.

But another emotion overrode the relief and her logic. On a concrete level, Kingston's work on the recital took priority over her swim lesson. She didn't want him looking like a fool on the dance floor, although she doubted he ever could. And they weren't really a couple, so he wasn't canceling a date. Still, she felt cast aside. Again.

"Are you sure?" He sounded hesitant. "I can call her back—"

"Positive." She shoved aside her ridiculous thoughts. "Go practice your tango."

He didn't respond, and they didn't say anything else the rest of the way back to her house. When he pulled into her driveway, he put the car in Park. "Are you okay?"

"Sure." She opened the door. "I'm fine." She wasn't, but she wasn't mad at him either. Just confused. Very, very confused. "We started the plan tonight, and that was the hard part. On Monday we put on another show."

"Don't forget Tuesday."

Oh. She had forgotten he was coming to read to the school-age kids that afternoon. Drawing a blank on her schedule wasn't normal for her either. She couldn't wait until they ended this faux relationship. Then she wouldn't be so out of sorts. No more deception or fake hand-holding or pretend infatuation. No more close dancing or near kisses . . .

"And I guess we should sit next to each other in church," he pointed out. "If we don't, Anita and Tanner will wonder why."

"Right." She was kicking herself for not anticipating the snarls. "See you tomorrow."

"Can I pick you up?"

She almost nodded but stopped herself. This was getting complicated, and she hated complications. "I'll meet you there. That way you can go straight to the studio after service."

"Okay."

Quickly, she closed the door and hurried to her small front porch, the Audi's headlights illuminating her way. As she inserted her key into the lock, her phone started pinging. And pinging. And pinging.

Olivia stepped inside, shut the door, and fished in her purse for her phone while Kingston backed out of her driveway. She glanced at the screen. The group text she was in with Anita, Harper, and Riley was blowing up.

Harper: You and Kingston! Squee!

Riley: Congrats, Olivia. He's a great guy.

Anita: Of course he is. He's my brother.

Harper: When's your first official date? We have to keep tradition alive and give you a makeover.

Olivia: I don't need a makeover.

She started to text that she needed a swimsuit but held off. Although she'd said yes to his rain check, their fake relationship would end before that time would come, and after that there would be no reason for them to be together. They'd have to make it clear that the breakup was friendly, though. She didn't want things to be awkward when she was around the Bedfords.

Anita: If I had to get a makeover, you have to get one.

Riley: Agreed. Like Harper said, it's tradition.

Harper: Hey, it's not like I forced you two. I just gave you a nudge.

Riley: A hard nudge.

Olivia plopped on the couch and read the texts as her friends discussed the past. Harper had given Riley a makeover before her first date with Hayden, had dolled up Anita for a party she and Tanner had catered together, and before they were a couple, she'd even transformed her husband, Rusty, from a shaggy-bearded mechanic to a clean-cut entrant in a charity bachelor auction. Now that she thought about it, Olivia realized that all three makeovers had been the beginning of romance for the couples. No, she was definitely not letting Harper near her.

> **Anita:** You two are adorable together, Olivia. I'm so happy for you.
> **Harper:** Me too.
> **Riley:** Ditto.

Olivia groaned. This was what she got for stepping outside her comfort zone. And the fact she'd barely hesitated to agree to Kingston's idea bothered her. A lot. She was never impulsive.

I never will be again.

> **Harper:** Olivia? You still there?
> **Olivia:** Yes. Just got up to get a drink. It's late, so I'm calling it a night.
> **Anita, Riley, and Harper:** z^{Zz}

She looked at the screen and checked the time. Only ten o'clock? She'd thought it was much later than that. It sure felt like it. She stood and locked the front door, set her purse in its usual spot on a small table near the door, and headed for her room. She finished getting ready for bed and was pulling down the crisp white bedding when her phone pinged again. She sat on the edge and looked at the screen. The message was from Kingston.

She was tempted to ignore it. She hadn't had a chance to process the evening's events, and she needed to get her bearings. But she couldn't be rude either. She swiped over the message.

I had a great time tonight. Thank you.

Olivia paused. And because she'd lied enough for one night, she typed the truth:

Me too.
. . .

Kingston was typing. She waited for him to finish, but his message didn't appear. She started to set the phone on her nightstand when she finally saw it pop up.

Sweet dreams

Olivia set down the phone, turned off her lights, and slipped under the sheets. Despite everything, she smiled.

Chapter 15

On Sunday after church, Erma hung back at the BBs' table at the Orange Bluebird as the rest of her friends lined up at the brunch buffet. Bea had called for another emergency meeting, this time to celebrate their success. According to Karen, who had texted a full and detailed report to everyone Saturday night, after one manufactured date, Olivia and Kingston were a couple. Or at least they appeared to be during church this morning.

But Erma wasn't as excited as her comrades in matchmaking crime. Even Myrtle was enthusiastic about Maple Falls' latest pairing. "*Bea was right*," she'd said to Erma on the ride over. "*They do make a lovely couple.*"

As she watched Peg, Myrtle, Viola, Gwen, Bea, and Madge fill up their plates—Madge's was only half full and she'd hit the salad bar first—Erma pondered her reaction. She'd seen Olivia and Kingston walk into the sanctuary and had watched, along with the BBs, as they sat next to the other young couples. She'd even smiled when Bea elbowed her in the side and gestured with a nod of her head at the two new lovebirds holding hands. But something was off. Erma had spent far more time observing them than paying attention to Pastor Jared's sermon, trying to figure out what was bothering her. They seemed stiff. Like they were going through the motions.

She shook her head at her own nonsense. Olivia had always been reserved, and she wouldn't be comfortable with PDA, especially in the sanctuary. Erma didn't know Kingston as well as Riley's other friends, but he was a doctor and a professional. He probably wasn't eager to canoodle in front of everyone at Amazing Grace Church either. Maybe they were passionate behind closed doors. Either way, it wasn't her business. She should celebrate, because now the matchmaking was finally over.

Bea was the first one to arrive at the table, a big fried chicken breast taking up half her plate. She sat down, her grin stretching ear to ear, and not just because the Orange Bluebird had her favorite side dish—greens and ham hocks—on the menu today. "Too bad Karen couldn't make it," she said. "I've never met anyone who 'doesn't do buffets.' But she's just as ecstatic as we are about Olivia and Kingston." She sat down next to Erma. "I still can't believe it was so easy to get them together."

Right. So easy. Erma mentally shrugged off the thought as her cell phone rang. She fished for her phone in her handbag and saw Hayden's number pop up. "Hello?"

"Hi, Erma," he said, sounding like he was in a car. "I need a favor, please."

"For you, sugar, I'll do anything. Well, anything that's legal."

He chuckled. "Jasper and I were having lunch at the Orange Bluebird—"

"What a coincidence! I'm here too," Erma said. "If I'd known you were coming, I would have saved you some seats."

"It was, uh, a last-minute decision. Can you give him a ride home? I have to leave early."

"Why? Is something wrong?"

"Um, no. I just had some . . . business to attend to. Campaign stuff."

Hmm. It wasn't like Hayden to be cagey. Then again, Erma didn't have a clue how running for office worked. "Sure." She stood and glanced around the packed restaurant. "Where were y'all sitting—" As if on cue, she saw Jasper Mathis amble toward the buffet. "Never mind. I see him."

"Thanks, Erma," Hayden said, sounding relieved. "I appreciate it."

"No problem." She watched as Jasper perused the buffet selections. "Did y'all get a chance to eat?"

"No, we'd just sat down when I got the phone call."

Phone call? She was tempted to ask him who had called, but it was none of her business. Phooey, now her curiosity was up.

"Gotta go, Erma. Again, thanks for taking him home."

"You're welcome." She hung up and counted the chairs situated around the large table. There was an extra one since they had half expected Karen to show up.

"Is that Jasper over there?" Bea asked, craning her neck to see around the person standing in front of the table.

"Yes." Erma realized she was in a bit of a pickle. Her

friends would be here any minute, plates of food in hand and ready to celebrate. If she invited Jasper to join them, the BBs couldn't be open about their matchmaking scheme. But she couldn't abide him eating alone either. He did enough of that at the diner.

"Yoo-hoo!" Bea waved her paper napkin in the air. "Over here, Jasper."

He startled and looked in their direction, pausing when he met Erma's gaze. He frowned.

She frowned right back. Just because they'd shared sweet tea and hummingbird cake didn't mean they were going to be chummy.

"I don't think he heard me, Erma," Bea said. "Go tell him to join us."

Well, at least her conundrum was solved. She threaded her way through the crowd. Good grief, had everyone from Hot Spring County come here today? She finally reached Jasper after dodging someone with a mountain of mashed potatoes on his plate.

"Jasper."

"Erma."

She didn't respond, waiting for the flutter she'd experienced the other night to return. When it didn't, she almost sighed with relief. "Hayden asked me to take you home after lunch."

He scowled. "I can catch a cab."

"You won't pay to get your car fixed, but you'll waste money on unnecessary cab fare?"

Averting his gaze, he said, "Don't want anyone to go to any trouble on my behalf."

Lord, give me strength. "It's no trouble. We're going to the same town."

Jasper tugged on the collar of his dress shirt. His black jacket, while appearing almost new, hung on his slim frame, half covering his old jeans. "Let's get some meat on those bones," she said and headed for the buffet, glancing over her shoulder to see if he was following her. When he didn't, she crooked her finger at him. With another scowl, he joined her at the buffet. She passed him a warm plate.

"Ain't never been here before," he said, taking it from her.

"You haven't?" She thought everyone in Maple Falls had been to the Orange Bluebird at least once. It, along with the Sunshine Diner, was one of the few dine-in establishments between Maple Falls and Malvern. There was a pizza place down the road, but they were closed on Sundays.

"No. What's good?"

"Everything. Just follow me." She selected a slice of prime rib, a fried chicken leg, and a piece of smoked sausage cooked with sauerkraut. After that she added mashed taters with white gravy, green beans and bacon, buttered sweet corn off the cob, and honeyed carrots, and topped it off with a big yeast roll and three pats of butter.

"Where you gonna put all that, Erma Jean?"

She turned and looked at Jasper's plate. He had a chicken leg, a glob of potatoes, and three green beans on his plate. "Is that all you're eating?"

"Yeah—"

Erma put carrots and corn on his plate, along with two rolls and a cornbread muffin. "There. Now that's a meal."

While she was at it, she added three more butter pats to her own plate.

He stared at his plate, as if sizing up the food, the short gray whiskers on his cheeks sinking into the wrinkles around his mouth. But he didn't say anything and let her go ahead of him as they went back to the table. The crowd was winding down, clearing a path for them to cross the dining room.

When they were a few feet from the BBs, she froze.

Every single woman was grinning at her. No, they were grinning at *them*.

"What are y'all smiling at?" Jasper sat down next to Bea.

"Oh, nothing," they all said in unison. Bea gave Erma a wink.

Now wait just one minute. Just because the Bosom Buddies were successful in getting Olivia and Kingston together didn't mean they could target her and Jasper. She shot a glare sharp enough to cut steel at each one of them. There was no way she was going to be a victim of their monkey business.

Her dirty look worked, because they all dug into their food. She sat down, calmly opened up her napkin and placed it on her lap, passed two pats of butter to Jasper, and took a sip of her sweet tea.

"I want to thank you all so much." Bea set down her fork, a rare occurrence for her so early in a meal. "Because of y'all, my Olivia is happy."

So much for not being candid. Oh well. She took a bite of the sausage. Delicious.

"Karen did the hard part," Myrtle pointed out.

"And I'll thank her the next time I see her. I appreciate everyone's moral support."

Jasper set down the chicken leg bone he'd been chewing on. Not a speck of meat was left. "What'd y'all do?"

The women looked at him. "We, uh," Bea said, turning to Erma for help.

"We got Olivia and Kingston together." Viola squeezed some honey on her corn muffin. "Just like Bea asked us to."

"As Myrtle pointed out," Madge said, "his mother was chiefly responsible."

Jasper leaned back in his chair and looked at all of them. "Y'all seem pretty proud of yourselves."

Bea beamed. "We are."

"Humph." He picked up his roll and tore it in half.

Erma turned to him. "What do you mean, 'humph'?"

He shrugged and crammed the roll into his mouth.

The BBs proceeded to ignore him and discuss other happenings in and around Maple Falls. But Erma only half listened. Why would Jasper have an opinion either way about Olivia and Kingston? The man remained silent during the rest of the meal, except to say thanks when Bea brought him back a bowl of chocolate pudding from the dessert section of the buffet.

They finished lunch, paid the bill, and walked up front together. Myrtle told Erma she was catching a ride with Gwen—they'd decided to see the latest superhero movie playing that afternoon at the cinema in Hot Springs. Gwen did like her muscled heroes. After telling her friends good-bye, Erma hit the bathroom before heading to the parking lot. As she walked out the door, she saw Jasper standing outside, his hands in the pockets of his baggy jeans.

She pulled her keys out of her purse. They dangled

from a purple key chain in the shape of a yarn ball. Riley had ordered them last year, and they were so popular that she had trouble keeping them in stock at the store. "Ready to go?"

"Naw. I'm just standing out here for my health."

Ooooh. He had some nerve getting snarky with her since she was his ride home. She had half a mind to leave him here to get a cab, but she wouldn't go back on her promise to Hayden and Riley. She turned to him, ready to shoot off a remark equally as caustic, when she saw that little lift of the corners of his mouth again, this time accompanied by a twinkle in his eye. *Flut—*

"Are we goin' or not?"

His expression turned surly, and now she questioned her own eyes. Had he shown a softer side of himself for a brief moment, or had she imagined it? Or wished for it? "Yeah," she said, charging toward her car two rows over. "We're going."

She walked to her vehicle and turned on the air as soon as she got inside. It was late August, and it would be hot clear to the end of September.

Jasper had moseyed behind her, unhurried. Without a word he got into the passenger seat. Equally silent, she drove toward Maple Falls.

After a few minutes, the quiet wore on her. Even when she drove by herself, she had the music on or was talking on the phone through her Bluetooth. She glanced at him, and he shifted, as if he felt her eyes on him. Finally she said, "What was all that about during lunch?"

"All what?"

"Humph." She tried as hard as she could to imitate the cranky old man's harrumph. She must have been successful, because he didn't look at her like she was crazy.

"Don't think it's right to poke into other folks' affairs. Especially those of the romantical kind."

Well, that was one thing they could agree on. "You saw Olivia and Kingston together. What did you think?"

He rubbed his stubby thumb over the hem of his jacket. "Didn't pay them much mind." He side-eyed her. "Looks like you paid them too much."

Jasper had her there, confound it. She sighed as they crossed the Maple Falls city limits. "Bea is positive those two are meant for each other."

"Maybe they are. Maybe they ain't. Probably best to let it happen on its own."

The world had to be upside down right now. There was no other explanation for her and Jasper having a civil conversation and agreeing with each other on every point. Especially about romance, and particularly since he was a lifelong bachelor.

"Why didn't you ever get married?" Erma blurted. It was a question she'd always had but never asked, even though she'd known the man for decades. He'd been very private about his private life.

"Ain't never met the right woman at the right time."

"Maybe someone should have set you up."

He scoffed. "If they had, they would have gotten an earful from me. Probably a fistful, in my younger days."

She chuckled. He had been pugnacious back in the day. Now he was worn down. That was another thing she could relate to. The body cooperated less and less with the mind at their age.

Erma pulled into Jasper's driveway. She expected him to bolt from her car as soon as she put the engine into Park. Instead, he cleared his throat.

"You, uh, wouldn't want to come inside for a spell, would ya? Tanner sent me home with a gallon jug of fresh-squeezed lemonade he said was left over from supper last night. Can't drink all that on my own."

He'd gobsmacked her, all right. She opened her mouth to tell him no. They might be getting along now, but that would change any minute. He was cantankerous, she was stubborn, and they had nothing in common except that they liked to dig at each other. Oh, and they both disliked being the target of matchmaking.

She flinched, realizing how hypocritical she was being. In her defense, she had tried to stop the BBs and their antics for a little while. And she still didn't know why she had an off feeling about Olivia and Kingston.

"Never mind." He dug into his back pocket and pulled out his wallet. "Twenty enough for the ride?"

"Put that away." She turned off the engine and looked at him. "Is that lemonade cold?"

"Been in the fridge all day."

"You got sugar in case it's too tart? I can't abide sour lemonade."

He frowned. "It ain't tart, but if you aim to sweeten it up, I got you covered."

"All right. But just for one cup. That's all. I'm a busy woman, and I have a lot of things to do."

He peered at her. "On the Lord's day? You don't fool me, Erma Jean McAllister. You were gonna go home and take a nap. Same as I was gonna do."

Rats. He was right about that too. That's exactly what she had planned to do—after putting aside all thoughts of matchmaking and Olivia and Kingston. She opened the car door. "Come on, you old coot. Let's go inside."

If she didn't know any better, she would have sworn she saw him crack a genuine smile.

Olivia pushed her chopsticks into a carton of vegetable fried rice and scooped out a small amount. She couldn't remember the last time she'd had Chinese food, or when she and the Chick Clique—she had to come up with a better name before that one stuck in perpetuity—had gathered after church for lunch. They were sitting at Riley's kitchen table, and like her art, the space was bright, colorful, and eclectic.

Using a fork, Harper dunked a steamed dumpling into soy sauce. "I really miss our lunches, ladies. Thanks, Riley, for suggesting this."

Anita nodded. "Tanner didn't put up too much of a fuss when Rusty suggested they play nine rounds this afternoon. He's not a golf fan, but maybe it will grow on him." She grinned and sprinkled her egg foo yung with brown sugar. "Dad's hoping it will."

Olivia looked at her friend's concoction and blanched. Harper and Riley did the same. "How long are pregnancy cravings supposed to last?"

Harper shrugged. "Mine are tapering off, oddly enough. I'm thankful they stopped early. Rusty was threatening to eat in a different room."

"Tanner already has. A couple of times." Anita pushed away her dish. "I'm sorry. I don't mean to gross y'all out."

"It's okay." Riley patted her arm and put the plate back in front of her. "You eat what you and the baby want. We're made of stronger stuff than the men."

They all laughed, and Olivia went back to her fried rice.

"I figured you and Kingston would be spending the afternoon together," Harper said to her with a wink.

"Y'all sure were cuddly last night." Anita cut off a piece of the sweetened egg foo yung. "Now that you're official, tell us when you first started to like him."

Olivia stilled. Here was another curve she hadn't anticipated. Her closest friends would want to know details. Out of the four she was the least romantic—and she had always been fine with that. Maybe it's why she hadn't thought about coming up with a story for her and Kingston. She should have.

"He swept you off your feet, didn't he?" Harper picked up another dumpling.

Olivia's mind went back to their make-out session on his car. *He sure did.*

"Aww, you're blushing." Anita sighed. "This is so sweet."

No, it was torture. She crammed her chopsticks into the container.

Riley put a spring roll on her plate. "I'm surprised he has time for a girlfriend. As long as I've known him, he's always been busy. Busier than Hayden, even, and I didn't think that was possible."

Anita nodded. "Up until two weeks ago, we rarely saw him. He's on an extended vacation right now. Right, Olivia?"

She nodded as she shoveled rice into her mouth.

"Where is he this afternoon?" Harper asked. "You didn't say."

Olivia swallowed and set the container down, the rice settling into a lump in her stomach. "He's practicing with Sunny for the showcase."

"That's the recital at the end of dance lessons," Anita explained to Harper and Riley.

"Why aren't you there?" Riley asked. Harper nodded.

"Why would I be?"

Harper raised a perfectly groomed eyebrow. "To keep an eye on them."

"Why?"

All three of them looked at her in disbelief. "You and Kingston are brand-new," Anita said in the gentle tone she used with her toddler Sunday-school class. "Like, not even twenty-four hours. I'm not saying you can't trust him, but—"

"You need to stake your claim on your man, Olivia." Harper gave her a pointed look. "Kingston's a catch. Scratch that. He's an über-catch."

"He's always had women chasing after him," Anita said.

"I'm sure he's trustworthy," Riley added. "But if Sunny is interested in him, she needs to know she's wasting her time."

Olivia blinked. Of all the things she hadn't foreseen—and

she was sure there would be more—her friends' concern was one of them. "It's just a dance," she said. But even as the words came out of her mouth, an ugly feeling spread across her chest. "Sunny's a professional."

"She's also human."

Olivia turned to Anita. If his own sister was uneasy . . . She shook her head. "I don't see the problem."

Her friends exchanged baffled glances. Harper leaned forward. "Sweetie, if you can't see the problem, then you have an even bigger one."

"When Tanner and I were dating, I wanted to spend every moment with him." Anita sipped her water.

"Same with Hayden," Riley said. "I almost lost him because of my stupidity—"

"You had extenuating circumstances," Harper said, referring to Riley's wayward mother. Her eyes filled with compassion. "Tracey had your head spinning."

"Yeah, let's not bring her up." Riley waved her hand. "Anyway, once we started our relationship, we couldn't wait until the end of the day to see each other." She let out a rare swoony sigh. Unlike Harper and Anita, she kept her emotions close. "Those were the days. Before mayoral campaigns—"

"And babies," Anita and Harper said at the same time.

"There's nothing sweeter than the first blushes of love." Riley grinned.

"Wow, that's really poetic," Anita said. "And very true."

Harper got up from the table and went to Olivia. She picked up her fried-rice container and folded the top.

"What are you doing?" Olivia grabbed at the container, but Harper held it out of reach.

"Helping you. Riley, hand me that bag. Oh, and two of those fortune cookies."

Riley gave her one of the white plastic bags that had held their takeout. Harper put the food in the bag and gave it to Olivia. "Go."

"Go where?"

"To the dance studio." Anita made a shooing motion with her fingers. "Tell Sunny you want to cut the lesson short so you can spend time with your man."

"But—"

"Out!" They all pointed to the kitchen exit.

Olivia frowned, gave each of them a bewildered look, and pushed back from the table. "I—"

They kept pointing at the doorway.

Lifting her hand in a baffled wave, she left the kitchen and went to her car. Now what? Her friends were being ridiculous, but then again, they didn't know the truth about her and Kingston. If they really were together, her friends' actions would make sense. But there was no need to "stake her claim" or to be worried about Sunny Abernathy.

She also didn't need to be jealous. They were just two people dancing a tango for a few minutes. Two beautiful people, not that it mattered. And whatever the sour ache emerging in her heart was, it wasn't jealousy. Probably heartburn from slamming down the fried rice.

Kingston and Sunny? Not a big deal.

Olivia got into her car and set the takeout on the passenger seat. She needed to go home and work on her paper. She still hadn't finished it, and it was due tomorrow. She had only two more pages left, but every time she thought about writing them, she found another distraction. Putting off an assignment had always been anathema to her, and now she was too close for comfort to the deadline.

She turned on the engine and was about to back out when her phone rang. She took it out of her purse and glanced at the screen. Surprised, she answered it. "Hi, Mom."

"Hello, Olivia."

"Is something wrong? Is Dad okay?" She shifted the car back to Park. She had just talked to her mother last week, and they never spoke to each other two weeks in a row.

"Your father is fine. There's nothing wrong."

"Thank goodness." She fell back against the seat.

"I heard you have a new development in your life. One you failed to mention to me last week."

Olivia sighed. Everything had to have an objective. Would it be too much to ask of her mother to call "just because"? "What new development would that be?"

"Your boyfriend."

Her temple started to throb. "Where did you hear that?" she asked faintly, suspecting the answer.

"Bea called me after church. She said you were dating Kingston Bedford. I guess you're too busy to let your parents know such important news."

She sat up in the seat. There was a hint of emotion in the way her mom phrased the words, but Olivia couldn't define it. Was she offended? Hurt? Mad?

Even worse, she hadn't anticipated her parents finding out. She should have, though, the minute she'd seen her aunt's beaming face as she and Kingston sat next to each other in church. He'd been the one to reach for her hand, and although he'd startled her and made her nervous knowing so many eyes were watching them, she was glad he did. Like last night, his touch calmed her. They might not be a real couple, but they were in this mess together.

And it was turning into a big mess. Aunt Bea wasn't the only one who had smiled at them—all the BBs had. And now her parents knew. Her aunt must be spreading the news everywhere.

She should just tell her mother the truth. But that would lead to more questions—and more lies. Ugh, she wanted to throw up. "I'm not sure he and I are going to work out." There. A half-truth.

"Olivia, you can't enter a relationship with that attitude. You're sabotaging yourself and your partner before you've given things a chance. Bea reminded me that Kingston is a doctor. Is he a surgeon? A specialist? Or is he in the mental-health field?"

"Pediatrics." She turned up the air-conditioning and aimed one of the vents straight at her face. Her parents had left Maple Falls after Olivia and Anita's graduation, while Kingston was getting his bachelor's.

"That's an acceptable discipline," her mother said. "However, your father and I had hoped you'd connect with a professor at one of the universities you attended."

"Really? You never mentioned that."

"We decided when you hit puberty not to interfere with your social life. Fortunately, you've always been a rule follower, so we didn't have to worry about you doing something impulsive or stupid. If you did, however, we would have applied appropriate consequences."

"How reassuring," she muttered.

Anita knocked on her window. "Is everything all right?" she said through the glass.

Olivia gave her a feeble thumbs-up and pointed to the phone. Anita smiled and went back to the house.

"Mom, I have to go. I can call you later." And she would, after she and Kingston broke up, something that should happen sooner rather than later before things really got out of hand. Then everything would go back to normal. She was craving some normalcy right now.

"Off to see your doctor?" Mom asked.

She opened her mouth to tell her no, that she was going to finish up her final. Then the stress of the last twenty-four hours hit her. Her friends, Aunt Bea, the BBs, and now her parents were involved in their deception. It wouldn't be long before the entire town was talking about her and Kingston.

Then the image of Sunny and Kingston dancing together, him holding her close, popped into her mind. The unfortunately familiar stab of jealousy hit her again, along with the realization that if she didn't go "claim her man" like her friends insisted she do, she would never hear the end of it. "Yes. I'm going to see Kingston," she said, wanting to bang her head against the steering wheel. "He's, uh, expecting me."

"I can't say I'm surprised you're eager to see him."

Olivia sounded anything but eager, but her mother was never good at reading emotions.

"Once I determined your father had genetic potential, we spent the requisite amount of time together to form a hormonal bond."

"Dad was okay with you genetically assessing him?"

"He did the Punnett square on our first date."

Now I know where I get it from. "Gotta go. I'll call you later."

"Goodbye, Olivia."

Her mother hung up the phone, and Olivia tossed her own on top of the takeout bag. She still intended to finish her final this afternoon, but she could at least make an appearance at the dance studio. She'd drop by, say hi, make a googly eye or two at Kingston for good measure, then get back to coursework—something she should have been doing all along.

As she drove to downtown Maple Falls, she thought about him again—more accurately, about the two of them last night, before Anita and Tanner had shown up. The way he'd held her in his arms, the yearning she thought she saw in his eyes as they danced, the scent of his cologne. It all made the tingles go haywire. It had been different from their first encounter in the Sunset parking lot. That had been hormones going haywire for both of them. The tender kiss they'd shared in the supply closet during Anita's reception had been different too. Even though she had accepted his apology then, her guard was still up.

But last night was different. Natural. Comfortable. She'd felt so secure in his arms she had almost lost her mind and kissed him. Thank goodness they'd been interrupted. If she had kissed him, that would have added another complication, and she didn't want any more of those. Besides, she would have been rebuffed. He saw her only as a friend now, and that was the way things had to be. She needed to remember the reason he was at the dance studio today was that Sunny had asked him to come, even though they had already made plans to swim. Ever since that fateful night at the theater, she'd come in second, even in a pretend relationship.

Olivia pulled up in front of the dance studio, her eyes burning. This was stupid. She was getting upset over nothing. Kingston was free to do what he wanted, and she was sure what he didn't want was her hovering and watching his every move.

She squealed out of the parking space and drove home.

Chapter 16

I'm sorry, Sunny," Kingston said as he miscounted his steps for the fourth—or was it fifth? sixth?—time since they started practicing.

"It's okay." She stepped out of his arms and went to her phone on top of the piano. "Let's take a little break."

He nodded, rubbing the back of his neck. He and Sunny had been practicing for almost an hour, and he was still making mistakes. She gestured for him to sit down on one of the folding chairs near the front window, then picked up a pink water bottle and joined him.

He slouched in the chair. The short dance she'd choreographed wasn't hard, but he couldn't remember the steps. "I don't know what I'm doing wrong."

"Your concentration is off." She took a calm sip of the water. "Or maybe you'd rather be dancing with someone else? Olivia, perhaps?"

Kingston turned to her. She'd nailed it. He kept thinking about Olivia. Their dance together last night, holding her hand in church this morning . . . Oh. He guessed Sunny, along with most of Maple Falls, had seen them holding hands. He wasn't upset about it either. That was the point—to let everyone know that they were together so when they broke up, his mother would leave them alone.

He frowned. That had sounded good in theory. He'd known it would be hard to resist Olivia, but he hadn't anticipated her being constantly on his mind.

Sunny adjusted the buckle on her dance shoe. "If I'd known you and Olivia were together, I would have planned a spotlight dance for the two of you. I must admit, I thought you two had chemistry when I saw you dancing together last week."

He almost laughed. How did she not notice how angry Olivia was with him? "We were a little on the outs that night."

"It looked like passion to me." Sunny straightened and smiled. "It's not too late to plan a dance for the two of you, if you're interested."

That sounded like a great idea. He imagined their practice sessions, all the opportunities he'd have to hold her . . . He smiled. He was being a little selfish, and he'd have to keep himself in check. But ultimately, he wanted to spend time with Olivia. He'd just seen her less than three hours ago and he was already missing her.

"Just think about it," Sunny said as her phone started to ring. "And talk it over with her. Excuse me for a minute. I'll be right back."

While she crossed the room and picked up her phone off the piano, he pulled out his cell and called Olivia. There would still be time to swim after he was finished here, and maybe they could go out for a bite to eat afterward. If nothing else, it would make his mother happy. When he'd told her they weren't coming over this afternoon, she'd sounded disappointed. "Oh well, there are plenty of other days you two can swim. The pool will be open until mid-October."

The buzz of his phone ringing Olivia's sounded in his ear. Mid-October. That would be around the time he would be going back to work. After that he wouldn't have as much free time as he had now, so he needed to make the best of it. *With Olivia.* They still hadn't discussed when they were going to break up, and he wasn't in any hurry to have that conversation. He wanted to enjoy their relationship as long as it lasted.

His call went to voice mail, and he smiled at her crisp, no-nonsense recording.

"This is Olivia Farnsworth. Please leave a message."

"Hey, it's me." He glanced up to see that Sunny wasn't in the room. "I'm almost finished here. If you're up for it, we can still have that swim lesson today. Call me when you can."

He hung up. She must still be with her girlfriends. After church he'd overheard them talking about getting Chinese and going to Riley's house. But her not answering brought up something he hadn't realized—that outside of library hours, he didn't know her schedule.

Sunny entered the dance room from the back of the studio where her office and the restroom were located. "I hate to cut this short, but something cropped up at the last minute. Don't worry about our dance. It's going to be fine. You can practice with Olivia."

Now that was a homework assignment he could get enthused about.

He noticed Sunny had changed out of her leotard and dance skirt into jeans and a purple short-sleeved blouse. She'd also taken down her bun and had tied her long hair into a ponytail at the nape of her neck, and she was turning out all the lights, apparently in a hurry. "Everything okay?"

"Sure." She pulled down the front shade, then faced him, blushing a little. "Bubba just called."

"Oh?"

"Yeah." She picked up her dance bag and flung the strap over her thin shoulder. "We've been kind of talking. He just invited me to see his niece in her first play at the high school. It's my favorite musical—*South Pacific*. I couldn't tell him no. The matinee starts in an hour."

Her and Bubba? That was a surprise. "No worries. I understand."

"Thanks." She opened the door just as Bubba's army-green pickup came to a stop out front. "See you tomorrow night!" she said. Bubba was already out of the truck, ready to open the passenger-side door for her. She grinned as she climbed inside, and he shut the door. He looked at Kingston and did a little fist pump, then jumped back into his truck and sped off.

As Kingston started for his Audi, his phone buzzed. He glanced at the screen and smiled. "Hey, Olivia," he said, slowing his steps. "Thanks for calling me back."

Silence.

"Olivia?" His smile dimmed when she didn't respond.

"We need to talk."

"Sure. I can pick you up and we can talk on the way to my parents' place—"

"No." Her voice sounded small.

"Somewhere else?" His jaw jerked. "Just let me know, and I'll be there."

"The library. The door is unlocked."

"I'm on my way." He hung up, not missing the fact that she'd chosen a neutral location. The library wasn't open on Sundays, so there would at least be some privacy. Dread stirred in his gut, but it was quickly overridden by worry. Olivia was not fine, and he had to find out why.

Kingston whipped into the library parking lot and parked across two empty spaces right in front of the building. He jumped out and hurried toward the entrance, stopping short as he saw Olivia through the glass door. She was standing on the other side, waiting for him. But she didn't open the door right away. He could see her distraught expression, and his heart pinched. Only glass and steel separated them, but it might as well have been a chasm.

He knocked on the door, even though she knew he was there. Finally, she moved and let him in. He went to her. "Olivia, sweetheart—"

"Don't." She held up her hand and moved away from him.

The "sweetheart" had been a slip. An unfortunate one,

considering her expression and mood. He kept his distance. "What's wrong?"

"I can't do this." She clasped her hands in front of her, her small feet close together.

"Our relationship?"

"It's not a relationship!" she snapped. "It's not real. And now I'm lying to my friends, my family, my . . ." She pressed her hand over her chest. "*Myself.*"

He couldn't stop from moving closer to her, and this time she didn't resist. He cradled her cheek. "Olivia . . ."

"You don't have to pretend," she said, finally looking at him. "No one's here to watch."

"I know."

Olivia couldn't move. He was gently running his thumb over the top of her cheek, sending her tingles into overdrive. They were the only ones here. There was no reason for him to be touching her. Unless he wanted to. What had made her ever think she could fake being attracted to him? It was impossible. And despite her vow to resist, she melted into his touch.

He pulled back, as if her skin burned his. "Sorry," he mumbled, moving away.

She was jerked back to reality. She never should have called and asked him to meet her here. She wasn't even sure why she was here and not at home. But when she'd left the dance studio, she couldn't bear to go home to her empty house. Aunt Bea wasn't a viable alternative, since

Olivia was sure all her aunt would want to talk about was her relationship with Kingston. Her fake relationship that, despite everything, she wished was real.

He stood in front of her, his head tilted, eyes filled with concern. She hadn't bothered to turn on the lights when she arrived, and she couldn't feel the calm she always experienced when she was around books. All she felt was pain.

"Do you still want to talk?" he asked.

No, she didn't want to talk. She wanted what she couldn't have—him. "I can't do this anymore," she said, barely able to speak above a whisper. "I can't keep pretending and lying to everyone."

Kingston nodded. "I don't like lying to them either."

"We never should have gone through with the plan in the first place. It was an impulsive decision, and now everything is a mess."

He took a step forward. "Olivia . . ."

She backed away. "Don't. I'm confused enough as it is."

"About the plan? Or how you feel about me? Because I'm tired of pretending too. I thought I could handle my feelings for you. That we could be friends and it wouldn't be a problem to keep up the ruse, and that we were being underhanded for a good reason. But if things were different, if you felt the same way about me that I feel about you . . ." He half smiled. "I'd be kissing the daylights out of you right now."

Her heart thumped in her chest. She hadn't expected *that*.

This time when he moved closer to her, she didn't step away. When he took her hand in his, she didn't resist. "I'm crazy about you, Olivia. I want to teach you to swim and watch old movies with you. I want to talk about books and dance with you. I want to learn everything about you and be a part of your life." He lowered his head until he was close enough to kiss her. "We can make this real, right here, right now."

Her pulse was galloping now, and she couldn't tear her gaze from his. She wanted to dance and talk and be with him too. She could throw caution to the wind and be in an honest relationship with him. All she had to do was tell him yes. Like she had after they watched *The Quiet Man*. Like she had at Anita's wedding.

Just say yes.

And then she realized what was really holding her back. It wasn't her rut or her aversion to impulsivity. She needed something from him, something he couldn't give her. "And then what?"

Confusion and hurt flashed across his face. "What do you mean?"

"What happens when you go back to work? When your calendar is filled again and you don't have time to breathe, much less have time for me. For *us*."

He paused. "I promise I won't let that happen."

Her throat constricted. "Can you promise I won't come in second in your life? Or third? Or *last*?"

He raked his hand through his hair. "I want to promise that you won't. You have to believe me."

"I do." His inability to make that promise showed his sincerity. It also broke her heart.

Silence hung between them. Then Kingston slowly

nodded. "We can stage the breakup tomorrow," he said tightly, putting distance between them. "End the charade quickly."

"We can do it now." She fought back tears. "No need to make a scene." Her emotions were shredded. The thought of faking a breakup in front of everyone was untenable.

"Word will get out anyway. It always does." He drew in a breath. "After I fulfill my obligation to read to the kids on Tuesday, I won't bother you anymore. We'll go our separate ways . . . again."

She nodded. She couldn't speak. She was getting what she wanted. To be left alone, to go back to her scheduled, uncomplicated life. She didn't need Kingston toying with her emotions anymore. And as he walked out the door, she told herself one more lie.

I don't need him.

Erma rubbed the dice in her hands, then let them fly on the Parcheesi board. "C'mon, lucky three!" The dice stopped, showing double sixes. Phooey. She'd been trying to make her winning move for the last fifteen minutes so she could sweep the best of three games.

Jasper chuckled and picked up the dice. "Looks like your luck is runnin' out." He tossed the dice. A six and a two. He moved his last piece home and sat back in his chair, arms crossed, a wide grin on his face. "I win."

She couldn't help but smile back. "Don't get too cocky, you old coot." She glanced up at the clock. Seven o'clock already? Had she really stayed here all afternoon and through supper? She'd had no idea it was so late.

"How about another round?" He was putting the pieces back at the starting point. Red for him, yellow for her.

"Sorry, but I have to get back home." She had a load of laundry she'd been ignoring for the past couple of days. She needed to wash it tonight. She was running out of clean unmentionables. She stood and picked up the empty lemonade glasses and took them to the sink. They'd polished off Tanner's lemonade in the middle of game three.

Jasper didn't have a dishwasher, so she quickly washed the dishes as he packed up the game. After drying them, she put them away in the cabinet where he'd taken them out. She folded the damp towel in half and draped it over the side of his single basin sink. When she turned around, he was standing there.

"Sure you got to get goin'?" he asked.

She was surprised at the hope in his eyes. "Unfortunately, yes."

He nodded. Took one step forward. Looked at his shoes again. Then back at her.

He wasn't looking at her with hope in his eyes this time. Something else was there, something she hadn't seen from a man since Gus passed. Butterflies danced a jig in her stomach.

He cleared his throat into his hand. "I wondered if we could do this again sometime."

The butterflies intensified. She'd enjoyed herself today, more than she anticipated. She and Jasper had gotten their digs in, but they'd also fallen into an easy camaraderie.

When he'd suggested playing a board game, she jumped at the chance. She loved playing games of all kinds, but the opportunities to do so were few and far between as of late.

While they played, she'd seen things about him she'd never noticed before. Like how his hands, although wrinkled, arthritic, and with one crooked pinky finger, were still strong enough to open a jar of peanuts with little effort. He'd worked construction for forty-five years, and she remembered he had been one of the workers who had erected the building that housed Knots and Tangles. When she brought it up, he'd told her several entertaining stories about his work and even mentioned his parents, who had moved from Mississippi to Maple Falls when he was ten. He'd outlived most of his family and friends. That had saddened her and made her even more grateful for the BBs.

He was old and crochety, and his eyebrows still needed trimming. He was also funny, a good conversationalist, and when he truly, genuinely smiled . . . *yowza*.

Yowza? About Jasper?

"Never mind." He turned his back to her.

She was never at a loss for words, and she didn't understand why she was now. She also didn't understand the butterflies. "Jasper, I—"

"You can see yourself out." He didn't turn around.

She took her purse off one of the kitchen chairs and walked through his small living room—he really did have a worn recliner right across from a console TV—and left the house. She got in her car, sped out of the driveway, and fought to get her bearings.

By the time she reached home, she wanted to kick herself.

Why hadn't she given him an answer? She'd wanted to tell him yes. Not because she felt sorry for him or because they were from the same generation. She wanted to be around him, to see his incredible smile. To feel those butterflies again.

And that terrified her. He was a long-standing bachelor, and she was a committed bachelorette. She hadn't been interested in a romantic relationship since Gus, and she had never seen Jasper as relationship material. Other than a fleeting, enticing look she thought she'd seen in his eyes, she didn't even know what his intentions were. Most likely he simply intended to beat her at Parcheesi again.

Erma turned off the car and rested her head against the steering wheel. One thing she was sure of—she'd hurt his feelings, and she had to make amends. Which she would do at dance lessons tomorrow. After he accepted her apology—because she was sure he would—they could get back to their normal squabbling.

Because anything else between her and Jasper didn't make sense. And Erma Jean McAllister was a sensible woman . . . most of the time.

Chapter 17

"Guess we should have checked the weather report this morning." Kingston set down two cups of coffee on the table near a huge window overlooking the Breezeway Golf Course. Sheets of rain battered down, and as he sat down, a flash of lightning lit up the clubhouse.

Dad shook a packet of artificial sweetener and shrugged. "According to my weather app, this should pass quickly. If it doesn't, we'll find something else to do. It's such a rare occasion both of us have the same day off during the week." He grinned and stirred his coffee. "Thanks for suggesting we get together."

Kingston nodded and took a sip of his coffee, barely flinching at the huge *boom* of thunder rattling the window. He'd called his father early this morning and asked if he wanted to play golf sometime this week. Dad was off today, and he never refused an opportunity to hit the links. Other than the staff, they were the only ones in the dining area of the club. Everyone else had either done the smart thing and checked the weather or given up and gone home.

"Looks like the Razorbacks might have a decent season this year," Dad said. "The coach recruited a fine quarterback. He's young but has huge potential. Hope springs eternal, anyway."

"That's good." Kingston stared at the heavy downpour.

"Something's on your mind, son. Your sabbatical going okay?"

"Yeah. Perfect."

"From what I've heard, you're enjoying your time off. You went from one dance lesson to being an instructor, and you're also seeing someone." His father grinned.

"I see you've been talking to Mom," Kingston mumbled.

"More like she's talking to me. She's been over the moon since Saturday night."

Kingston stared at his coffee. At least his mother was happy. She wouldn't be for long, once she discovered that her matchmaking had lasted exactly twenty-four hours. He wasn't looking forward to her reaction tonight at the dance studio. He wasn't looking forward to dancing at all.

"Olivia's a lovely girl," his father continued. "Smart too. She'll give you a run for your money in that department."

The rain hammered down even harder, the sky turning dark as the storm continued.

"Kingston."

He looked at his father. "Yeah?"

"What's eating at you?"

He turned from the window and faced his father, cradling the full coffee cup. For two supposedly smart people, he and Olivia had been dumb, especially him. He had pushed her yesterday, and he should have known better. She was

100 percent right about their fake relationship being a horrible idea. But he didn't want it to end. He'd been selfish and blurted out his feelings, then blown it when he couldn't promise to put her first.

"I did something stupid, Dad. Really stupid." He scrubbed his hand over his face. "Stupid" didn't even begin to cover it. Even "imbecilic" didn't come close. Taking a breath, he explained everything to his father, including how badly he'd handled his other two opportunities with Olivia.

"So you and Olivia aren't together?" Dad asked, confused.

Kingston shook his head. "No. We never have been. And it's my fault. The first two times I let work get in the way. Or rather my inability to manage my schedule. This third time, I knew we were just pretending and that our fake relationship was only going to last a short time."

"But you weren't faking it."

"I tried." He sat back, looking at the rain again. "But I couldn't."

"You really care about her." His father rubbed his chin.

"I do. A lot."

"Then why are you letting her get away?"

"I don't have a choice." Kingston rubbed the back of his neck. "I couldn't give her what she wanted."

"Which was?" When Kingston couldn't answer, Dad slowly took another sip of his coffee. Set it back down just as gradually. "How do you see your life in ten years? Are you married? Have a family? Or single and devoted to your career?" He looked Kingston straight in the eye. "Have you ever thought about what *you* want?"

Kingston paused. "I always wanted to follow in your footsteps. I'd planned to go into cardiology too."

Dad frowned. "I wondered if we put too much pressure on you. I didn't want you to be a carbon copy of me, Kingston."

"I'm not. I love being a pediatrician. Once I did my pediatric rotation, I knew that was the field I wanted to go into. I wanted to be successful. Respected. And I am."

"At what cost?" Now it was his dad's turn to stare out the window.

It had almost cost him the job he loved. It had cost him Olivia.

After a few moments of silence, his father turned to him. "Looks like the rain has dried up. Ready to play?"

Kingston nodded, but golf was the last thing on his mind, and it showed as they played nine holes. His score was abominable, but his father had the good grace not to say anything. He also didn't press him for anything else about Olivia or his job, and Kingston was grateful. As they parted ways, he started to shake his father's hand. To his surprise, his dad put his arm around Kingston's shoulder.

"You'll figure it out, son," he said. "You always do."

Kingston nodded, although he was doubtful. He might get a grip on his professional life, but he'd lost his chance with Olivia. Three strikes, he was out. And he deserved to be.

Erma sat behind the counter of Knots and Tangles and sighed. Her crochet project lay beside her, a shawl similar to the ones Riley and her friends were making. But she hadn't touched it all day, even though business was slow. She hadn't slept well last night, and this morning she'd woken up in a grumpy mood. *Sigh*.

Riley came out from the back and stopped by the counter, giving Erma an odd look. Then she glanced at the front door. "Why are we still open?" she asked, going to turn the Open sign to Closed and lock the door.

Erma barely glanced at the clock. Almost six thirty. They always closed at five thirty, and usually she was home by now, sitting in her recliner and watching Pat and Vanna. She leaned on the counter and set her chin in her hand.

"Mimi?" Riley was in front of her now, peering at her. "Are you all right?"

"Yes." That was a fib of biblical proportions. She hadn't been all right since yesterday's butterflies. She couldn't get her mind off Jasper, and not only because she felt guilty about hurting his feelings yesterday. She couldn't stop thinking about his smile. The way he casually rolled the dice. How he tipped small handfuls of peanuts in his mouth without dropping a single one.

The fact that the butterflies had come back . . . and this time they didn't go away.

"You're going to be late for your dance lesson," Riley said.

"I'm not going." That was the other thing bothering her. She wasn't a coward. She owed Jasper an apology, and she needed to give it to him. But for some reason, she wanted to hide instead. Knots and Tangles was the perfect place to do just that.

"Why not?" Her granddaughter frowned.

"I don't feel like it." *Sigh*.

"You're acting weird. Do I need to call 911?"

Erma straightened at Riley's panicked tone. "I'm not ill. I'm fine."

Riley stared at her for a long minute. "Does your current oddball mood have anything to do with Jasper?"

"Who?" Erma grabbed her crochet and started hooking, even though she couldn't remember the stitch pattern. Oh well, that's what frogging was for.

"Jasper. Your dance partner? The man you've been clashing with my entire life?"

Erma ducked her head down so she didn't have to look at her granddaughter. Talk about yellow-bellied. She might as well slap a lemon-colored streak of paint down the middle of the T-shirt she was wearing, which said *I might be wrong but it's highly unlikely.*

"I thought you liked dance lessons," Riley said.

"I do." Erma finally lifted her head. She was acting ridiculous, but she didn't know what else to do. "I just don't want to go tonight."

Riley frowned. "I told them this wasn't a good idea."

"Told who about what?"

"The BBs. And Hayden."

Erma dropped her crochet. "What's going on?"

Now it was Riley's turn to sigh. "The BBs wanted to set you up with Jasper."

"*Excuse* me?" How dare her friends meddle in her life like this?

"Bea and Viola approached me and Hayden, and when I told him you were taking dance lessons, he came up with the plan to convince Jasper to take them too."

"Why, that sneak." Now her dander was getting up. "You didn't try to talk him out of it?"

Riley took a step back. "Yes. A little."

"I suppose Hayden abandoning Jasper at the Orange Bluebird was also part of the shenanigans."

"Yes. I'm sorry, Mimi. But you two have always been so adorable together—"

"*What?*" Erma came around from the back of the counter and scowled at her granddaughter.

"We just thought it would be fun to do a little harmless matchmaking. That's all."

"Harmless, huh?" Erma went back to the counter and grabbed her phone, then clicked on Group Chat.

> Every single one of you better hightail it to
>   Ms. Abernathy's Studio right now. Am I clear?

She waited.

> **Gwen:** Uh-oh.
>
> **Viola:** Oh dear.
>
> **Madge:** Why?
>
> **Erma:** Not you, Madge. I know you're not a part of this nonsense.
>
> **Peg:** Girls, I think we're in trouble.
>
> **Bea:** I'm already here. Erma, be reasonable. We only want you to be happy.
>
> **Erma:** Poppycock. You people are out of control, and I'm nipping this in the bud now.
>
> **Myrtle:** Erma, they wouldn't listen to me.

Erma: Why didn't you tell me?
Myrtle: . . .

While Myrtle was typing, Erma pointed at a sheepish Riley. "I want to see you and Hayden at the studio too."

"Why?"

"You'll see!" Oh, they'd gotten her blood boiling all right. She went to the back room and heard the pinging sound of another text. She stopped to read it.

Myrtle: Because you two have been tap-dancing around each other for years. We had to do something.
Gwen: I'm in Little Rock. I won't be back until ten or so.
Viola: Lucky you.

Erma shoved her phone in her bag and unlocked the front door. She marched onto the sidewalk to the crosswalk. The coast was clear, and she crossed the street. Her best friends and even her own family thought they knew her heart better than she did. So what if she and Jasper were always ribbing each other? It wasn't like they were in grade school, him pulling on her hair and her chasing him around the playground.

She came up short in front of Petals and Posies, the shop directly across the street from hers. Oh. *Oh.* No, they couldn't be right.

Could they?

The butterflies were a swarm now.

There was only one way to find out. She gripped her purse and headed for Ms. Abernathy's.

Kingston entered the dance studio at six twenty-nine and was immediately faced with his mother's disapproving look. This was one reason he'd stayed in his car and waited until the last minute to come inside. He ignored her and glanced around the studio, looking for the other reason he'd lagged behind. Olivia. He didn't see her, but everyone else was here from last week, along with some new students. Bea and Bill Farnsworth. Bill gave Kingston a nod in greeting, but Bea ignored him as she wrung her hands. Olivia must have told them about their "breakup." Bea would probably never speak to him again.

In addition to the Farnsworths, there was a young couple he didn't recognize. Sunny was talking to Bubba, Kingston's mother was showing Pastor Jared an intermediate rumba step, and Senior was standing next to Myrtle, who looked a little pale. Jasper was sitting by himself, his arms crossed over his chest, glowering at everyone.

Kingston walked over and sat next to him, mimicking the old man's posture. He didn't want to be here, even though it looked like Olivia was a no-show. She'd been a little late last week, but he doubted she would be two weeks in a row.

"What's got you in a dither?"

He looked at Jasper. The man was still scowling, but there was a spark of curiosity in his eyes. "I'm not in a . . ." He shook his head. *No more lies.* "I'm tired of pretending. That's all."

The door opened and in walked the two older women

he'd seen at the diner last week. He never had remembered their names. Like Myrtle, they looked upset, and soon they and Bea were huddled in a circle. When the door opened again, Riley and Hayden walked inside, both wearing hangdog expressions. Everyone seemed to be in a bad mood tonight.

Sunny clapped her hands, her smile bright and cheery. She was either oblivious to the atmosphere in the room or determined to change it. "Welcome, new students! I'm thrilled we have so many participating tonight."

Myrtle raised her hand. "Could we wait a little longer before we start?"

Sunny's smile dipped a little. "I'm sorry, we're already running late—"

The door flew open and Erma stormed in. She glared at Riley and Hayden, who were now standing by her friends. Well, more like standing behind them, Kingston realized.

Erma looked around the room, her gaze locking on Jasper for a second before she turned to Sunny.

"I'm sorry, this will only take a minute. Jasper Mathis." She walked over to him.

Kingston glanced at the man's shocked face. What was going on?

Erma stopped in front of them. "Jasper, I owe you an apology. I'm sorry I hurt your feelings yesterday. I didn't mean to, and I shouldn't have. And I'm not the only one who needs to apologize." She snapped her fingers and pointed to the empty space next to her.

Moving as a unit, Erma's friends and family walked over to Jasper. "I'm sorry, Jasper," Myrtle started. This continued for the next two people until Jasper held up his hand. "What in tarnation is all this? Why are y'all apologizing?"

"You and I have been set up, Jasper," Erma said.

"Huh?"

"I'll explain later. Right now we need to get these *public* apologies out of the way so we don't hold up Sunny's class any longer."

"We don't mind," Senior said. "No offense, Ms. Abernathy, but this is more entertaining."

"Perhaps I should make some popcorn," Sunny muttered, crossing her arms over her chest.

The rest of the group made their amends. When they finished, Erma turned to them. "What lesson have we learned?"

"No more matchmaking," they said in unison.

"Correct." She turned to Sunny. "Thank you for your patience."

"All right, everyone, get in your places." Sunny looked at the group. "You're all welcome to join us."

Hayden looked at Riley. "It's the least we can do," he said. She nodded.

"I don't mind learning a few steps," Viola added.

"Let's take our spot, Bill." Bea led him over to stand by Myrtle and Senior.

Everyone took their places, with Sunny helping the new students. Jasper stood in front of Erma as if nothing out of the ordinary had happened. Kingston took turns dancing with Peg and Viola, who had volunteered their names to him.

When the dance lesson was finished, everyone started talking about how much fun they'd had. Kingston remained silent.

"We should all get some pie at the diner," Bea said. "It's still open."

"Excellent idea," Erma said, every trace of her earlier anger gone. She turned to Jasper. "Will you join us?"

The two of them locked gazes, and if Kingston had been in better spirits, he would have smiled. Looked like the matchmaking had worked, even if Erma and Jasper hadn't figured it out yet.

Everyone except his mother and Sunny ended up agreeing to go. "We have some planning to do," his mom explained.

Bubba gave Sunny a wave of his hand and a toothy grin and left the studio along with the rest of the group.

Bea went to Kingston. "I thought Olivia would be here," she said with a small frown. "Did something come up?"

"I don't know." That was the truth.

"Didn't you two talk today?"

He started to shake his head, then realized Olivia must not have told her aunt about the breakup. And if she hadn't told her aunt, then as far as everyone knew, except for his father, they were still together. "She's had a busy day." Again, the truth, because all her days at the library were busy.

Bea nodded. "I'll give her a call and tell her to meet us at the diner. I'll save you both a seat."

"Um, I'm sorry. I can't come tonight. But thanks," he said, making sure he added a quick smile of appreciation.

"Oh." Bea frowned. "Okay. Maybe next week."

"Maybe."

She gave him a puzzled look and walked away. Bill held the door open for her and they left.

"King!" his mother shouted, even though she was only

a few feet from him. She and Sunny were sitting in the folding chairs in front of the picture window. She waved him over.

The last thing he wanted to do was deal with his mother tonight, but duty called. He walked over to them, but he didn't sit down.

"I have a splendid idea, King." She looked up at him, a small frown on her face. "Please sit down. I'm straining my neck looking at you."

He sank down on a chair, the headache that had started at the beginning of the dance lesson intensifying.

"Sunny was just telling me that she gets nervous speaking in front of crowds."

"A *little* nervous," Sunny said, pressing her bottom lip. "I can do it—"

"I told her not to worry, that you'll be the emcee of the showcase. It's perfect! You have excellent public-speaking skills, and you're such a charmer. You still own a tux, don't you?"

"Karen," Sunny said, touching Mom's shoulder. "I don't think that's necessary—"

"Of course it is! Do you have a tux, King?"

"Yes." He nodded, rubbing the back of his neck. The tension wouldn't ease.

"We'll take Olivia with us so you can get a tie and cummerbund to match her dress. Better yet, we can dress-shop with her, too, so you can both have the perfect outfits."

Kingston turned to Sunny, who looked overwhelmed and helpless. The Karen Effect. He was beyond familiar with that malady.

His mother was looking at her phone calendar. "What day is good for you? Oh, and we need to coordinate with Olivia too. I have several stores in mind where we can shop."

His head started to spin. This was his sabbatical. Not hers. But she was taking control of it anyway. He still hadn't told her how much time he had off, other than six weeks for the dance course. He didn't want to be emcee or wear a tux. He didn't even want to dance anymore. The only thing he wanted was a relationship with Olivia, and that was permanently out of reach.

"King? King!"

His mother's face came into view. "What day is good for you this week?"

He started to tell her to pick a day. He didn't care. But as he opened his mouth, something clicked inside him.

I don't have to do this. I can tell her no.

He turned to Sunny. "Can you excuse us for a minute?"

"Sure. I have a phone call to make anyway." Their instructor jumped out of her seat and scurried into the back room of the studio.

Mom faced him. "Good, I wanted to talk to you alone anyway."

"What about?"

"Your and Olivia's party." She lifted her phone and started tapping on the calendar.

"What party?"

"Just a little celebration. A chance for your colleagues and our friends to meet her and vice versa."

"Mom—"

"It will be semicasual. Cocktails and finger foods. She

can wear that cute dress she had on last week, the fuchsia one. It brings out her olive skin tone—"

"No."

Her head lifted. "What?"

"There will be no party, no tuxes and cummerbunds, no shopping or emceeing."

His mother blinked. "I don't understand."

His patience was wearing thin. "I'm on vacation."

"I know—"

"Do you? Do you understand that this is my sabbatical? That I need a break?"

"A break from what?"

"Work. All this." He spread out his arms. "Remember we were only going to do one dance lesson? And now you've got me doing all these things. Things I don't want to do."

Her chin lifted as she closed her calendar. "Then why don't you tell me what you want to do?"

Escape. It was the first word that came to mind. He wanted to be free of obligations and expectations. He'd spent most of his life doing everything he could not to disappoint anyone. Now that was all he seemed to do lately. "Go to Fiji," he said.

"You want to go to Fiji." Disapproval crept into her eyes. "With Olivia?"

It suddenly dawned on him that his mother was also in the dark about their breakup, like everyone else. "No. I'm going by myself."

"Do you think that's wise, considering you just started a relationship?"

He should tell her the relationship was over. But not right

now. He wanted to give Olivia the time she needed to break it to Bea and her friends. "She's fine with me leaving for a while."

"How long will you be gone?"

He shrugged. "Until I get back."

"Kingston, this isn't like you." Irritation laced his mother's tone. "You have responsibilities here."

"Responsibilities I didn't ask for. Or want. You just assumed I would say yes. This time I'm saying no. To all of it." He stood.

"Kingston! Come back here!"

He ignored her and walked out the door. Eventually he'd have to apologize for walking out on her, but right now he never felt freer.

Chapter 18

"He's a handsome one, isn't he? How do you know him?"

Olivia ignored Flo's question and began checking in the large stack of children's books that always showed up right before Tuesday's youth class. There weren't as many books as there were for toddler story time, since those parents usually checked out their limit of books and finished them in a week. But she had plenty to go through and little patience for Flo's commentary, which had started the minute Kingston walked into the library.

Flo sighed as she watched him with the kids in the young-adult section. There were eight children between the ages of nine and twelve, split evenly between boys and girls, and they were seated at two round tables while Kingston stood in front of them and read a book about hurricanes and tornadoes, complete with sound effects and added weather trivia that most adults knew but kids didn't.

Olivia continued checking in the books, trying to close her

ears to his resonant voice and engaging demeanor. This was the first time she'd witnessed the excellent rapport he had with children. Naturally he was good with them. He was good at everything. And it was starting to dawn on her that the only time she'd seen him stumble was when she was personally involved.

"Is he single?" Flo asked.

"Go shelve these." Olivia pushed a stack of books in her direction.

Flo frowned at her sharp tone. "You've been grouchy for the past two days. What's got your underwear in a clump?"

She shot Flo a hard look that had the older woman holding up her hands, then lifting her chin and grabbing the books. "Good thing RaeAnne's on vacation," she muttered as she walked away. "She doesn't have to deal with *this*."

Olivia slumped, guilt gathering in her chest. She shouldn't have snapped at Flo, and while the woman sometimes got on her nerves, it was usually only when she was trying to set Olivia up with her nephew, whom she'd found out yesterday had not only moved out of his parents' house but also started a new job in IT management and was engaged to be married. "*She's a darling girl,*" Flo had said the minute she'd arrived at work. "*The wedding is in December.*"

She got the distinct impression that Flo wanted to say, "You missed your chance." Or maybe Olivia was projecting her own disillusionment. It didn't matter, and good for Beau for starting a new chapter in his life.

The kids erupted in laughter, and Olivia fought to stay focused on her task. Unless she was in a meeting or on the phone, she always checked in the books that were returned before story time. But it took everything in her not to look at or listen to Kingston. Even some of the mothers, who usually perused the stacks during the hour-long class, were sitting at the adjoining table. Probably drooling over him, just like Flo was. She didn't dare look.

When Flo returned, Olivia had checked in only three books. "Finish this, please," she said, hoping she didn't sound as caustic as she felt.

"Uh, sure." Flo moved closer to her. "Are you feeling all right? Maybe you're coming down with something."

"I'm fine. I just have something to do in the office." Before Flo could ask more questions, Olivia hurried to the back. She rushed inside and shut the door, then plopped down at her desk. Her head drooped as she rubbed her temples, staring at the desk calendar in front of her. She'd missed the due date for her first assignment. She'd been unable to focus on her essay after her talk with Kingston. She never missed an assignment, and now she was thinking about dropping the class, something she never would have considered before. But she had no interest in eighteenth-century English literature. She'd taken the class only because she had *always* taken classes.

She also avoided her laptop and her phone. Aunt Bea had left two voice mails after yesterday's dance lesson had passed—Olivia had spent that time torturing herself by watching the romance movie channel all night—and she'd called Olivia three times already today and it wasn't even noon. Even though she and Kingston were officially not in a fake relationship anymore, she hadn't told anyone, even Aunt Bea. She didn't want to answer a bunch of questions. She didn't want to tell any more lies.

As if on cue, her phone buzzed. Anita's text showed up on their group chat.

> Can't wait to see y'all tonight. I'm almost done with my shawl.

Olivia stared at the message. She'd completely forgotten that tonight was their weekly Chick Clique meeting.

> **Harper:** I made ten baby washcloths. Is that excessive?
> **Anita:** I don't think so.
> **Riley:** I guess y'all heard about Erma and Jasper.
> **Harper:** What? I'm always out of the loop! Are they finally realizing they're in love?
> **Riley:** Um, about that . . .

Olivia opened her desk drawer, dropped her phone inside, and slammed it shut. The last thing she wanted to read about was a couple in love, even if it was Jasper and Erma.

A knock sounded at the door. "I'm busy," she barked. Then closed her eyes. It wasn't like her to be so touchy and terse. "I'll be with you in just a second."

"Olivia, sugar. It's me."

She should have known Aunt Bea wouldn't be ignored.

She went to the door and opened it. "I don't have a lot of time, Aunt Bea. I'm very busy today." Then she noticed her aunt's face. Aunt Bea wasn't concerned. Or sad. She was angry.

The older woman entered the office in a huff. "I won't take up too much of your time."

Dread pooled in Olivia's stomach. She couldn't remember

the last time she'd seen Aunt Bea this fired up. Probably because she'd never gotten in trouble before. Like, ever.

"What's wrong?" she asked, going to her. Aunt Bea couldn't be this upset over her and Kingston. It had to be something else.

"Why are you avoiding my calls?" Her aunt whirled around and faced Olivia, a flash of hurt in her eyes.

She walked back to her desk, taking the few seconds to regain her composure. "Like I said, I've been busy."

"Does this have anything to do with you and Kingston?"

Did her aunt know? "What did he tell you?"

"Nothing. But it was obvious he was out of sorts last night at the dance studio." Aunt Bea lifted her chubby chin. "Extremely out of sorts. And when I asked him why you weren't at the dance lesson, he didn't have any idea. That doesn't sound like a couple in love."

Her gaze jumped to Aunt Bea. "Who said anything about love?"

"You didn't have to." Aunt Bea went to her. "It was plain as day on both y'all's faces. At my house, at church on Sunday. Everyone could see it."

Love? Was that what she was feeling for Kingston?

Had felt, she tried to tell herself.

Not only was her inner monologue not working, but she was more confused than before. Tears filled her eyes. "I don't . . . understand."

At the sight of her tears, Aunt Bea's face fell. "Oh, honey. I'm so sorry." She bustled over to Olivia and pulled her into her big, soft embrace. "I shouldn't have snapped at you like that."

Olivia started to cry . . . and she couldn't stop.

"Let's sit down." Aunt Bea led Olivia to the chairs in front of her desk and sat in one. As Olivia followed suit, her aunt grabbed a handful of tissues from the box next to her work computer. "Here. Your nose needs a little blow."

Olivia used a tissue, then swiped her upper lip. "I'm sorry," she said, taking a clean tissue and wiping her eyes. "I don't know what happened."

"It's okay. Sometimes we all need a good cry."

"I don't cry." She sniffed. It was true. She couldn't remember the last time she'd cried, even over a sad movie, although she tended to avoid those. She hadn't even cried when her parents moved away.

"Then you're overdue, sugar." Aunt Bea smiled, every trace of her earlier anger gone. "Tell me what's going on."

There was nothing else she could do but tell the truth. "Kingston and I aren't together."

"Oh, honey." Bea reached for a tissue and dabbed her own eyes. "I'm so sorry—"

"We never were." She glanced at her blueberry-colored skirt, ashamed. "We pretended to be together."

Her aunt's hand flew to her chest. "Why on earth would you do that?"

"Because Karen Bedford was trying to get us together."

Aunt Bea's eyes bulged. "Um, she was?" She started shredding the tissue with her fingers.

"We thought the best way to circumvent that would be to go along with it. Then after a few days we would break up—"

"And everyone would leave you both alone."

Kathleen Fuller

"Exactly."

Aunt Bea desperately looked around the room. "You wouldn't happen to have any snacks around here, would you?"

Olivia peered at her aunt. "You're acting suspicious again." *Oh boy.* "Did you have anything to do with Karen's scheme?"

"Um . . . possibly?"

"I don't believe this." Olivia gritted her teeth together. "I told you I was doing fine."

"But when you and Kingston came over for peach pie, you were having such a lovely time. I'd never seen you so lively around another man. Or any man, for that matter."

"You promised me you would let me live my life."

"And I meant it at the time . . . Oh bother." Aunt Bea hung her head. "I'm so sorry. I shouldn't have interfered."

Olivia didn't doubt her sincerity. She sighed. "It's okay."

Her aunt met her gaze, her expression slightly brighter. "Well, it's all water under the bridge now, right? Since you and Kingston don't have feelings for each other, no one got hurt."

Olivia tried to nod. She needed to confirm Aunt Bea's statement before the older woman got any more crazy ideas about Olivia's love life. She also wanted to believe it. Instead, she stayed still and silent.

Aunt Bea tilted her head, also not saying anything. Then she took Olivia's hand. "I promise," she said, making an X motion across her heart with her other hand, "that I will never, ever meddle in your business again. Or Erma's."

"Erma?"

Her aunt's eyes grew wide again as she let go of Olivia.

"Oh, nothing. We sorted it all out last night. You should really keep some snacks here. Just in case."

Olivia finally managed to smile. "I'll think about it."

Aunt Bea rose. "Now that I know you're okay, I'll let you get on with your day. Just a reminder, tomorrow night before church I'm making grilled chicken and tomato-and-cucumber salad."

"Sounds delicious. I'll be there."

As Aunt Bea walked out the door, Olivia said, "Keep it open." She felt slightly better, but not much. At least her aunt wasn't mad at her. And now that she'd told her the truth, soon everyone in Maple Falls would know too. Mission accomplished.

She heard another light rap at the door and turned around. Kingston.

"Just letting you know I'm leaving," he said.

She glanced at the clock. The class had ended ten minutes ago. She turned into Olivia Farnsworth, head librarian. "The students sounded like they had a good time."

"I hope so. I sure did."

Her heart thumped. He stood in the doorway. She didn't invite him in. "Thank you for volunteering." She forced a smile and put the children first. "Next week's topic is blizzards. Would you be interested—"

"I'll be in Fiji. Hopefully scuba diving, but I might try snorkeling first."

"By . . . by yourself?"

He nodded.

"What about your dance lessons?"

"I talked to Sunny last night and put in my notice."

At some point she must have moved because she was now standing in front of him. "Are you leaving town because of me?" She sounded so self-centered. But she had to know, because if he was, she would do everything she could to stop him.

"I'm leaving because of *me*. I have a lot to think about, and I can't do it here." He averted his gaze. "Too many distractions."

"When are you coming back?"

"I don't know." His eyes shifted to hers. "Take care, Olivia. You've got a great thing going here. The moms couldn't stop singing your praises about how much they and their kids enjoy the library." His expression was impassive. "See you around."

"See . . . you." But he was already gone.

She went back to her desk. Stared at her closed laptop. That was that. He was going to Fiji, and she was sure he'd forget about her the moment he got on the plane and set off on his new adventure. He was doing her a favor. Now she didn't have to worry about running into him. She could even go back to dance lessons again if she wanted to, because the only reason she hadn't gone last night was that he was there. She could also refocus on her class. To make up for the late assignment, she would work extra hard and turn in everything early.

He would live his life. She would live hers.

A sharp pain hit her square in the chest. She ignored it. Opened her laptop document, brought up her late assignment, and began to type. Her life was recalibrating back to normal. Exactly how she wanted it to be.

Kingston finished packing his carry-on bag and set it on the floor next to his larger suitcase. When he called Sunny last night and explained that he couldn't help her or be a part of the showcase, she'd understood. *"Your mom and I can handle the class,"* she'd said.

"Are you sure you can handle her, though?"

Sunny laughed. *"I will now that I'm getting to know her. The key is knowing when to agree and when to say no."*

He was glad Sunny had it figured out. He wished he would have before now.

He sat down at the kitchen table and opened his computer. He still had websites about Fiji on the screen. He'd also booked a hotel for the next few days and had information on other places to stay in case he wanted to change abodes. He didn't want to be locked into anything. Even though the idea of winging it made him nervous, it was a good kind of anxiety. He was looking forward to this, particularly the relaxation.

He stared at the photo of blue water and a sandy beach on the screen and thought about Olivia's question. He'd been truthful when he told her he needed to leave for his own sanity, but it wouldn't hurt to have thousands of miles between them. He just hoped the adage that absence made the heart grow fonder wasn't true, because that was the last thing he needed.

His doorbell rang. He frowned, having no idea who wanted to see him at this time of night. When he opened the door, his mother stood there, her eyes puffy as if she'd been crying.

"Can I come in, King?"

He inwardly groaned. His resolve, and his newfound ability to say no, was being tested very quickly.

His mother must have noted his ambivalence. "If you don't want me here, I'll go. Just say the word."

Kingston hesitated. "You will?"

She nodded. "I only came by to apologize to you before you go on your trip. That's all. I promise."

He opened the door wider and let her in. When he offered her a drink, she refused. He gestured to the kitchen table, and they both sat down. "I need to apologize too," he said. "I shouldn't have walked out on you."

"You were right to do that." She pulled a tissue out of her purse and blotted under her nose. "After you left, I went home, furious that you would do something so insubordinate to me. Your father pointed out that I was being overbearing, as usual. Once I calmed down, I knew he was right. You would think with my degree and experience in counseling, I could figure out how to stop vexing my children."

That sounded harsh, but it was also true. "Mom, it's okay."

"No, it's not. Out of my three children, I've been the hardest on you. You're my golden child, right down to your hair. The fact that you were smart and handsome and accomplished—"

"Mother, don't—"

"And humble! Also easygoing, and I took advantage of that. I should have been teaching you how to set boundaries, not always breaking yours." She sniffed. "I made an appointment with a counselor, something I should have done a long time ago."

He stilled, completely stunned by her revelations.

"I need help, Kingston," she said. "And I'm going to get it."

He smiled and took her hand. "We both need to learn a few things. I love you, Mom. Quirks and all."

"Thank you, dear." She covered his hand with her own. "I love you too."

"But there will be times when I tell you no. Can you accept that?"

"Yes," she said. "I can't promise I'll like it, but I'll respect your decisions."

"I appreciate the honesty." He knew this was going to be a process, for both of them. He might even consider some counseling, too, once he got back from his travels. His mother wasn't the only one who needed to learn about boundaries.

She got up from her chair, and he stood. "Enjoy your time in Fiji," she said, giving him a hug.

"I plan to." He smiled.

She turned to leave, then stopped. "You and Olivia?"

His jaw jerked. "Over." She didn't need to know anything else.

She sighed. "I had an inkling when she didn't show up last night. And then you were fine leaving her for an indefinite time. I shouldn't have tried to force you two together. Lesson learned."

He hoped so. He gave her a last hug goodbye and walked her to the car. As she pulled out, he gazed up at the night sky. This time tomorrow he would be looking at a different part of the sky, perhaps while lying on the beach or from the balcony of his hotel room. But something would be missing: Olivia. Eventually he'd get over her, but it would take time, and a trip to Fiji or anywhere else would only be a Band-Aid. But he would heal. Someday.

⁂

That evening, Olivia picked up her knitting bag, her purse, and a box of wheat crackers to share at tonight's Chick Clique. She had to get back to her routine as soon as possible. Before she left the library, she'd finished her assignment and had started on the next one. Hopefully as the course progressed, she would gain some interest in the subject matter. Even if she didn't, she would finish the class with an A.

Like I always do.

She went to the door, reached for the doorknob . . . and stopped. Her future flashed in front of her—Mondays once a month at the Sunset Cinema, weekly Tuesday meetings with her friends, Wednesday-night suppers with Aunt Bea and Uncle Bill, and the rest of her time filled with work and school. The pattern would repeat over and over and over, like it had for the past several years.

Isn't this what I want? Isn't it what I need?

Then why did it feel so wrong? Why did the idea of going back to her rut cause such chaos in her heart?

She turned and set her stuff on the kitchen counter, then took her cell out of her purse.

Sorry, can't come tonight.

One of the girls pinged her, but she ignored it. She needed advice from an unlikely source. She needed a different perspective. She dialed her mother's number.

"Hello, Olivia."

She closed her eyes, her mother's monotone washing over her like a calming wave. "Hello, Mom."

"I'm puzzled to hear from you. This isn't our scheduled time."

"I know." Olivia sat down on the love seat. "I wanted to talk to you."

"Regarding what topic?"

"My relationship with Kingston."

Taking a deep breath, she explained everything to her mother, including the moments after the movie and coffee shop and at Anita's wedding. She told her about the matchmaking Kingston's mother had plotted and that she was sure Aunt Bea was in on it. Then she told her what she'd been afraid to admit to herself. "I have feelings for him. Deep feelings. I'm afraid they'll never go away."

"I see."

Olivia could imagine her mother sitting in her favorite chair in a sparsely decorated living room, listening intently. For years people had said she was the spitting image of her mother, down to her olive skin tone and black hair, although Mom wore hers in a practical pixie cut.

"If I understand you correctly, you're dissatisfied with your life."

"I didn't say that exactly—"

"That's exactly what you said. You were finding your extremely confining life stifling until you found excitement with Dr. Bedford. When he neglected to fulfill his promises, you were hurt and retreated to your carefully structured existence. Then when you were given another chance with him to be a couple—"

"A pretend couple," she corrected.

"Are you saying you didn't take advantage of the opportunity to be closer to Kingston?"

"I . . ." She couldn't deny it, although she sure did rationalize it. *Why did I want to call my mother again?* "No. I'm not saying that."

"Don't be hard on yourself, Olivia. Your actions, while illogical on the surface, are completely reasonable considering how much you care for Dr. Bedford."

That made her feel a little bit better. "But how do I stop those feelings?"

"A better question is, why do you want to?"

She pinched the bridge of her nose. "Because they're fruitless. He couldn't guarantee I would be his priority after he went back to work."

"Does life give us any guarantees?"

Her mother's habit of giving answers in the form of questions was becoming tiresome. "Mom, I don't know what to do."

"Perhaps you should give him another chance."

She shook her head, even though her mother couldn't see it. "I already did. Twice."

"Are the circumstances the same now?"

No. They weren't.

"I'd also posit that you haven't been fair to Dr. Bedford."

"What? He's the one who ghosted me, remember?"

"Why didn't you call him?"

She winced. "He said he would call me." But the point hit home. She'd written him off both times when she hadn't heard from him. She knew he was busy, but she'd immediately jumped into thinking he'd cast her aside. Although he had, she'd made it easy for him.

"It seems you're at a crossroads," Mom continued. "You can take the path of least resistance and zero risk and continue to live a life you don't find personally fulfilling."

Olivia mulled over her words, hating the fact that her mother was right about her disillusionment. "What's the other path?"

"If you truly care for Dr. Bedford and want to pursue a possible romantic connection, you should tell him."

"What if I end up being rejected?" she whispered. He might not do it now, but she was sure once he was busy with work, he would fall into his old habit of overworking and leave her behind. She believed that because they were alike in that way, retreating to what was familiar and predictable.

"That's the risk you take," Mom said. "Only you can decide if it's worth it or not."

She let that sink in. Was Kingston worth the risk of getting hurt a third time?

I'm hurting now.

"Olivia?"

"I'm here. You've given me a lot to ponder."

"Is there anything else you'd like to discuss? We have plenty of time to converse."

After she'd asked her mother the standard small-talk questions and half listened to her small-talk answers, her mother said, "I believe it would be prudent for me to end our phone call so you can contemplate your decision."

"Thanks, Mom."

"You're welcome. I'm gratified I was able to help. I'll admit there were times during your growth and development that your father and I felt out of our depth. But your aunt Bea was always helpful."

"She's been a little too helpful lately," Olivia said. But she knew her aunt's intentions were always good. "Good night, Mom. Tell Dad I said hello."

"I will. And, Olivia?"

"Yes?"

"It would be acceptable if we spoke outside our scheduled time, if you're so inclined."

She smiled. "I'd like that."

After she hung up the phone, she stared at the screen. After everything that had happened between them, she wasn't sure Kingston would be open to a simple date, much less a relationship. Then it hit her. For the most part, she had been seeing their interchanges from only her point of view, not his. Her mother was absolutely right—she wasn't being fair to Kingston. She'd hidden behind her hurt and fear and had given up the minute things didn't go her way.

Was it too late to start over? There was only one way to find out.

Chapter 19

Erma sat across from Jasper, a mancala board on the table between them. She'd brought it over a few minutes ago, part of the olive branch she needed to extend to him. But the marbles were still in the burgundy velvet pouch as they both stared at each other. After a few more minutes, she said, "Are we gonna play or not?"

He sniffed, his gaze still on her, but he didn't say anything.

She shouldn't be surprised he would make this hard on her. A part of her wondered why she'd even come. She and the other partners in crime had apologized to him, and this morning Riley had promised never to interfere again. Erma told her that as long as she held Hayden to that standard, too, everything was fine. Although she had to admit she deserved the comeuppance for her own machinations three years ago.

But Erma had also learned a lesson along the way. Her feelings for Jasper had irrevocably changed, and she had to acknowledge them. Blast it, her friends were right, at least in part. She didn't love Jasper, but she did enjoy his company and their sparring. She hadn't realized how much until she'd almost wrecked their friendship.

Jasper still hadn't said anything, so she picked up the bag and started dumping marbles into the indented cups on the mancala board. "Blue or yellow?" she asked.

"I ain't said I'd play," he groused.

"You *ain't* said you wouldn't either." She finished sorting the colors. "I'll take blue this time." She gathered up her marbles.

"Dagnabbit." He grabbed the yellow ones, and soon they were involved in a competitive game of mancala.

After he'd bested her in three out of four games—dagnabbit, indeed—she started collecting the marbles, then stopped. It was nearly 9:00 p.m. She should go home. Normally she was getting ready for bed by this time. But she was having too much fun, and going back to her empty house didn't appeal. When Jasper yawned, though, she bagged up the pieces. He was eight years older than her, and she didn't want to keep him up too late.

Once she had gathered up the game, she stood. "Have a good evening, Jasper."

He sprang from his chair and went to her, faster than she thought he could move. "Why'd you come over tonight, Erma Jean?"

That was a strange question. Certainly he wasn't getting senile. He had all his marbles, pun intended. "To play mancala."

"And?" When she found herself at a loss for words *again*, he grinned. "I think you like me."

She stumbled back a step as his eyes locked on hers. "Stop being presumptuous. And ridiculous." But the lack of verve behind her words only made him smile wider.

"You've been a good friend to me over the years, Erma. Even when we're insultin' each other, which I never minded too much. Kept me sharp, it did." His expression turned serious. "But lately, there's been something . . . I reckon I can't describe it." He rubbed his thick thumb over the edge of his old round table. "Tarnation, I'm not good at this."

"Jasper, just spit it out," she said softly. "What are you trying to say?"

"I like ya, Erma Jean. I like sippin' lemonade with ya. I like dancin' together. I like playin' games and matchin' wits with you." He met her eyes. "I want to court ya. That's what I'm trying to say."

Oh. My. She almost giggled. *Court* was such an old-fashioned word. Then again, she and Jasper were old, so it suited.

His expression was muted, even a little defiant. But she glanced at his thumb, now rubbing so fast she was sure he'd take the finish off the table if she didn't stop him. *This man . . .*

She moved closer to him. There were no butterflies crashing in her stomach. Just a sense of peace and the knowledge that this was right. The good Lord certainly enjoyed throwing her a curveball occasionally.

"Well?" he barked. "What's takin' ya so long to answer?"

"You're right, Jasper. I do like you." Erma took his hand. Squeezed it. One lone butterfly leapt for joy. "My answer . . . is yes."

Due to his flight being so early in the morning and the fact he had an hour's drive to the Little Rock airport, Kingston decided to turn in for the night, even though it was barely past nine. He'd already gone through his condo to make sure everything was set for him to be gone for a few weeks and had taken out the trash. He went inside and washed his hands and was just about to turn off the lights when he saw headlights shining through his front window. Had his mother changed her mind about staying out of his business? He hoped not, but he wouldn't put it past her.

He opened the front door in time to see Olivia on the second step of his front stoop. She froze midstride, looking at him, then finished the motion. When she was in front of him, she said, "Hi."

"Hi." He frowned, unable to fathom why she was here. They'd said their goodbyes at the library, and he'd been positive they'd never see each other again except when they were both in Anita's orbit. But here she was. Her hands were in front of her, and she was wringing them in a manner similar to that of her aunt Bea last night at the dance studio. "Is something wrong?"

"No."

He waited for further explanation, but she had started rocking back and forth on her heels. "Do you want to come in?" She nodded, and he gestured for her to go inside. After shutting the door, he said, "Olivia, are you all right?"

She nodded, but she didn't look all right.

he was sitting apart from her, and as he talked, he seemed distant. No, that wasn't it. More like clinical.

"I have a lot of changes to make," he continued. "I need to gain some balance in my life. I can't do that here." He gave her a half-hearted grin. "I need a plan. My own plan."

She nodded. If anyone understood the value of a plan, she did.

He stared straight ahead at the multicolored watercolor print hanging on the wall. "Our timing is terrible, isn't it?"

Olivia let out a cheerless chuckle. "It certainly is."

Then he turned to her and moved a little closer. "For the record, I care about you, Olivia. Enough to walk away, even though I don't want to. But you deserve to be with someone who has his act together. I don't. I like to pretend I do, and I've put on a good show all these years. But the real me is still a mess." He took her hand, looked at it, and lifted his gaze to hers. "I never wanted to hurt you. I'm sorry if I'm doing it again."

She was hurting, but she didn't blame him. Everything he said made sense. If he couldn't be the man she needed, it didn't matter how she felt. In fact, he was proving how much he cared, and that was more important than anything else.

"It's okay," she said, placing her other hand on his. "I want what's best for you too. I hope you find that someday."

He unclasped her hand. "I've got an early flight in the morning."

That was her cue to leave. There wasn't anything else to say. They both stood, and he walked her to the door. She turned to him. "Have a good trip, Kingston. Promise me something, okay?"

"Name it."

"Enjoy yourself."

A grin spread on his face. "I will."

She moved to leave, but she couldn't go until she did one last spontaneous thing. She reached up on her tiptoes and kissed him, then rushed back to her car and drove off.

Only then did she let her tears fall.

Chapter 20

Five weeks later

Olivia clapped as Aunt Bea and Uncle Bill finished their showcase dance. Harper stood up and wolf whistled, and soon her friends and their husbands were urging a standing ovation. The rest of the audience obliged with gusto.

After the applause ended and everyone sat back down, Olivia glanced around the community center again as they waited for the next pair of dancers to appear. As always Karen had outdone herself, and the center was perfectly decorated for the recital. White lights twinkled everywhere, making the ladies' sparkly dresses shimmer even more. Everyone sat at round tables on the perimeter, giving the audience a good view of the dancers.

Olivia was proud of her aunt and uncle, who'd had the courage to dance in front of a crowd. Olivia herself had tried one more dance lesson, but despite copious amounts of encouragement from Sunny and everyone else in the class, she was hopelessly inept. Ballroom dancing wasn't for her. She had more fun watching the dancers than she did actually dancing.

A few minutes later, Jared and Karen took their place on the floor. The sound of fifties-era music started to play, and they danced an East Coast swing. Olivia could tell how much Jared had improved since his first lesson, and Karen was light on her feet, not missing a step.

The rest of the couples were fun to watch too. Myrtle had gone to the Florida Keys for vacation, so Senior danced with both Peg and Viola. He was totally in his element, hamming it up and working the crowd. Bubba and Sunny were the spotlight dance, and while their tango wasn't perfect, he'd given his all, wearing a powder-blue suit and putting a long-stemmed rose between his teeth. The crowd loved it.

The final couple, Erma and Jasper, danced a rather sweet waltz. When they finished their dance, everyone erupted into applause.

With the showcase over, the DJ Karen had hired urged everyone onto the dance floor. Soon the room was filled with couples, some who had taken lessons and some who were just there to watch the showcase.

Olivia sat at a table with the Chick Clique and their husbands. Yes, Chick Clique. When her friends had offered to come up with something else, she'd declined. The name was growing on her.

Harper gestured to Erma and Jasper, who were sitting close together at a nearby table. "They're so cute, Riley."

"Nauseatingly so, sometimes." Riley grinned. "I love it, though. Mimi always said she'd be single for the rest of her life. And she didn't mind if she was. But ever since she and Jasper started dating, she's been giddy."

"So has Jasper," Hayden added. "Even at work he's got a new pep in his step."

"Do you think they'll make things official?" Anita asked. Everyone at the table looked to Riley.

"Yes," she said. "I'm positive it will happen. They were both happy being alone, but they're even happier together."

Olivia looked at the elderly couple again and smiled. Erma was brushing something off Jasper's tie. He batted her hand away, but he was grinning. Harper was right. They were cute, and Olivia was glad they'd found each other.

As for herself, it still hurt to think about Kingston, so as usual she'd thrown herself into her work. But she'd also done a few spontaneous things, like dropping her literature class. For the first time in almost her entire life, she didn't have an impending deadline, and it was wonderful. She'd also taken an afternoon off to go shopping with Harper. She'd even let her friend do her makeup tonight. Normally she didn't wear any, but Harper had used a light touch when she applied the cosmetics. The effect was subtle, and Olivia liked the neutral pink lipstick Harper had chosen.

During their spree, she'd purchased a modest, hip-flattering swimsuit from the clearance rack at one of the department stores. She'd even investigated swim lessons at the Hot Springs Aquatic Center but hadn't signed up yet. The idea of taking swim lessons made her think of Kingston.

But she needed to move on, despite knowing it would take a long time for her to get over him.

But even though her heart was still aching, her friends and family eased some of the pain.

She put Kingston out of her mind and speared one of the bacon-wrapped dates on the small plate in front of her. This was her second one, and they were delicious. She wondered if Tanner, who had catered the event, would consider adding them to the diner menu.

She'd started to take a bite when Karen, still dressed in her elegant dance costume, appeared. "This is for you." She slipped a folded piece of paper into Olivia's hand, then went back to circulating around the room.

Olivia opened the note.

Sunset Cinema. Eight p.m.

She frowned at the cryptic words. The note was typed, so she didn't know the sender . . . or did she? She glanced at Karen, who was at the next table. When she winked at Olivia, her suspicion was confirmed. Her heart danced in her chest.

"Sorry, y'all. I gotta go," she said, popping up from her seat.

None of her friends looked surprised, and no one questioned why she was making a hasty exit. They were all smiling, though, and that made her think they were up to something. For once, she didn't care.

Grabbing her shawl and the sparkly rose-pink wrist purse Riley had crocheted for her and the other Chicks, she headed out the door to the parking lot. She took a quick glance at her watch. Almost 8:00 p.m. She didn't want to be late.

A few minutes later she pulled into the theater's empty parking lot and frowned again. The Sunset showed the latest movies on Saturdays, and she'd expected the place to be filled with moviegoers.

When she got out of her car, she wrapped her shawl around her. Fall had arrived, and the mid-October evening air was crisp and dry. She was wearing her fuchsia dress and the high heels Harper had insisted she wear. To her surprise, they didn't hurt her feet as much as she'd thought they would. Still, although she wanted to run, she had to watch her step in the gravel lot.

The interior of the theater was dark, but when she reached the front door, the lights turned on. She went inside. The scent of freshly popped corn filled the air, but no one was in sight. She rushed through the empty lobby to the screening room. As she slowed her steps, she opened the door and entered the dimly lit theater.

Her breath caught. Every seat was empty except one. Seventh row, *eleventh* seat. Even in the dim lighting of the antiquated sconces lined up on opposite walls, she could see him. The back of his head, at least.

Kingston.

She took a deep breath and tried to slow down the hammering heartbeat in her chest. She also didn't want to trip gracelessly over her feet—a good possibility considering her impractical footwear.

When she reached the seventh row, he stood up. Turned. Looked at her and smiled.

The tingles returned with a vengeance. She made her way down the row, stopping a few feet in front of him. "Hi," she said, giving up on trying to control her racing pulse. Oh, how she'd missed him while he was gone. And even though they were just friends now, she was so happy to see him.

"Hi."

The tingles turned into tiny explosions, but she held her composure. "Welcome back."

"I'm glad to be back." He took her in. "Nice outfit."

She blushed. "I didn't want to be underdressed at the showcase."

"How did it go?" He sat down and motioned to the seat on the opposite side. Number ten. Her seat.

She looked at it, then sat down on number twelve. Hmm, just as good as ten. "It was terrific." She filled him in on the event. "Why didn't you come if you were back in town?"

"If I did, I wouldn't have been able to do this." He lifted his hand, and an usher appeared with a bucket of popcorn and two drinks. He handed one of the sodas to Olivia.

She sipped. Diet Coke, of course.

After Kingston took his drink and the popcorn, she asked, "How did you manage this?"

"I won't divulge all my secrets, but let's just say the owner has a soft spot for surprises." He turned to the usher. "Give us ten minutes. Then you can start the show."

"I'll let Fred know." The young man hustled to the back of the theater and exited.

"What show?" she asked.

He offered her popcorn, and she accepted. "You'll see."

She smiled. "I think I already know."

He arched a brow and smirked. "Maybe you do; maybe you don't." He looked at her. "It's so good to see you."

"Same here."

Her pulse settled. The conversation was a step above small talk, as to be expected between friends. While he was gone, she'd held on to a sliver of hope that when he returned, they could . . . She extinguished the thought. They had both agreed to keep things platonic, and she needed to temper her expectations.

"How was Fiji?" Olivia knew Anita hadn't heard from him other than when he checked in periodically to let his family know he was okay.

"Productive. I learned how to scuba dive. Snorkel. Did some deep-sea fishing. After a week and a half, I flew back to the US and did a tour of the northwest and up into Canada. But mostly I relaxed and had fun."

"I'm glad." And she was. She was also grateful that things weren't awkward between them anymore.

"I also did a lot of soul-searching. I came to the conclusion I don't like everything I do. I had figured since I'm good at teaching, I should teach. I'm a good practitioner, so I needed to join a clinic that had two locations. I'm a good speaker, so I should do the convention circuit."

"The curse of being so talented," she said, completely serious.

"Or just overly ambitious."

"See, you're even good at being humble."

A slight blush tinted his cheeks. "Anyway, those things aren't what I'm passionate about. Once I was away from the office and the university and the travel, I didn't miss it that much. I realized there were only two things I truly missed while on sabbatical. One was volunteering at the health department. So when I came back, I had a talk with their HR department. They're looking to hire a pediatrician. The hours are less. So is the pay. It's not a glamorous job, but there's a need, and I want to fill it. I've already put in my notice at the clinic."

"How did they react?"

"Better than I expected. Lawrence said he was sorry I was leaving, but he agreed it was the right decision, and the door would always be open if I decided to return. I also canceled my spring class and took my name off the available speaker list. I start at the health department on Monday." He grinned. "Mom doesn't know yet. I figured I'd tell her at brunch on Sunday. That seems to be the preferred time to drop bombshells on her."

As Kingston talked, Olivia could see how relaxed he was. "I'm so happy you've found your niche. What's the other thing?"

He pulled his phone out of his pocket, swiped the screen a couple of times, and then showed it to her.

She glanced at it and hid her frown. So nothing had changed. Disappointment filled her. Next week he was going back to work with a full schedule—and there was no room for her, or their friendship. Every single square was filled, even though he'd just said he was cutting back on his work and activities. Was this his way of telling her goodbye?

"Looks like you'll be busy," she said, trying to stem her confusion.

He glanced at the screen. "Oops. That's not the right

one. That was my old schedule. I need to get rid of that." He ran his thumb over the screen. "Here's my new one."

She took the phone again. Her eyes widened. Her name was written all over the month of October, along with activities. There was "Movie at Sunset," "Walk through Garvin Gardens," and "Teach Olivia how to golf," among others. On each Saturday night the words "Olivia's choice" appeared. "What is this?"

"Our calendar."

The tingles returned. "'Our'?"

He turned in his seat and faced her. "I missed you, Olivia. Every day I was in Fiji, I wished you were there with me. I know we agreed to be friends, and if friendship is all we have, then I'll accept it. But I want to show you how committed I am to spending time with you. No excuses, no ghosting, no conflicting obligations."

Olivia stilled. He'd just made the closest thing to a commitment other than actually showing up for the planned events. But would he follow through? Could she trust him a third time?

Is he worth the risk?

She took the phone from him and started swiping on the screen.

He leaned over. "What are you doing?" When she handed the phone back to him, he glanced at the screen, his brow lifting. "You erased 'Olivia's choice.'"

She nodded. "We'll wing it on Saturdays." And to show him her commitment to spontaneity, she leaned over and kissed him. When they parted, she murmured, "Yeah. Totally worth it."

"What?"

"Never mind," she said with a smile.

He gazed at her. "That wasn't a friendly kiss."

"It wasn't supposed to be." She held her breath, waiting to see how he would respond.

"I was hoping you'd say that."

This time he kissed her, just as the lights dimmed in the theater and *The Quiet Man* started rolling. "The movie's beginning," he said in a low voice.

"I already know how it ends."

Happily ever after.

Epilogue

One year later

Olivia stood in front of the mirror and touched the string of pearls around her neck. The beautiful necklace had belonged to her mother, who had given it to her last night before her and Kingston's wedding earlier that day. Mom had worn the pearls when she married Dad, and Olivia was touched by the special gift.

Just remembering the unexpected emotion in Mom's eyes made Olivia emotional. Again. She teared up when she and her bridesmaids Harper, Riley, and Anita were getting ready for the ceremony. Harper's daughter, Claire, and Anita's son, Wyatt, had been sitting with their proud grandparents. She cried when she saw Kingston standing at the end of the aisle. She swallowed her tears as she told her friends and Aunt Bea goodbye before leaving with him on their simple honeymoon to Gatlinburg—he'd taken a 75 percent pay cut when he went to the health department and had zero regrets—and now that they were in their hotel, she was getting emotional again.

Soft music suddenly drifted into the room, and in the mirror she saw Kingston walking up behind her. Quickly she wiped the corner of her eye. He slipped his arms around her waist, his black wedding band shining in the low light. "You okay?"

"Yeah. Just an emotional day, in a good way. Where's the music coming from?"

"I packed a Bluetooth speaker." He turned her in his arms so they faced each other. "I know we had our first dance during the reception—"

"Thank goodness I talked you out of the tango." She smiled and moved closer to him.

"I still think you can learn it. Maybe sometime you'll let me teach you." He drew her close. "I wanted to dance with you alone for a while. Just you and me, husband and wife."

That sounded so good to her. They danced, not ballroom or anything fancy, just rocking back and forth together. She leaned her head against his chest, closed her eyes, and sighed. Perfect.

When the song ended, she looked up at him. "I brought something too." She walked out of his embrace and over to her carry-on, opened a zippered compartment, and pulled out her laptop.

"You're kidding me," he said, his disappointment clear in his tone of voice. "You're not going to work on our honeymoon, are you? Didn't you learn from my mistakes?"

She laughed and opened it. "This isn't for work." She

pulled up a recording of his favorite movie, *Casablanca*, and set it on their bedside table. "A bit of nostalgia," she said.

He laughed and sat down on the bed, pulling her onto his lap. "You really think we'll be watching movies?" He shook his head, his gaze turning serious as he touched his forehead to hers. "Thank you for giving me another chance. I love you, Olivia Bedford."

"I love you too." He didn't have to thank her. Over the past year he'd more than proved his commitment to her, while she had learned to embrace her spontaneous side. She still liked to keep a schedule, and there were days when he had to put in some overtime at work. But together they had found balance in their lives . . . and love.

She put her arms around his neck. "Are you sure you don't want to watch the—"

His kiss silenced her.

Sigh.

"That sure was a nice weddin' yesterday."

Erma gave Jasper a surprised look. They sat in her kitchen, and she was just about to jump over three of his checker pieces, plus get kinged, making her wonder if he'd thrown a few of the games on purpose, because she was winning this round far too easily. "Wow" was all she could say.

He took a sip of decaf coffee and arched his brow. "'Wow' what?"

"You making a positive comment about a wedding." Olivia and Kingston's wedding was the third one they'd attended over the past year. The first had been Myrtle and Javier—they'd had a simple wedding at Amazing Grace, with Myrtle's children as the bridal party and the BBs and their spouses and plus-ones also in attendance. The other one had surprised the entire town—except for the students at Ms. Abernathy's School of Dance. Sunny Abernathy had become Mrs. Bubba Norton back in January. Sunny was still giving ballroom dance lessons, but Erma and Jasper had decided to take a break from the latest six-week program.

He squinted. "I ain't never said nuthin' bad about weddin's."

"You never say anything good either." She picked up the red checker piece and held it over his black one, ready to strike.

"Maybe we should have one."

The checker hit the game board and sailed over the side of the table. Erma gulped. "Um, what?"

Jasper fiddled with the handle on his mug. "I reckon we should have a weddin'."

Her jaw fell open. "*We* should have a wedding?"

He hooked his fingers around the handle, not looking at her. "Yup."

"Jasper Eugene Mathis, are you proposing to me?"

He lifted his gaze and met hers, and what she saw in his eyes made her gulp again. Over the past year and some change, they had settled into a routine with each other. Thursdays were still set aside for meeting with her BBs, but she and Jasper spent every other weeknight at each other's houses, and usually did something together on Saturday. Sunday was church, where she would sit next to him during the service, then they would usually go to the Orange Bluebird for lunch, then back to her house for checkers. The butterflies she'd felt at the beginning of their relationship had simmered down, and she'd figured that was normal considering their ages. She didn't expect him to paw her, but they hadn't even really kissed yet, other than the perfunctory peck on the cheek before they left each other for the night.

But the way he was looking at her now . . . whoa.

He got up slowly—basically the only speed he knew— and moved to stand in front of her. He put his left hand on the table and started to bend down.

"Wait wait wait!" She put out her hands. "Are you kneeling?"

"I'm tryin' to," he grumbled. "But yer gettin' in the way."

She shot up from her seat and took his hands, tears glazing her eyes. "You old coot," she said, her voice thick. "Don't you know if you get down on the floor, it'll be a lot harder to get back up?"

He grimaced. "I wanted to do right by ya, Erma, and propose all proper-like. But I guess this will have to do." He fished in the pocket of his blue jeans and pulled out a small white box.

Her hand went to her mouth. She'd given up on him asking her to marry him, since there was nothing really keeping them from getting married and yet he'd never said anything. She figured he was fine with the way things were, and she was too—for the most part. And now he was surprising her with a proposal. What was it young people said nowadays?

Squee!

He held out the box and started opening the lid. "Will you ma—"

"Hey, Mimi," Riley said, entering the kitchen. She froze.

Hayden, who was right behind her, bumped into her. "What's going on—"

Jasper glared at him. "You're interruptin' me. You might be mayor now, but that don't mean you have the right to come burstin' into someone else's kitchen."

Erma cringed. Jasper knew Riley and Hayden always made themselves home here. She wouldn't have it any other way. "It's okay," she said, moving to Jasper's side and whispering to him. "We can do this later."

"No." He lifted his chin. "I don't mind havin' witnesses." Then he paused. "Unless you do, Erma."

She shook her head as Mayor Hayden Price—as of five months ago when he'd swept the Maple Falls mayoral election—put his arm around Riley's waist. "Happy to be of service," he said with a grin.

"I thought you two would have done this months ago." Riley smiled. "Go on."

Jasper scowled. "Now I don't remember what I was gonna say."

Erma took the box from him and opened it. Inside lay a simple gold band. No stones or fancy engraving. A wedding band, not an engagement ring. She smiled. He'd never done this before, so she wasn't surprised he was being untraditional.

She took the band out of the box and handed it to him. Later she'd explain the difference in rings to him, but she wasn't going to take this one off until the day of their wedding, when he would put it on her finger again.

And that's going to happen soon.

"Erma Jean," he said, meeting her gaze. "Will you marry me?"

"Of course I will, you crazy man." She put her arms around him and gave him a kiss—on the lips this time.

His cheeks turned scarlet, and he slid the ring onto her finger. "You've made me a happy man, Erma."

"That's good, because I'm a happy woman!" She hugged him again, and Riley and Hayden clapped.

The four of them celebrated with some leftover blondies courtesy of Bea, who was still baking and cooking too much but who enjoyed sharing the leftovers with her friends. Hayden had come over to talk to Jasper about his new schedule at work, giving him more responsibility since Hayden had to focus on his mayoral position. Erma and Riley went into the living room while the men talked. Erma sat in her recliner and Riley on the couch, like they always had when Riley lived with her during her teen years.

"How does it feel to be engaged?" her granddaughter asked.

Erma sighed and looked at the band. "It feels a little unreal. But right. Very right. If you'd told me a year and a half ago that I'd be in love with Jasper Mathis, I would have sent you to the doctor to get your head examined."

"And if you'd told me three years ago that I'd not only be living in Maple Falls but would love it here, be married to Hayden, have the best friends in the world, and be the mayor's wife, I'd have done the same thing. Our lives have changed so much, Mimi."

"Good changes, all of them." Erma wished for only one

more, and that was for Riley's mother, Tracey, to return home, clean and sober. That had always been her prayer, and she would continue praying for her daughter until her last day. Riley rarely talked about Tracey, but Erma knew her granddaughter had the same hope.

Riley kicked off her gray tennis shoes and tucked her legs underneath her. "Any idea when the wedding will be?"

Erma shook her head. "This was a complete surprise." A little bit of panic set in. "There will be so much to do! We have to set a date, talk to Pastor Jared—"

"Don't forget the wedding shower," Riley said. "You'll need to find a dress—and it's not going to be your prom dress from the late sixties."

"Drat. That would have been perfect. I can still fit into it—"

"No."

"It's my wedding." She crossed her arms. "If I want to wear a potato sack, I will."

"And that would be better than your hideous prom dress."

Hayden and Jasper came into the room. Riley stood up. "You two just saved us an argument." At Hayden's questioning look she said, "Prom dress."

"Oh no." Hayden shook his head. "Not that thing again."

"Excuse me? What do you have against sixties fashion?"

"You'll get a proper weddin' gown." Jasper moved to her and took her hand. "I'll see to it."

She turned to him. "You can't see me in the gown before the ceremony. That's bad luck."

"And we're out of here." Riley shoved her feet into her shoes and hugged Erma. She held out her hand to Jasper. "Welcome to the family."

Jasper nodded as they shook hands.

After Riley and Hayden left, Erma and Jasper sat on the couch, knees touching. She turned to him. "Are you sure about this?"

"Yep." He met her gaze. "You?"

"Absolutely." She leaned her head on his slim shoulder. There was a lot to do, but she had her BBs to help, along with Riley and the CCs. She couldn't wait to get started.

"Love you." His whisper was gruff and tender. "Even though you drive me crazy."

Erma smiled. "Ditto, you old coot. Ditto."

Acknowledgments

My deepest appreciation to my editors, Becky Monds and Leslie Peterson. This book was a challenge in many ways, so thank you for always keeping me on the right track! A big thank you to my agent, Natasha Kern, for her endless support. I also want to thank my dear friend Laura Larimore, who helped brainstorm Olivia's passion for literacy.

Thank you, dear reader, for going on another journey with me. This book was so much fun to write, especially Erma and Jasper's happily ever after! I hope you enjoyed this trip to Maple Falls, and as always, happy reading!

Discussion Questions

1. Olivia and Kingston first knew each other as kids—he was her best friend's brother—and they are surprised to find themselves attracted to each other as adults. Have you ever begun to see someone in a different light as you've gotten to know him/her in a different setting or at a later age?

2. Kingston struggles with overscheduling. How do you balance your professional and personal commitments?

3. Kingston twice broke promises to Olivia. Do you think she was right to give him not only a second but a third chance? Why or why not?

4. Bea goes to the Bosom Buddies when she needs advice. Who do you go to for advice and why?

5. Why do you think Kingston had such a difficult time establishing boundaries with his mother? How do you establish boundaries in your relationships?

6. The Bosom Buddies, Karen, Riley, and Hayden all try to matchmake for their loved ones. Do you think

they were right to get involved, or should they have stayed out of it?

7. Have you ever tried to matchmake or been set up on a date by a family member or friend? What were the results?

8. The author met her husband at a ballroom dance class. If you have a significant other, how did you meet? What are the most interesting ways couples you know have met?

9. The town of Maple Falls is growing and new businesses are coming to Main Street. What has been your experience watching your community develop or going back to a community where you used to live and seeing the differences?

10. The characters in *Two to Tango* take ballroom dance lessons, most of them without any prior experience. Is there any new skill you'd like to learn or hobby you'd like to take up?

About the Author

With over a million copies sold, Kathleen Fuller is the *USA TODAY* bestselling author of several bestselling novels, including the Hearts of Middlefield novels, the Middlefield Family novels, the Amish of Birch Creek series, and the Amish Letters series as well as a middle-grade Amish series, the Mysteries of Middlefield.

Visit her online at KathleenFuller.com
Instagram: @kf_booksandhooks
Facebook: @WriterKathleenFuller
Twitter: @TheKatJam

LOOKING FOR MORE GREAT READS? LOOK NO FURTHER!

THOMAS NELSON

Since 1798

Visit us online to learn more:
tnzfiction.com

@tnzfiction